Phaedra Patrick qualified first as a stained-glass artist before gaining her professional marketing qualifications. She has worked as a waitress, stained-glass designer, film festival organiser, and communications manager. Her first real writing success came when she entered and won several short story competitions, and she now writes full-time. Phaedra lives in Saddleworth, near Manchester, with her husband and son, where she enjoys walking, eating chocolate, and arts and crafts. Her idea for *The Curious Charms of Arthur Pepper* emerged as she showed her own childhood charm bracelet to her young son and told him the stories behind each of the charms.

You can discover more about the author at www.phaedra-patrick.com

THE CURIOUS CHARMS OF
ARTHUR PEPPER

Arthur Pepper gets up every day at 7:30 a.m. He eats his breakfast, waters his plant, Frederica, and does not speak to anyone unless it is absolutely necessary. Until something disrupts his routine. On the first anniversary of his beloved wife Miriam's death, he finally sorts through her wardrobe and finds a glistening charm bracelet that he has never seen before. Upon examination, Arthur finds a telephone number on the underside of a gold elephant. Uncharacteristically, he picks up the phone. And so begins Arthur's quest — charm by charm, from York to Paris to India — as he seeks to uncover Miriam's secret life before they were married. Along the way, he will find hope, healing, and self-discovery in the most unexpected places.

PHAEDRA PATRICK

THE CURIOUS CHARMS OF ARTHUR PEPPER

Complete and Unabridged

CHARNWOOD
Leicester

First published in Great Britain in 2016 by
Harlequin Mira
an imprint of
HarperCollins*Publishers*
London

First Charnwood Edition
published 2017
by arrangement with
HarperCollins*Publishers*
London

A catalogue record for this book is available
from the British Library.

ISBN 978–1–4448–3251–8

Published by
F. A. Thorpe (Publishing)
Anstey, Leicestershire

Set by Words & Graphics Ltd.
Anstey, Leicestershire
Printed and bound in Great Britain by
T. J. International Ltd., Padstow, Cornwall

Acknowledgements

Firstly, hats off to Super-Agent Clare Wallace for her insight, expertise and all round loveliness. Also, to all at Darley Anderson for their warm welcome and support — especially Mary Darby, Emma Winter and Darley himself. Thanks also to Vicki Le Feuvre for early feedback.

Behind every book is a great editor and I am fortunate to have two of the best in my corner. To my UK editor Sally Williamson and to Erika Imranyi in the US, many thanks for your thoughtfulness, creativity and championing of Arthur. A special acknowledgment also goes to Sammia Hamer, who originally gave Arthur his home in the UK.

All the team at Harlequin Mira and Harper Collins have been wonderful, with fantastic input from Alison Lindsay, Clio Cornish, Nick Bates and Sara Perkins Bran, to name just a few.

To friends who read an early draft of this book without rolling their eyes, thanks to Mark RF, Joan K, Mary McG and Mags B.

My mum and dad have always encouraged my love of books and reading, so to Pat and Dave — this couldn't have happened without you!

The biggest shout out goes to Mark and Oliver for supporting me on every step on this journey, believing it was possible and for always being there.

Thanks also to my friend, Ruth Moss, whose bravery and spirit of fun I think of often.

For Oliver

The Surprise in the Wardrobe

Each day, Arthur got out of bed at precisely 7:30 a.m. just as he did when his wife, Miriam, was alive. He showered and got dressed in the grey slacks, pale blue shirt and mustard tank top that he had laid out the night before. He had a shave then went downstairs.

At eight o'clock he made his breakfast, usually a slice of toast and margarine, and he sat at the pine farmhouse table that could seat six, but which now just seated one. At eight-thirty he would rinse his pots and wipe down the kitchen worktop using the flat of his hand and then two lemon-scented Flash wipes. Then his day could begin.

On an alternative sunny morning in May, he might have felt glad that the sun was already out. He could spend time in the garden plucking up weeds and turning over soil. The sun would warm the back of his neck and kiss his scalp until it was pink and tingly. It would remind him that he was here and alive — still plodding on.

But today, the fifteenth day of the month, was different. It was the anniversary he had been dreading for weeks. The date on his *Stunning Scarborough* calendar caught his eye whenever he passed it. He would stare at it for a moment

1

then try to find a small job to distract him. He would water his fern, Frederica, or open the kitchen window and shout 'Gerroff' to deter next door's cats from using his rockery as a toilet.

It was one year to the day that his wife had died.

Passed away was the term that everyone liked to use. It was as if saying the word *died* was swearing. Arthur hated the words *passed away*. They sounded gentle, like a canal boat chugging through rippling water, or a bubble floating in a cloudless sky. But her death hadn't been like that.

After over forty years of marriage it was just him in the house now, with its three bedrooms and the en-suite shower room that grown-up daughter, Lucy, and son, Dan, recommended they had fitted with their pension money. The recently installed kitchen was made from real beech and had a cooker with controls like the NASA space centre, and which Arthur never used in case the house lifted off like a rocket.

How he missed the laughter in the home. He longed to hear again the pounding of feet on the stairs, and even doors slamming. He wanted to find stray piles of washing on the landing and trip over muddy wellies in the hallway. *Wellibobs* the kids used to call them. The quietness of it being just him was more deafening than any family noise he used to grumble about.

Arthur had just cleaned his worktop and was heading for his front room when a loud noise pierced his skull. He instinctively pressed his back against the wall. His fingers spread out against magnolia woodchip. Sweat prickled his underarms. Through the daisy-patterned glass of his front door, he saw a large purple shape looming. He was a prisoner in his own hallway.

The doorbell rang again. It was amazing how loud she could make it sound. Like a fire bell. His shoulders shot up to protect his ears and his heart raced. Just a few more seconds and surely she'd get fed up and leave. But then the letterbox opened.

'Arthur Pepper. Open up. I know you're in there.'

It was the third time this week that his neighbour Bernadette had called around. For the past few months she had been trying to feed him up with her pork pies or home-made mince and onion. Sometimes he gave in and opened the door; most of the time he did not.

Last week he had found a sausage roll in his hallway, peeking out of its paper bag like a frightened animal. It had taken him ages to clear up the flakes of pastry from his hessian welcome mat.

He had to hold his nerve. If he moved now she would know he was hiding. Then he'd have to think of an excuse; he was putting out the bins, or watering the geraniums in the garden. But he felt too weary to invent a story, especially today of all days.

'I know you're in there, Arthur. You don't have to do this on your own. You have friends who care about you.' The letterbox rattled. A small lilac leaflet with the title 'Bereavement Buddies'

3

drifted to the floor. It had a badly drawn lily on the front.

Although he hadn't spoken to anyone for over a week, although all he had in the fridge was a small chunk of cheddar and an out-of-date bottle of milk, he still had his pride. He would not become one of Bernadette Patterson's lost causes.

'Arthur.'

He screwed his eyes shut and pretended he was a statue in the garden of a stately home. He and Miriam used to love visiting National Trust properties, but only during the week when there were no crowds. He wished the two of them were there now, their feet crunching on gravel paths, marvelling at cabbage white butterflies fluttering among the roses, looking forward to a big slice of Victoria sponge in the tea room.

A lump rose in his throat as he thought about his wife, but he held his pose. He wished he really could be made of stone so he couldn't hurt any more.

Finally the letterbox snapped shut. The purple shape moved away. Arthur let his fingers relax first then his elbows. He wriggled his shoulders to relieve the tension.

Not totally convinced that Bernadette wasn't lurking by the garden gate, he opened his front door an inch. Pressing his eye against the gap, he peered around outside. In the garden opposite. Terry, who wore his hair in dreadlocks tied with a red bandanna and who was forever mowing his lawn, was heaving his mower out of his shed. The two redheaded kids from next door were running

4

up and down the street wearing nothing on their feet. Pigeons had pebble-dashed the windscreen of his disused Micra. Arthur began to feel calmer. Everything was back to normal. Routine was good.

He read the leaflet then placed it carefully with the others that Bernadette had posted for him — 'Friends Indeed', 'Thornapple Residents Association', 'Men in Caves' and 'Diesel Gala Day at North Yorkshire Moors Railway' — then forced himself to go and make a cup of tea.

Bernadette had compromised his morning, thrown him off balance. Flustered, he didn't allow his tea bag enough time in the pot. Sniffing the milk from the fridge, he winced at the smell and poured it down the sink. He would have to take his tea black. It tasted like iron filings. He gave a deep sigh.

Today, he wasn't going to mop the kitchen floor or vacuum the stairs carpet so hard that the threadbare bits grew balder. He wasn't going to polish the bathroom taps and fold the towels into neat squares.

Reaching out, he touched the fat black telescope of bin liners that he'd placed on the kitchen table and reluctantly picked them up. They were heavy. Good for the job.

To make things easier he read through the cat charity leaflet one more time: 'Cat Saviours. All items donated are sold to raise funds for badly treated cats and kittens.'

He wasn't a cat lover himself, especially as they had decimated his rockery, but Miriam liked them even though they made her sneeze.

5

She had saved the leaflet under the telephone and Arthur took this as a sign that this was the charity he should give her belongings to.

Purposefully delaying the task that lay ahead, he climbed the stairs slowly and paused on the first landing. By sorting out her wardrobe it felt as if he was saying goodbye to her all over again. He was clearing her out of his life.

With a tear in his eye, he looked out of the window onto the back garden. If he stood on tiptoe he could just see the tip of York Minster, its stone fingers seeming to prop up the sky. Thornapple village, in which he lived, was just on the outskirts of the city. Cherry blossom had already started to fall from the trees, swirling like pink confetti. The garden was surrounded on three sides by a tall wooden fence that gave privacy; too tall for neighbours to pop their heads over for a chat. He and Miriam liked their own company. They did everything together and that was how they liked it, thank you very much.

There were four raised beds, which he had made out of railway sleepers and which housed rows of beetroots, carrots, onions and potatoes. This year he might even attempt pumpkins. Miriam used to make a grand chicken and vegetable stew with the produce, and home-made soups. But he wasn't a cook. The beautiful red onions he picked last summer had stayed on the kitchen worktop until their skins were as wrinkly as his own and he had thrown them in the recycling bin.

He finally ascended the remainder of the stairs and arrived panting outside the bathroom. He used to be able to speed from top to bottom, running after Lucy and Dan, without any problem. But now, everything was slowing down. His knees creaked and he was sure he was shrivelling. His once-black hair was now dove white (though still so thick it was difficult to keep flat) and the rounded tip of his nose seemed to be growing redder by the day. It was difficult to remember when he stopped being young and became an old man.

He recalled his daughter Lucy's words when they last spoke, a few weeks ago. 'You could do with a clear-out, Dad. You'll feel better when Mum's stuff is gone. You'll be able to move on.' Dan occasionally phoned from Australia, where he now lived with his wife and two children. He was less tactful. 'Just chuck it all out. Don't turn the house into a museum.'

Move on? Like to bloody where? He was sixty-nine, not a teenager who could go to university or on a gap year. *Move on.* He sighed as he shuffled into the bedroom.

Slowly he pulled open the mirrored doors on the wardrobe.

Brown, black and grey. He was confronted by a row of clothes the colour of soil. Funny, he didn't remember Miriam dressing so dully. He had a sudden image of her in his head. She was young and swinging Dan around by an arm and leg — an aeroplane. She was wearing a blue polka dot sundress and white scarf. Her head was tipped back and she was laughing, her mouth inviting him to join in. But the picture vanished as quickly as it came. His last memories of her were the same colour as the clothes in the wardrobe. Grey. She had aluminium-hued hair in the shape of a swimming cap. She had withered away like the onions.

She'd been ill for a few weeks. First it was a chest infection, an annual affliction which saw her laid up in bed for a fortnight on a dose of antibiotics. But this time the infection turned into pneumonia. The doctor prescribed more bed rest and his wife, never one to cause a fuss, had complied.

Arthur had discovered her in bed, staring, lifeless. At first he thought she was watching the birds in the trees, but when he shook her arm she didn't wake up.

Half her wardrobe was devoted to cardigans. They hung shapeless, their arms dangling as if they'd been worn by gorillas, then hung back up again. Then there were Miriam's skirts; navy, grey, beige, mid-calf length. He could smell her perfume, something with roses and lily of the valley, and it made him want to nestle his nose into the nape of her neck, *just one more time please, God*. He often wished this was all a bad dream and that she was sat downstairs doing the *Woman's Weekly* crossword, or writing a letter to one of the friends they had met on their holidays.

He allowed himself to sit on the bed and wallow in self-pity for a few minutes and then swiftly unrolled two bags and shook them open. He *had* to do this. There was a bag for charity and one for stuff to throw out. He took out armfuls of clothes and bundled them in the charity bag. Miriam's slippers — worn and with a hole in the toe — went in the rubbish bag. He worked quickly and silently, not stopping to let emotion get in the way. Halfway through the task and a pair of old grey lace-ups went in the charity bag, followed by an almost identical pair. He pulled out a large shoe box and lifted out a pair of sensible fur-lined brown suede boots.

Remembering one of Bernadette's stories about a pair of boots she'd bought from a flea market and found a lottery ticket (non-winning) inside, he automatically slid his hand inside one boot (empty) and then the other. He was surprised when his fingertips hit something hard. Strange. Wriggling his fingers around the thing, he tugged it out.

He found himself holding a heart-shaped box. It was covered in textured scarlet leather and fastened with a tiny gold padlock. There was something about the colour that made him feel on edge. It looked expensive, frivolous. A present from Lucy, perhaps? No, surely he would have remembered it. And he would never have bought something like this for his wife. She liked simple or useful things, like plain round silver stud earrings or pretty oven gloves. They had struggled with money all their married life, scrimping and squirrelling funds away for a rainy day. When they had eventually splashed out on the kitchen and bathroom, she had only enjoyed them for a short while. No, she wouldn't have bought this box.

He examined the keyhole in the tiny padlock. Then he rummaged around in the bottom of the wardrobe pushing the rest of Miriam's shoes around, mixing up the pairs. But he couldn't find the key. He picked up a pair of nail scissors and jiggled them around in the keyhole, but the lock remained defiantly closed. Curiosity pricked inside him. Not wanting to admit defeat, he went back downstairs. Nearly fifty years as a locksmith and he couldn't bloody get into a heart-shaped box. From the kitchen bottom drawer he took out the two-litre plastic ice cream carton that he used as a tool box; his box of tricks.

Back upstairs, he sat on the bed and took out a hoop full of lock picks. Inserting the smallest one into the keyhole, he gave it a small wriggle. This time there was a click and the box opened by a tantalising few millimetres, like a mouth about to whisper a secret. He unhooked the padlock and lifted the lid.

The box was lined with black crushed velvet. It sang of decadence and wealth. But it was the charm bracelet that lay inside that caused him to catch his breath. It was opulent and gold with chunky round links and a heart-shaped fastener. Another heart.

What was more peculiar was the array of charms, spread out from the bracelet like sun rays in a children's book illustration. There were eight in total: an elephant, a flower, a book, a paint palette, a tiger, a thimble, a heart and a ring.

He took the bracelet out of the box. It was heavy and jangled when he moved it around in his hand. It looked antique, or had age to it, and was finely crafted. The detail on each charm was sharp. But as hard as he tried he couldn't remember Miriam wearing the bracelet or showing any of the charms to him. Perhaps she had bought it as a present for someone else. But for whom? It looked expensive. When Lucy wore jewellery it was new-fangled stuff with curls of silver wire and bits of glass and shell.

He thought for a moment about phoning his children to see if they knew anything about a charm bracelet hidden in their mother's wardrobe. It seemed a valid reason to make contact. But then he told himself to reconsider as they'd be too busy to bother with him. It had been a while since he had phoned Lucy with the excuse of asking how the cooker worked. With Dan, it had been two months since his son had last been in touch. He couldn't believe that Dan was now forty and Lucy was thirty-six. Where had time gone?

They had their own lives now. Where once Miriam was their sun and he their moon, Dan and Lucy were now distant stars in their own galaxies.

The bracelet wouldn't be from Dan anyway. Definitely not. Each year before Miriam's birthday, Arthur phoned his son to remind him of the date. Dan would insist that he hadn't forgotten, that he was about to go to the post box that day and post a little something. And it usually was a *little* something: a fridge magnet in the shape of the Sydney Opera House, a photo of the grandkids, Kyle and Marina, in a cardboard frame, a small koala bear with huggy arms that Miriam clipped to the curtain in Dan's old bedroom.

11

If she was disappointed with the gifts from her son then Miriam never showed it. 'How lovely,' she would exclaim, as if it was the best present she had ever received. Arthur wished that she could be honest, just once, and say that their son should make more effort. But then, even as a boy, he had never been aware of other people and their feelings. He was never happier than when he was dismantling car engines and covered in oil. Arthur was proud that his son owned three car body repair workshops in Sydney, but wished that he could treat people with as much attention as he paid his carburettors.

Lucy was more thoughtful. She sent thank you cards and never, ever forgot a birthday. She had been a quiet child to the point where Arthur and Miriam wondered if she had speech difficulties. But no, a doctor explained that she was just sensitive. She felt things more deeply than other people did. She liked to think a lot and explore her emotions. Arthur told himself that's why she hadn't attended her own mother's funeral. Dan's reason was that he was thousands of miles away. But although Arthur found excuses for them both, it hurt him more than they could ever imagine that his children hadn't been there to say goodbye to Miriam properly. And that's why, when he spoke to them sporadically on the phone, it felt like there was a dam between them. Not only had he lost his wife, but he was losing his children, too.

He squeezed his fingers into a triangle but the bracelet wouldn't slip over his knuckles. He liked the elephant best. It had an upturned trunk and small ears; an Indian elephant. He gave a wry smile at its exoticness. He and Miriam had discussed going abroad for a holiday but then always settled upon Bridlington, at the same bed-and-breakfast on the seafront. If they ever bought a souvenir, it was a packet of tear-off postcards or a new tea towel, not a gold charm.

On the elephant's back was a howdah with a canopy, and inside that nestled a dark green faceted stone. It turned as he fingered it. An emerald? No, of course not, just glass or a pretend precious stone. He ran his finger along the trunk, then felt the elephant's rounded hind before settling on its tiny tail. In places the metal was smooth, in others it felt indented. The closer he looked though, the more blurred the charm became. He needed glasses for reading but could never find the things. He must have five pairs stashed in safe places around the house. He picked up his box of tricks and took out his eyeglass: every year or so it came in handy. After scrunching it into his eye socket, he peered at the elephant. As he moved his head closer then further away to get the right focus, he saw that the indentations were in fact tiny engraved letters and numbers. He read and then read again.

Ayah. 0091 832 221 897

His heart began to beat faster. Ayah. What could that mean? And the numbers too. Were they a map reference, a code? He took a small pencil and pad from his box and wrote them down. His eyeglass dropped onto the bed. He'd watched a quiz programme on TV just last night. The wild-haired presenter had asked the dialling code for making calls from the UK to India — 0091 was the answer.

Arthur fastened the lid back onto the ice cream box and carried the charm bracelet downstairs. There, he looked in his *Oxford English Pocket Dictionary*; the definition of the word 'ayah' didn't make any sense to him — *a nursemaid or maid in East Asia or India.*

He didn't usually phone anyone on a whim; he preferred not to use the phone at all. Calls to Dan and Lucy only brought disappointment. But, even so, he picked up the receiver.

He sat on the one chair he always used at the kitchen table and carefully dialled the number, just to see. This was just silly, but there was something about the curious little elephant that made him want to know more.

It took a long time for the dialling tone to kick in and even longer for someone to answer the call.

'Mehra residence. How may I help you?'

The polite lady had an Indian accent. She sounded very young. Arthur's voice wavered when he spoke. Wasn't this preposterous? 'I'm phoning about my wife,' he said. 'Her name was Miriam Pepper, well it was Miriam Kempster before we married. I've found an elephant charm with this number on it. It was in her wardrobe. I was clearing it out . . . ' He trailed off, wondering what on earth he was doing, what he was saying.

The lady was quiet for a moment. He was sure she was about to hang up or tell him off for making a crank call. But then she spoke. 'Yes. I have heard stories of Miss Miriam Kempster. I'll just find Mr Mehra for you now, sir. He will almost certainly be able to assist you.'

Arthur's mouth fell open.

The Elephant

Arthur gripped the receiver tightly. A voice in his head told him to put it down, to forget about this. Firstly, there was the cost. He was on the phone to India. That couldn't be cheap. Miriam was always so careful about the phone bill, especially with the cost of phoning Dan in Australia.

And then there was the gnawing feeling that he was prying on his wife. Trust had always formed a great part in their marriage. When he travelled around the country selling locks and safes, Miriam had voiced her concerns that on overnight stays he might succumb to the charms of a comely landlady. He had assured her that he would never do anything to jeopardise his marriage or family life. Besides, he wasn't the type that women would find attractive. An ex-girlfriend had compared him to a mole. She said that he was timid and a bit twitchy. But, surprisingly, he *had* been propositioned a few times. Though it was probably because of the loneliness or opportunism of the ladies (and once a man), rather than his own appeal.

Sometimes his working days had been long. He travelled around the country a lot. He especially enjoyed showing off new mortice

locks, explaining the latches, snibs and l[   ]
his clients. There was something about lo[   ]
intrigued him. They were solid and reliab[   ]
protected you and kept you safe. He loved how
his car always smelled of oil and he enjoyed
chatting to his customers in their shops. But then
along came the internet and online ordering.
Locksmiths didn't need salesmen any longer.
The shops that remained open started to order
their stock by computer and Arthur found
himself confined to a desk job. He used the
phone to talk to his clients rather than talking
face-to-face. He had never liked the phone. You
couldn't see people smiling or their eyes when
they asked questions.

It was hard being away from the kids too,
sometimes getting home when they were already
in bed. Lucy understood, delighted to see him
the next morning. She would fling her arms
around his neck and tell him she missed him.
Dan was trickier. On the rare occasion that
Arthur finished work early, Dan seemed to
resent it. 'I like my time with Mum better,' he
once said. Miriam told Arthur not to take it to
heart. Some kids were closer to one parent than
the other. It didn't stop Arthur from feeling
guilty about working so hard to provide for his
family.

Miriam had vowed that she would always be
faithful, no matter what hours he worked, and he
trusted that she had been. She never gave him
cause to think otherwise. He never saw her flirt
with other men or found any evidence that she
might ever have strayed. Not that he was looking

or it. But sometimes when he got home after working away, he wondered if she'd had company. It must have been hard being alone with the two kids. Not that she ever complained. She was a real trouper was Miriam.

Swallowing a lump that formed in his throat as he thought about his family, he began to move his ear away from the receiver. His hand trembled. Best just to leave this be. Hang up. But then he heard a tinny voice calling out to him. 'Hello. Mr Mehra speaking. I understand that you are phoning about Miriam Kempster, yes?'

Arthur swallowed. His mouth had gone dry. 'Yes, that's right. My name is Arthur Pepper. Miriam is my wife.' It felt wrong to say that Miriam *was* my wife, because although she was no longer here they were still married, weren't they?

He explained how he'd found a charm bracelet and the elephant charm with the engraved number. He had not expected anyone to answer his call. Then he told Mr Mehra that his wife was now dead.

Mr Mehra fell silent. It was over a minute before he spoke again. 'Oh, my dear sir. I am so sorry. She looked after me so well when I was a boy. But that was many years ago now. I still live in the same house! There is little movement in our family. We have the same phone number. I am a doctor and my father and grandfather were doctors before me. I have never forgotten Miriam's kindness. I hoped that one day I might find her again. I should have tried harder.'

'She looked after you?'

18

'Yes. She was my *ayah*. She looked after me and my younger sisters.'

'Your childminder? Here in England?'

'No, sir. In India. I live in Goa.'

Arthur couldn't speak. His mind went numb. He knew nothing of this. Miriam had never mentioned living in India. How could this be? He stared at the pot pourri stuffed leaf in the hallway twirling and hanging by a thread.

'May I tell you a little about her, sir?'

'Yes. Please do,' he murmured. Anything to fill in some gaps, tell him that this must be some other Miriam Kempster they were talking about.

Mr Mehra's voice was soothing and authoritative. Arthur didn't think about his phone bill. More than anything he wanted to hear from someone else who might have known and loved Miriam, even if this man was a stranger to him. Sometimes not talking about her made it feel like her memory was fading away.

'We had many *ayahs* before Miriam joined us. I was a naughty child. I played tricks on them. I put newts in their shoes and chilli flakes in their soup. They didn't last long. But Miriam was different. She ate the hot food and didn't say a word. She picked the newts out of her shoes and put them back in the garden. I studied her face but she was a fine actress. She never gave anything away and I didn't know if she was annoyed with me, or amused. Slowly I gave up teasing her. There was no point. She knew all my tricks! I remember that she had a bag of wonderful marbles. They were as shiny as the moon and one was like a real tiger's eye. She

19

didn't care if she kneeled in the dust.' He gave a throaty laugh. 'I was a little in love with her.'

'How long did she stay with your family?'

'For a few months, in India. I was very broken-hearted when she left. It was my entire fault. That is something I have never told anyone before. But you, Mr Pepper, deserve to know. It is a shame I have carried with me for all these years.'

Arthur shifted nervously in his seat.

'Do you mind if I tell you? It would mean a great deal to me. It is like a secret burning a hole in my stomach.' Mr Mehra didn't wait for a response before he carried on his story. 'I was only eleven but I loved Miriam. It was the first time I had noticed a girl. She was so pretty and always wore such classy clothes. Her laughter, well, it sounded like tiny bells. When I woke up in the morning she was the first thing I thought about and when I went to bed I looked forward to the next day. I know now that this was not true love like when I met my wife, Priya, but for a young boy it was very real. She was very different to the girls I went to school with. She was exotic, with her alabaster skin and hair the colour of walnuts. Her eyes were like aquamarines. I probably followed her around a little too much, but she never made me feel foolish. My mother had died when I was very young and I used to ask Miriam to sit with me in her room. We would look through my mother's jewellery box together. She loved the elephant charm. We used to look through the emerald and see the world in green.'

So, it is a real emerald, Arthur thought.

'But then Miriam began to go out on her own twice a week. We spent a little less time together. I was old enough not to need an *ayah* but my two sisters did. She was there for them but not so much for me. I followed her one day and she met with a man. He was a teacher at my school. An English man. He came around to the house and he and Miriam took afternoon tea. I saw that he liked her. He picked a hibiscus flower from the garden to give to her.

'Mr Pepper. I was a young boy. I was growing and had hormones roaring around my body. I felt very angry. I told my father that I had seen Miriam and the man kissing. My father was a very old-fashioned man and he had already lost one *ayah* because of similar circumstances. So there and then he went to find Miriam and told her to leave. She was so surprised but she acted with dignity and packed her suitcase.

'I was devastated. I had not meant this to happen. I took the elephant from the jewellery box and ran to the village to have it engraved. I pushed it into the front pocket of her suitcase as it stood by the door. I was too much of a coward to say goodbye, but she found me hiding and gave me a kiss. She said, 'Goodbye, dearest Rajesh.' And I never saw her again.

'From that day, Mr Pepper, I swear I have tried never to tell a lie. I only tell the truth. It is the only way. I prayed that she could forgive me. Did she say that to you?'

Arthur knew nothing about this part of his wife's life. But he knew this was the same woman that they had both loved. Miriam's laughter did sound like tiny bells. She did have a bag of marbles, which she gave to Dan. He was still reeling from astonishment, but he could hear the longing in Mr Mehra's voice. He cleared his throat. 'Yes, she forgave you long ago. She spoke of you kindly.'

Mr Mehra laughed out loud. A short 'Ha ha!' Then he said, 'Mr Pepper! You have no idea how happy your words make me feel. For years this has felt like a huge weight for me. Thank you for taking the trouble to ring me. I am so sorry to hear that Miriam is no longer with you.'

Arthur felt a glow in his stomach. It was something that he hadn't felt for a long time. He felt useful.

'You were a lucky man to be married for so long, yes? To have a wife such as Miriam. Did she have a happy life, sir?'

'Yes. Yes, I think she did. It was a quiet life. We have two lovely children.'

'Then you must try to be happy. Would she want you to be sad?'

'No. But it's hard not to be.'

'I know this. But there is much to celebrate about her.'

'Yes.'

Both men fell silent.

Arthur turned the bracelet around in his hand. He now knew about the elephant. But what about the other charms? If he didn't know about Miriam's life in India, what stories did the other charms hold? He asked Mr Mehra if he knew anything about the bracelet.

'I only gave her the elephant. She did write to me once, a few months after she left, to say thank you. I'm a sentimental fool and I still have the letter. I always told myself that I would get in touch, but I felt too ashamed about my lie. I can see what address is on the letter if you like?'

Arthur swallowed. 'That would be most kind.'

He waited for five minutes until Mr Mehra returned to the call. He reached out to stop the pot pourri leaf from twirling. He flicked through the leaflets Bernadette had posted through the door.

'Ah, yes, here it is — Graystock Manor in Bath, England, 1963. I hope this helps with your search. She talks in the letter about staying with friends there. There's something about tigers in the grounds.'

'There is a tiger charm on the bracelet,' Arthur said.

'Aha. Then that might be your next port of call. You will find out the stories of the charms one by one, yes?'

'Oh, this isn't a search,' Arthur started. 'I was just curious . . .'

'Well, if you are ever in India, Mr Pepper, you must look me up. I will show you the places that Miriam loved. And her old room. It hasn't changed much over the years. You would like to see it?'

'That's very decent of you. Though I'm afraid I've never left the UK before. I can't see myself travelling to India any time soon.'

'There is always a first time, Mr Pepper. You bear my offer in mind, sir.'

Arthur said goodbye and thank you for the invitation. As he placed the receiver down, Mr Mehra's words rolled over and over in his head: . . . . *next port of call . . . finding out the stories of the charms one by one . . .*

And he began to wonder.

The Great Escape

It was still dark the next morning when Arthur woke. The digits on his alarm clock flicked to 5:32 a.m. and he lay for a while staring at the ceiling. Outside a car drove past and he watched the reflection of the headlights sweep over the ceiling like the rays of a lighthouse across water. He let his fingers creep across the mattress, reaching out for Miriam's hand knowing it wasn't there and feeling only cool cotton sheet.

Each night, when he went to bed, it struck him how chilly it was without her. When she was next to him he always slept through the night, gently drifting off, then waking to the sound of thrushes singing outside. She would shake her head and ask did he not hear the thunderstorm or next door's house alarm going off? But he never did.

Now his sleep was fitful, restless. He woke up often, shivering and wrapping the duvet around him in a cocoon. He should put an extra blanket on the bed, to stop the cold from creeping around his back and numbing his feet. His body had found its own strange rhythm of sleeping, waking, shivering, sleeping, waking, shivering, which, although uncomfortable, he didn't want to shake. He didn't want to drop off and then wake with the birds and find that Miriam was no longer there. Even now that would be too much of a shock. Stirring through the night reminded him that she had gone and he welcomed those constant reminders. He didn't want to risk forgetting her.

If he had to describe in one word how he felt this morning, it would be *perplexed*. Getting rid of Miriam's clothes was going to be a ritual, freeing the house of her things, her shoes, her toiletries. It was a small step in coping with his loss and moving on.

But the newly-discovered charm bracelet was an obstacle to his intentions. It raised questions where once there were none. It had opened a door and he had stepped through it.

He and Miriam differed in how they saw mysteries. They regularly enjoyed a Miss Marple or a Hercule Poirot on a Sunday afternoon. Arthur would watch intently. 'Do you think it's him?' he would say. 'He's being very helpful and his character adds nothing to the story. I think he might be the killer.'

'Watch the film.' Miriam would squeeze his knee. 'Just enjoy it. You don't have to psychoanalyse all the characters. You don't have to guess the ending.'

'But, it's a mystery. It's supposed to make you guess. We're supposed to try and work it out.'

Miriam would laugh and shake her head.

If this were the other way round and (he hated to think this) he had died, Miriam might not have given finding a strange object in Arthur's wardrobe much thought. Whereas here he was, his brain whirring like a child's windmill in the garden.

He creaked out of bed and took a shower, letting the hot water bounce off his face. Then he dried himself off, had a shave, put on his grey trousers, blue shirt and mustard tank top and headed downstairs. Miriam liked it when he wore these clothes. She said they made him look *presentable*.

For the first weeks after she died, he couldn't even be bothered getting dressed. Who was there to make an effort for? With his wife and children gone, why should he care? He wore his pyjamas day and night. For the first time in his life he grew a beard. When he saw himself in the bathroom mirror he was surprised at his resemblance to Captain Birdseye. He shaved it off.

He left radios on in each room so he wouldn't have to hear his own footsteps. He survived on yoghurts and cans of soup, which he didn't bother to heat. A spoon and a can opener were all he needed. He found himself small jobs to do: tightening the bolts on the bed to stop it squeaking, scratching out the blackened grout around the bath.

Miriam kept a fern on the windowsill in the kitchen. It was a moth-eaten thing with drooping feathery leaves. He despised it at first, resenting how such a pathetic thing could live when his wife had died. It had sat on the floor by the back door waiting for bin day. But, out of guilt, he relented and set it back in its place. He named it Frederica and began to water and talk to it. And slowly she perked up. She no longer drooped. Her leaves grew greener. It felt good to nurture

27

something. He found it easier to chat to the plant than to people. It was good for him to keep busy. It meant he didn't have time to be sad.

Well, that's what he told himself, anyway. But then he'd be going about his daily tasks, kind of doing okay, holding it together. Then he'd spy the green pot pourri fabric leaf hanging in the hallway or Miriam's mud-encrusted walking shoes in the pantry, or the lavender Crabtree & Evelyn hand cream on the shelf in the bathroom — and it would feel like a landslide. Such small meaningless items now tore at his heart.

He would sit on the bottom step of the stairs and hold his head in his hands. Rocking backward and forward, squeezing his eyes shut, he told himself that he was bound to feel like this. His grief was still raw. It would pass. She was in a better place. She wouldn't want him to be like this. *Blah blah*. All the usual mumbo-jumbo from Bernadette's leaflets. And it did pass. But it never vanished completely. He carried his loss around with him like a bowling ball in the pit of his stomach.

At these times he imagined his own father, stern, strong: 'Bloody 'ell. Pull yerself together, lad. Crying's for sissies,' and he would lift his chin and try to be brave.

Perhaps he should be getting over it by now.

His recollections of those dark early days were foggy. What he did recall was like seeing it on a black-and-white TV set with a crackly picture. He saw himself shuffling around the house.

If he was honest, then Bernadette had been a great help. She had turned up on his doorstep like an unwelcome genie and insisted that he bathed while she cooked lunch. Arthur hadn't wanted to eat. Food held no taste or pleasure for him.

'Your body is like a steam train that needs coal,' Bernadette said as he protested against the pies, soups and stews she carried over his threshold, heated and then placed in front of him. 'How are you going to carry on your journey without fuel?'

Arthur wasn't planning any journey. He didn't want to leave the house. The only trip he made was upstairs to use the bathroom or go to bed. He had no desire to do anything more than that. For a quiet life he ate her food, blocked out her chatter, read her leaflets. He really would prefer to be left alone.

But she persisted. Sometimes he answered the door to her, other times he wriggled down in the bed and pulled the blankets over his head or thrust himself into National Trust statue mode. But she never gave up on him.

* * *

Later that morning, as if she knew he was thinking of her, Bernadette rang his doorbell. Arthur stood in the dining room, still for a few moments, wondering whether to go to the door. The air smelled of bacon and eggs and fresh toast as the other residents of Bank Avenue enjoyed their breakfasts. The doorbell rang again.

'Her husband Carl died recently,' Miriam had

29

told him, a few years ago, as she spied Bernadette on a stall at a local church fete, selling butterfly buns and chocolate cake. 'I think that bereaved people act in one of two ways. There are those who cling with their fingertips to the past, and those who brush their hands together and get on with their lives. That lady with the red hair is the latter. She keeps herself busy.'

'Do you know her?'

'She works at LadyBLovely, the boutique in the village. I bought a navy dress from there. It has tiny pearl buttons. She told me that, in her husband's memory, she was going to help others through her baking. She said that if people are tired, lonely, heartbroken, or have simply run out of steam, then they need food. I think it's very courageous of her to make it her mission to help others.'

From then on Arthur noticed Bernadette more — at the local school summer fair, in the post office, in her dressing gown tending roses in her garden. They said *hello* to each other and not much else. Sometimes he saw Bernadette and Miriam chatting on the street corner. They would laugh and talk about the weather and how strawberries were sweet this year. Bernadette's voice was so loud that he could hear the conversation from inside the house.

Bernadette had attended Miriam's funeral. He had a hazy memory of her appearing beside him and patting his arm. 'If you ever need anything, just ask,' she said and Arthur wondered what he might possibly ever ask her for. Then she had started to turn up announced on his doorstep.

At first he felt irritated by her presence, then he began to worry that she had set her sights on him, perhaps as a potential second husband. He wasn't looking for anything like that. He never could do after Miriam. But in all the months she had been knocking on his door, Bernadette hadn't ever given him cause to think her attention was anything more than platonic. She had a full roster of widows and widowers to call upon.

'Mince and onion pie,' she greeted him as he opened up. 'Freshly made.' She let herself into the hallway, pie-first. There, she ran her finger along the shelf over the radiator and nodded with satisfaction that it was dust free. She sniffed the air. 'It's a bit musty in here. Do you have air freshener?'

Arthur marvelled at how impolite she could be without realising and dutifully fetched one. A few seconds later and the cloying smell of Mountain Lavender filled the air.

She bustled into the kitchen and put the pie down on the worktop. 'This is a mighty fine kitchen,' she said.

'I know.'

'The cooker is wondrous.'

'I know.'

Bernadette was the polar opposite to Miriam. His wife had sparrow bones. Bernadette was fleshy, cushioned. Her hair was dyed post-box red and she wore diamanté studs on the tips of her nails. One of her front teeth was stained yellow. Her voice was big, cutting through the

31

quiet of his home like a machete. He jangled the bracelet nervously in his pocket. Since speaking to Mr Mehra last night, he had kept it with him. He had studied each charm in turn several times.

India. It was so far away. It must have been such an adventure for Miriam. Why had she not wanted him to know? Surely Mr Mehra's story wasn't enough for her to keep it secret.

'Are you okay, Arthur? You're in a dream world.' Bernadette's words broke his thoughts.

'Me? Yes, of course.'

'I called yesterday morning but you weren't in. Did you go to *Men in Caves*?'

Men in Caves was a community group for single men. Arthur had been twice to find a group of men with gloomy expressions handling chunks of wood and tools. The man who ran it, Bobby, was shaped like a skittle with a tiny head and large body. 'Men need caves,' he trilled. 'They need somewhere to retreat to and be at one with themselves.'

Arthur's neighbour with the dreadlocks had been there. Terry. He was busy filing a piece of wood. 'I like your car,' Arthur said to be polite.

'It's actually a tortoise.'

'Oh.'

'I saw one last week when I was mowing my lawn.'

'A wild one?'

'It belongs to the red-haired kids who wear nothing on their feet. It escaped.'

Arthur didn't know what to say. He had enough trouble with cats on his rockery without a tortoise being on the loose too. Returning to his own work, he made a wooden plaque with the number of his house on it — 37. The 3 was much bigger than the 7 but he hung it on his back door anyway.

It would have been easy to say yes, he was at *Men in Caves*, even though it had been too early in the morning. But Bernadette was standing and smiling at him. The pie smelled delicious. He didn't want to lie to her, especially after hearing Mr Mehra's regret over telling lies about Miriam. He would do the same and try not to he again. 'I hid from you yesterday,' he said.

'You *hid*?'

'I didn't want to see anyone. I'd set myself the task to clear out Miriam's wardrobe and so when you rang the doorbell, I stood very still in the hallway and pretended not to be at home.' The words tumbled off his tongue and it felt surprisingly good to be this honest. 'Yesterday was the first anniversary of her death.'

'That's very truthful of you, Arthur. I appreciate your honesty. I can see how that would be upsetting. When Carl died . . . well, it was a hard thing to let him go. I gave his tools to *Men in Caves*.'

Arthur felt his heart dip. He hoped that she wouldn't tell him about her husband. He didn't want to trade stories of death. There seemed to be a strange one-upmanship amongst people who had lost spouses. Only last week in the post office he had witnessed what he would describe as boasting amongst a group of four pensioners.

— 'My wife suffered for ten years before she eventually passed away.'

— 'Really? Well, my Cedric was flattened by a lorry. The paramedics said they'd never seen anything like it. Like a pancake, one said.'

— Then a man's voice, breaking. 'It was the drugs, I reckon. Twenty-three tablets a day they gave her. She almost rattled.'

— 'When they cut him open there was nothing left inside. The cancer had eaten him all up.'

They talked about their loved ones as if they were objects. Miriam would always be a real person to him. He wouldn't trade her memory like that.

'She likes lost causes,' Vera, the post office mistress, said to him as he took a pack of small brown manila envelopes to the counter. She always wore a pencil tucked into her round tortoiseshell glasses and made it her business to know everything and everyone in the village. Her mother had owned the post office before her and had been exactly the same.

'Who does?'

'Bernadette Patterson. We've noticed that she brings you pies.'

'*Who* has noticed?' Arthur said, feeling angry. 'Is there a club whose role it is to pry into my life?'

'No, just my customers having a friendly information exchange. That's what Bernadette does. She's kind to the hopeless, helpless and useless.'

Arthur paid for his envelopes and marched out.

He stood and switched on the kettle. 'I'm giving Miriam's things to *Cat Saviours*. They sell

34

clothes, ornaments and things to raise money to help mistreated cats.'

'That's a nice idea, though I prefer small dogs myself. They're much more appreciative.'

'I think Miriam wanted to help cats.'

'Then that's what you must do. Shall I pop this pie in the oven for you? We can have lunch together. Unless you have other plans . . . '

He was about to murmur something about being busy but then remembered Mr Mehra's story again. He had no plans. 'No, nothing in the diary,' he said.

Twenty minutes later as he dug his knife into the pie, he thought about the bracelet again. Bernadette could give him a woman's perspective. He wanted someone to tell him that it was of no significance and that, although it looked expensive, you could buy good reproductions cheaply these days. But he knew the emerald in the elephant was real. And she might gossip about it to Post Office Vera and to her lost causes.

'You should get out more,' she said. 'You only went to *Men in Caves* once.'

'I went twice. I do get out.'

She raised an eyebrow. 'Like to where?'

'Is this *Mastermind*? I don't remember applying.'

'I'm just trying to take care of you.'

She saw him as a lost cause, just as Vera had implied.

He didn't want to feel like this, be treated like this. An urge swelled in his chest. He needed to say something so she wouldn't think him

35

helpless, hopeless and useless, like Mrs Monton who hadn't left her house in five years and who smoked twenty Woodbines a day, or Mr Flowers who thought there was a unicorn living in his greenhouse. Arthur had some pride left. He used to have meaning as a father and a husband. He used to have thoughts and dreams and plans.

Thinking of the forwarding address Miriam had left on her letter to Mr Mehra, he cleared his throat. 'Well, if you must know,' he said hurriedly, 'I've been thinking about going to Graystock Manor in Bath.'

'Oh yes,' Bernadette mused. 'That's where the tigers roam free.'

Bernadette was a one-woman almanac of the UK. She and Carl had toured everywhere together in their luxury campervan. The back of Arthur's neck bristled as he prepared to hear where he should and shouldn't go, what he should and shouldn't do, at Graystock.

As she busied herself in his kitchen, straightening his scales and checking that his knives were clean enough, Bernadette recited what she knew.

No, Arthur didn't know that five years ago Lord Graystock had been mauled by a tiger, which sank its teeth and claws into his calf, and now he walked with a limp. He also didn't know that, as a younger man, Graystock kept a harem of women of all nationalities, like a hedonistic Noah's ark, or that he was renowned for hosting wild orgies at his manor in the sixties. He also didn't know that the lord only wore the colour electric blue, even his underwear, because he had once been told in a dream that it was lucky. (Arthur wondered if he had been wearing electric blue during the tiger attack.)

He also now knew that Lord Graystock tried to sell his manor to Richard Branson; however the two men had fallen out and refused to speak to each other ever again. The lord was now a recluse and only opened up Graystock Manor on Fridays and Saturdays and the public were no longer allowed to look at the tigers.

After Bernadette's tales, Arthur now felt well informed about Lord Graystock's life and times.

'It's just the gift shop and gardens that are open now. And they're a bit tatty.' Bernadette finished cleaning Arthur's mixer taps with a flourish. 'Why are you going there?'

Arthur looked at his watch. He wished he hadn't said anything now. She had taken twenty-five minutes to regale him. His left leg had grown stiff. 'I thought it would be a nice change,' he said.

'Well, actually, Nathan and I are going to be down in Worcester and Cheltenham next week. We're looking at universities. Tag along if you like. You could head off to Graystock on the train from there.'

Arthur's stomach felt fizzy. Going to Graystock had only been a mild consideration for him. He hadn't actually planned to go there. He only went on outings with Miriam. What was the point of going alone? He had only mentioned going to Graystock to show Bernadette that he wasn't useless. Now apprehension nagged him. He wished he could turn back the clock and not have pushed his hand into the boot and discovered the bracelet. Then he would never have phoned the number on the elephant. He wouldn't be sitting here discussing Graystock Manor with Bernadette. 'I'm not sure about it,' he said. 'Another time perhaps . . . '

'You should go. Try to move on with your life. Small steps. An outing might do you good.'

Arthur was surprised to feel a tiny kernel of excitement taking root in his stomach. He had found out something about his wife's past life and his inquisitive nature was compelling him to find out more. The only feelings he experienced these days were sadness, disappointment and melancholy, so this felt new. 'I like the idea of tigers walking around an English garden,' he said.

And he did like tigers. They were strong majestic colourful beasts, prowling around with the key purposes in life of hunting, eating and mating. Humans were so different with their lives of meekness and worry.

'Really? I'd have you down more as a small dog person, you know a terrier or something. Or you look like the kind of person who would like hamsters. Anyway, why don't you come with us in the car? Nathan is driving.'

'Are you not taking the campervan?'

'I'm selling it. It's too big for me to handle and I've been paying for storage since Carl died. Nathan's got a Fiesta. It's a rust bucket but reliable.'

'Shouldn't you ask him first? He might have other plans . . . ' Arthur instinctively found himself trying to get out of the trip. He should have kept his mouth shut. He couldn't carry out his daily chores if he went away. His timings would be up the shoot. Who would care for Frederica the fern and stop the cats crapping in his garden? If he went down south then he might have to stay overnight. He had never packed his own suitcase before. Miriam did that kind of thing for him . . . His brain ticked away trying to find excuses. He didn't want to pry on his wife but he did want to discover more about her life before they met.

'No, no. Nathan doesn't really do thinking. I do it all for him. It will do him good to have some self-responsibility. He won't have remembered that he has to look at universities. I know he won't need to apply for a few months but I want to start early. I will be so lonely when he goes. It will be strange being on my own again. I dread to think how he'll cope away from me. I'll visit him in his student digs and find his skeleton because he's forgotten to eat . . . '

Arthur had been about to say that, now he thought about it, he might go later in the year. He already knew that he didn't want to go on a trip with Bernadette and her son. He had met Nathan briefly once before when he and Miriam had bumped into Bernadette at a coffee morning. He seemed like a monosyllabic kind of young man. Arthur really didn't want to leave the security of his house, the smothering comfort of his routine.

But then Bernadette said, 'When Nathan leaves, I will be all on my own. A lonely widow.

Still, at least I have you and my other friends, Arthur. You're like family to me.'

Guilt twisted his gut. She sounded lonely. It was a word he would never have used to describe her. Every cautious nerve in his body told him not to go to Graystock. But he wondered what connection Miriam had there. It seemed a highly unlikely address for her. But then so was India. Lord Graystock sounded an intriguing character and his family had owned the manor for years, so there was a possibility that he might know or remember Miriam. He might know the stories behind more of the charms. Could Arthur really expect to be able to forget all about the charm bracelet, to put it back in its box and not discover more about his wife as a young woman?

'Do you mind if I'm honest with you?' Bernadette said. She sat down beside him and wrung a tea towel in her hands.

'Er, no . . . '

'It's been difficult for Nathan since Carl died. He doesn't say much but I can tell. It would be good for him to have a little male company. He has his friends but, well, it's not the same. If you could give him a bit of advice or guidance while we're travelling . . . I think that would do him good.'

It took all his might for Arthur not to shake his head. He thought about Nathan with his runner-bean body and black hair that hung over one eye like a mortuary curtain. When they met, the boy had hardly spoken over his coffee and cake. Now Bernadette was expecting Arthur to have a man-to-man talk with him. 'Oh, he won't

40

listen to me,' he said lightly. 'We've only met the once.'

'I think he would. All he hears is me telling him what and what not to do. I think it would do him the world of good.'

Arthur took a good look at Bernadette. He usually averted his eyes, but this time he took in her scarlet hair: her dark grey roots were springing through. The corners of her mouth drooped downwards. She really wanted him to say yes.

He could take Miriam's things to the charity shop. He could put the bracelet back in his wardrobe and forget about it. That would be the easy option. But there were two things stopping him. One, was the mystery of it. Like one of the Sunday afternoon detective stories that he and Miriam watched, finding the stories behind the charms on the bracelet would nag at his brain. He could find out more about his wife and feel close to her. And the second was Bernadette. In the many times she had called around with her pies and kind words, she had never once asked for anything in return — not money, not a favour, not to listen to her talk about Carl. But now she was asking him for something.

He knew that she would never insist, but he could tell by the way she sat before him, turning her wedding ring around and around on her finger, that this was important to her. She wanted Arthur to accompany her and Nathan on their trip. She needed him.

He rocked a little in his chair, telling himself that he had to do this. He had to silence the nagging voices in his head telling him not to go. 'I think a trip to Graystock would do me good,' he said before he could change his mind. 'And I think me and Nathan will get along just swell. Count me in.'

On the Way

Nathan Patterson existed in that he had a body and a head and arms and legs. But Arthur wasn't sure if there were any thoughts inside him making his body operate. He walked like he was on an airport conveyer belt, looking as if he was gliding. He was reed thin and dressed in tight black jeans that hung off his hips, a black T-shirt with a skull on it and bright white training shoes. His fringe obscured most of his face.

'Hello, Nathan. It's very nice to meet you again,' Arthur said brightly and offered his hand as they stood together on the pavement outside Bernadette's house. 'We met at a coffee morning once, do you remember?'

Nathan looked at him as if he was an alien. His hands hung by his sides. 'Nah.'

'Oh well, it was only briefly. I understand that you're looking at universities. You must be a very smart young man.'

Nathan turned his head and looked away. He opened the car door and got into the driver's seat without speaking. Arthur stared after him. This could be a long journey. 'I'll sit in the back, shall I?' he said, to no response as he got in the car. 'Give you and your mum a chance to talk in the front.'

Arthur had wheeled his suitcase over to Bernadette's house after lunch. He had given Frederica extra water and felt quite guilty leaving her behind. 'It will just be for a couple of days,' he muttered as he gave her leaves a wipe with a damp cloth. 'You'll be fine. Me and you, we can't just sit around any longer. Well, you can. But I have to go. I'm going to find things about Miriam that I didn't know. I think you would want this for me.' He examined Frederica for a sign, a shake of her leaves or a bubble of water in her soil, but there was nothing.

He packed a spare shirt and underwear, his toiletries, cotton pyjamas, an emergency carrier bag and a sachet of hot chocolate. Bernadette had booked him a single room at the Cheltenham bed and breakfast they were staying at that night. 'It looks nice,' she said. 'Some rooms have a view of Cheltenham Minster. It will just be like being in York, Arthur. So you won't feel homesick.'

Bernadette bustled out of her house. She wheeled out a navy blue suitcase and then a purple one, followed by four Marks and Spencer carrier bags.

Arthur wound the window down. He assumed that Nathan would rush out to help, but the young man sat with his feet on the dashboard eating a bag of crisps. 'Do you need a hand?'

'I'm fine. I'll just load this little lot into the boot then we can set off.' She slammed the boot door shut then took the front seat next to Nathan. 'Now, do you know where we're going?'

'Yes,' her son sighed.

'It should take us around three hours to get to our accommodation,' Bernadette said.

In the car Nathan turned up the radio so loud that Arthur couldn't think. Rock music blared out. A male singer screamed about wanting to kill his girlfriend. Periodically, Bernadette turned and gave Arthur a smile and mouthed, 'Okay?'

Arthur nodded and gave a thumbs-up. He was already tense about changing his morning routine. He hadn't shaved and he didn't remember washing out his teacup. When he got back from the trip it would have a thick collar of beige gunk inside. Perhaps he had over-watered Frederica. Had he swept up the crumbs from the worktop? He shuddered at the thought. And he had locked the front door properly, hadn't he?

To cancel out his worries, he tucked his hand in his pocket and wrapped his fingers around the heart-shaped box. He stroked the textured leather and felt the small padlock. It felt comforting to have something that belonged to his wife so close to him, even if he didn't know where it had come from.

As they drove along tree-lined roads toward the motorway, Arthur felt his eyes shutting. He widened them but then slowly they flickered and closed again. The shush of tyres on tarmac lulled him to sleep.

He dreamed that he was on a picnic with Miriam, Lucy and Dan at the seaside. He couldn't recall which town. Lucy and Dan were still young enough to be excited by a trip to the sea and a 99 ice cream. 'Come and have a paddle, Dad.' Dan tugged his hand. Sunlight

45

rippled like silver sweet papers on the surface of the sea. The air smelled of freshly cooked doughnuts and vinegar from the food vans on the promenade. Seagulls cawed and swooped overhead. The sun shone hot and bright.

'Yes, come on in, Arthur.' Miriam stood facing him. The sun was behind her and she looked as if she had a golden halo in her hair. He admired the silhouette of her legs through her translucent white dress. He sat on the sand, his trousers rolled up to his ankles. Perspiration formed under his mustard tank top.

'I'm a bit tired,' he said. 'I'll just have a lie down on the sand and watch you three. I'll catch up on the day's news.' He patted his newspaper.

'You can do that anytime. Come on in with us. We can relax tonight when the kids are in bed.'

Arthur smiled. 'I'll just stay here. You and the kids go paddle.' He reached up and ruffled Lucy's hair.

His wife and two kids stood and stared at him for a few seconds before giving up on their persuasion. He watched as they held hands and ran toward the sea. For a moment he almost stood up and raced after them, but they disappeared into a sea of beach umbrellas and coloured towels. He took off his tank top, rolled it up and put it under his head.

But because this was a dream, he was able to rewind events in his head. This time when his wife stood before him inviting him to paddle, he said yes. Because he knew he might never have this moment again. Because he knew that his time with the kids was precious, and in the future Dan would live thousands of miles away and Lucy would be distant. He knew there would be so many times over the coming years that he would long to be on the beach with his family again.

So this time, in his dream, he stood up and took Dan's and Lucy's small clammy, sandy hands in his own. They ran down the sand together, the four of them in a line, laughing and squealing. And he kicked the sea until it soaked his trousers to the thighs and made his lips salty. Miriam waded toward him. She laughed and trailed her fingertips in the water. Lucy clung to his legs and Dan sat with the sea lapping around his waist. Arthur wrapped an arm around his wife's waist and pulled her close to him. He saw that freckles had sprung to life on her nose and she had pink sun circles on her cheeks. There was nowhere he wanted to be more than this. He leaned in toward her, feeling her breath on his mouth and . . .

'Arthur. *Arthur!*'

He felt a hand on his knee. '*Miriam?*' He opened his eyes. His time with his wife and children vanished abruptly. Bernadette was leaning over from her front seat. Her door was open. He could see expanses of grey tarmac. 'You dropped off. We're at the services. I need to spend a penny.'

'Oh.' Arthur blinked, readjusting to the real world. He could still feel Miriam's hand in his. He wanted to be with her so badly, to kiss her lips. He wriggled out of his slump. 'Where are we?'

47

'We've almost reached Birmingham already. The roads are quiet. Come on out and stretch your legs.'

He did as he was told and got out of the car. He had been asleep for two hours. As he walked toward the grey slab of a building, he wished that he could slip back into his dream to be with his family again. It had seemed so real. Why hadn't he appreciated those moments when they were happening?

He meandered around WHSmith and bought a *Daily Mail* and then a coffee in a cardboard cup from a machine outside. It tasted of soil. The lobby rang with the sound of amusement machines, their coloured lights flashing and piping out jaunty electronic music. He could smell fried onion rings and bleach. He carefully placed his half-drunk coffee in the bin and went to the loo.

Back at the car he found himself alone with Nathan.

The boy was sitting with his feet on the dashboard again, displaying an expanse of milky ankle. In the back Arthur opened up his paper. There was going to be a heatwave over the next couple of days. The hottest May in decades. He thought of Frederica's soil and hoped it would stay moist.

Nathan took a yellow curl from his packet of crisps. After taking the longest time that Arthur had known anyone eat a crisp, he finally said: 'So are you and my mum, *you know* . . . ?'

Arthur waited for the next part of the sentence, which didn't arrive. 'I'm sorry, I . . . '

'You and Mum. Are you, y'know, getting it on?' He then affected a posh accent as he turned to face Arthur. 'Are you *dating*?'

'No.' Arthur tried not to sound aghast. He wondered how Nathan could possibly have got this idea. 'Definitely not. We're just friends.'

Nathan nodded sagely. 'So, you have a separate room at the B and B?'

'Of course I have.'

'I was just wondering.'

'We are definitely *just* friends.'

'I've noticed that she makes you the savoury stuff, pies and shit. Her others only get sweet things.'

Her other *lost causes*, Arthur thought. Mad Mr Flowers, housebound Mrs Monton and Co. 'I really appreciate your mother's efforts for me. I've been going through a tough time and she's been a great help. I prefer savoury to sweet.'

'Oh, yeah.' Nathan finished munching his crisps. He folded up the packet, tied it into a knot, then positioned it beneath his nose and wore it as a moustache. 'My mum gets off on helping people. She's a real saint.'

Arthur didn't know if he was being sarcastic or not.

'Your wife. She died, didn't she?' Nathan said.

'Yes, she did.'

'That must've been pretty shit, huh?'

For a second, Arthur felt like jumping over the seats into the front of the car and ripping the crisp packet out from under Nathan's nose. How easily young people could dismiss death, as if it was some far-off country that they'd never get to

49

visit. And how dare he talk so casually about Miriam like that. He dug his fingernails into the leather seat. His cheeks burned and he stared out of the window to avoid catching Nathan's gaze in the vanity mirror.

A woman wearing a black T-shirt printed with a badger was dragging her screaming toddler across the car park. The little girl clutched a Happy Meal bag. An elderly lady stepped out of a red Ford Focus and began to shout too. She pointed at the bag. Three generations of family arguing over a McDonald's hamburger.

Arthur had to answer Nathan because it would be rude not to, but he couldn't be bothered to describe how he felt. 'Yes. Pretty shit,' he responded, not even realising he had sworn.

'Here we are then.' Thankfully, the front door opened and Bernadette manoeuvred a series of stuffed carrier bags into the footwell of the car. She then tried curving into her seat to fit herself around them. 'Ready for off?' she asked, fastening her seat belt.

'What have you got in there, Mum? There's only a MaccieD.'s and a WHSmith in that place,' Nathan said.

'Just some magazines, drinks, chocolatey things for the journey. You and Arthur might get hungry.'

'I thought you had food in the boot?'

'I know, but it's nice to have fresh stuff.'

'I thought we'd be getting tea at the B and B,' Nathan said. 'We'll be there in an hour.'

Arthur felt uncomfortable. Bernadette was only trying to please. 'I'm a little peckish actually,' he said, trying to support her, even though he wasn't hungry at all. 'A drink and snack would be just the ticket.'

He was rewarded with a warm smile, a king-size Twix and a two-litre bottle of Coke.

His bedroom at the B and B was tiny with just enough space for a single bed, a rickety wardrobe and a chair. There was the smallest sink he had ever seen in the corner with a wrapped soap the size of a Babybel cheese. The toilet and bath (the landlady informed him) were on the next floor up. No baths after nine at night and you had to give the toilet a firm flush or else it wouldn't get rid of all the contents.

Arthur couldn't remember the last time he had slept in a single bed. It seemed so narrow and confirmed his status as a widower. The bedding was bright and fresh though and he sat on the side of the bed and looked through the sash window. A seagull strutted along the windowsill and there was a pleasant view of the park across the street.

Usually the first thing he and Miriam would do when they got to a room in a B and B was to have a nice cup of tea and see what type of biscuit graced the courtesy tray. They had devised a rating system together. Obviously, receiving no biscuits at all scored a big fat zero. Digestives scored a two. Custard creams were a little better, coming in at a four. Bourbons, he had originally rated as a five, but had grown to

51

appreciate them, so upgraded them to a six. Any biscuit that tasted of chocolate without containing any had to be admired. Further up the scale were the posh biscuits usually provided by the larger hotel chains — the lemon and ginger or chocolate chip cookies, which came in at an eight. For a ten, the biscuits had to be home-made by the proprietors, and this was very rare.

Here, there was a packet of two ginger nuts. They were perfectly acceptable but the sight of them in their packet made his heart sink. He took one out and munched on it then folded over the packet and put it back on the tray. The remaining ginger nut was Miriam's biscuit. He couldn't bring himself to eat it.

There were still two hours before he had arranged to meet Bernadette and Nathan for their evening meal in the restaurant downstairs. He and Miriam would usually put their anoraks on and go for a walk to explore and get their bearings, to plan what they would do the next day. But he didn't want to go out on his own. There didn't seem much point in discovering things alone. Out of the window he watched as Nathan sloped out toward the park. He had one hand dug in his pocket and smoked a cigarette. Arthur wondered if Bernadette knew about this bad habit.

He took the box from his pocket and opened it up on the windowsill. Even though he was used to seeing it now, used to handling it, he still couldn't relate the bracelet to his wife. He couldn't imagine something so chunky and bold dangling from her slender wrist. She had taken pride in having elegant taste and was often mistaken for being French because of her classic way of dressing. In fact, she often said that she admired the way French ladies dressed and that one day she would like to go to Paris. She said it was chic.

When she began to feel ill, felt her chest growing tight and the shortness of breath, she changed the way she dressed. Her navy-blue silk blouses, cream skirts and pearls were replaced by the shapeless cardigans. Her only aim was to keep warm. She even shivered when the sun beat down on her skin. She wore her anorak in the garden, her face bravely tilted toward the sun as if she were confronting it. *Ha! I can't feel you.*

'I just don't understand why you didn't tell me about India, Miriam,' he said aloud. 'Mr Mehra's story was unfortunate, but there was nothing for you to be ashamed of.'

A magpie stood on the other side of the window and stared in at him, and then it seemed to look at the bracelet. Arthur tapped the window. 'Shoo.' He held the box to his chest and squinted at the charms. The flower was made of five coloured stones surrounding a tiny pearl. The paint palette had a tiny paintbrush and six enamelled blobs to represent paint. The tiger snarled, baring pointed gold teeth. He looked at his watch again. There was still an hour and forty-five minutes to go before dinner.

If he was at home he would have eaten by now. He and Miriam always dined at five-thirty prompt and he carried on the tradition. He set the table while she cooked. After eating, he washed up and she dried the pots. Their only day off from this routine was Friday — chippy tea day when they sat in front of the TV and ate fish, chips and mushy peas straight from the polystyrene tray. He lay back on the bed with his hands behind his head. Food wasn't the same without his wife.

To fill his time, he started to think about the next day. He doubted that he'd get his cup of tea and breakfast at the usual time. He read through the train times he had scribbled down on a piece of paper, and memorised them. He imagined Lord Graystock striding toward him with his hand outstretched and greeting him like an old friend. Then he tried to picture Miriam kneeling in the dust, playing marbles with young children in India. It was too hard to comprehend.

Time had only ticked on ten minutes so Arthur picked up the remote control for the miniature television which hung wonkily on the bedroom wall. He switched it on, flicked through all the stations, and began to watch the last twenty minutes of an episode of *Columbo*.

Lucy and the Tortoise

Lucy Pepper stood on the doorstep of her old home and looked up at her old bedroom window. Each time she returned the house seemed to shrink in size. It had once seemed so spacious with her and Dan running up and down the stairs and Mum and Dad sat reading in the sitting room. They were always together, like those porcelain dogs that sat on the opposite ends of the mantelpiece.

Her father, once strong and upright, now seemed so much smaller too. His back curved where once it was straight. The black hair she used to love pulling on and watching spring back into place was now wiry and white. It had all happened so quickly. The innocence of being young and thinking that your parents would last for ever had been broken.

All Lucy had ever wanted was to be a mum. Even since she was little, when she used to pretend that her dolls were her babies, she had pictured herself with two kids. Whether that was a boy and a girl, two boys or two girls, she didn't care. At the age of thirty-six, she should be a mother with toddlers by now. On Facebook, one of her classmates was even a grandmother. She longed to feel the planting of small, sticky kisses on her cheeks.

These days it felt like a strange thing to admit to. Shouldn't she be striving for a glittering career, or wanting to travel the world? But she wanted to be like her mum, Miriam, who had been so happy raising her children. She and Dad had the perfect marriage. They never argued. They laughed at each other's jokes and they held hands. Lucy had found this something of an embarrassment when she was younger: her mum and dad strolling around with their arms wrapped around each other's waist as if they were teenage lovers. It was only when she started dating herself and couldn't seem to find someone who would put their hand on the small of her back when she crossed the road, as if she was precious, that she realised what her parents had. She didn't of course need protection as she had a brown belt in karate, but it would be nice to feel that way.

Her brother, Dan, had never shown any interest in becoming a parent. He was focused on setting up his business, on making a life for himself overseas. It seemed unfair that he and his wife, Kelly, had managed to pop out two gorgeous kids as soon as they tried. Dan always seemed to land lucky whereas Lucy felt she had to struggle to achieve anything, whether that was in her marriage, her relationship with Dad or her job.

When she lay in bed at night and thought about her ideal life, she saw herself at the park with her husband and kids, laughing and pushing the swings. Her mum would be there too with a ready supply of tissues and kisses for scuffed knees.

But Mum wasn't here and she never would be again. She would never see or hold the grandchildren that hadn't yet been born to Lucy.

As a schoolteacher at a local primary, Lucy had noticed that the mums dropping their kids off at the school were now younger than she was. She grimaced when she thought about wasting so much of her time on Anthony. He insisted that they should have just one more foreign holiday before she threw away her contraceptive pills. They should treat themselves to a new sofa before they started baby making. They had differing priorities.

She came off the pill anyway, without him knowing. In opposition to her usual cautious self, she knew she had to become a think-now act-later person in this situation. If Anthony had his way then he would be still musing about whether to have kids or not when he was fifty. Anyway, within a few weeks she was pregnant and then, a few months later, she was not.

Anthony was gone now and Mum had gone too. And with them, Lucy's dreams of family had evaporated like perfume spilled in the sun.

She still beat herself up that she hadn't gone to her mum's funeral. What kind of daughter did that make her? A crap one, that's what. She should have been there to say goodbye. But it was impossible. She hadn't even managed to tell her dad why she couldn't be there. The note she wrote and pushed through his door said:

Sorry, Dad, I can't go through with it. Say goodbye to Mum for me. Love, Lucy xxx.

Then she had gone back to bed and hadn't got up for a week.

Her father had settled into a routine. His life was regimented and together. When she did call, she felt like an inconvenience. He constantly looked at his watch and carried on with tasks around her as if she wasn't there, like the two of them existed in parallel universes. The last time she called, she put the kettle on and made two cups of tea. Her father then refused to drink it, saying that he only took his tea at eight-thirty in the morning, eleven, and sometimes a cup at three. It was like visiting Howard Hughes.

She wished her mum was still here to sort him out. Lucy still expected to find her sitting at the kitchen table or pruning the rose bushes in the garden. She found herself reaching out into thin air to place a gentle hand on her mother's diminishing shoulders.

Lucy wanted her brother to show more of an interest, in her life and Dad's. Dan and Dad's relationship always had an edge to it, as if the two men couldn't quite embrace each other's ways and personalities. They were like two jigsaw pieces with the same bit of sky on, but which didn't fit together. It was more evident now that Mum was gone, when Lucy had to remind Dad and Dan how and when to communicate.

When Lucy went home after a frustrating hour spent with her father, she wished she had someone there, waiting to hold her and tell her that things were going to be okay.

It had been six months now since Anthony had walked out on their marriage. It was such a

58

cliché but she had come home from work one day and found his suitcase in the hallway. At first she thought he might be working away and had forgotten to tell her. But when he appeared behind the case, she *knew*. He stared down at the ground. 'It isn't working, Luce. We both know it isn't.'

She hadn't wanted to beg. When she looked back it seemed so feeble. But she *had* begged. She told him that she wanted him to stay, that he was the future father of her children. That whatever crap they'd been through in the past year was all behind them. They could move on. She knew she had neglected him when her mother died. Since they lost the baby.

But he shook his head. 'There's been too much sadness. I want to be happy. I want you to be happy. But we can't be with all the history between us. We need to be apart so we don't dwell on it. I have to go.'

Just last month, under the stark white light of the Co-op confectionery aisle, she had spied Anthony pushing a shopping trolley with another woman. She looked a bit like Lucy, with her bobbed hair and long neck.

Lucy followed them around the fruit juice aisle and into frozen desserts but then gave up. If Anthony saw her then he'd think she was stalking him. He would introduce her to his new girlfriend and Lucy would have to smile and say that it was lovely to see him again but she had really just popped in for some fresh strawberries and now she had to dash. When she was out of earshot, Anthony would whisper and tell his new girlfriend, 'That was my estranged wife. She lost our baby when she was fifteen weeks pregnant and she was never the same again. It was like a light went off or something. I had to get out.' And his girlfriend would nod sympathetically and squeeze Anthony's hand to reassure him that she was massively fertile and if he wanted a family then her body wouldn't let things down.

Lucy held it together at the tills, but when she was in the trolley park she started to cry. She rammed her trolley over and over into the one in front to return it, but it wouldn't fit. She walked away leaving her token, with a white Yorkshire rose on it, still in the trolley slot. A man with a neck the same thickness as his waist offered her a tissue and she blew her nose, went home and drank half a bottle of vodka.

After that she changed her surname back to Pepper. Lucy Pepper sounded so much better than Lucy Brannigan anyway. She silently and swiftly swept the house of memories of Anthony and stuck all the leaflets for baby milk, nappy vouchers and breast pads in the recycling bin. Her old name made her feel stronger, more equipped to face life again.

And now she was standing in front of the house she grew up in, where her mum and dad had changed her own nappy thousands of times. A feeling of warmth flooded over her. She smiled and rang the doorbell. Through the daisy-patterned glass in the front door she could see her father's coat hung in the hallway. There was a pile of post on the doormat. Strange that he hadn't picked it up yet.

She rang the bell again and gave the knocker a rap. Nothing.

Looking up, she saw that all the windows were shut. She walked through the passageway at the side of the house to the back garden, but there was no sign of him.

She narrowed her eyes against the glare of the sun. Perhaps, if she found him, she could persuade him to go to the garden centre. It was a lovely day.

She'd finished work an hour early. It was the school sports day and really she should be there, putting plasters on knees or helping to serve orange squash. But as she had watched the kids stumbling along in the egg and spoon race, she felt a deep need to be with her dad. With Dan in Australia and Mum gone, he was her only close family left. She feigned a migraine and had driven away from the laughter and applause as the relay races started.

She stood on her tiptoes, cupped her hand around her eyes and peered in the back window. Frederica the fern looked a bit sorry for herself. Her leaves curled a little at the sides. Her dad had developed an obsession with that plant.

Then a terrible thought hit her. *He could be dead*. He might have fallen down the stairs or died in bed like Mum had. He might be sprawled on the bathroom floor unable to move. *Oh God*. Panic began to bubble in her stomach. She moved to the front of the house again.

'Can I help you?' a man shouted from the garden opposite. It was Dad's neighbour who wore a bandana. Lucy had seen him before. As he leaned on his lawnmower, he seemed to be carrying a small brown upturned bowl.

'I've called around to see my dad. I can't get a reply. I'm worried that he's fallen or something. It's Terry, isn't it?' Lucy looked both ways and then crossed the road.

'That's me. No need to worry. Your dad went out this morning with his suitcase.'

Lucy ran her hand through her hair. 'A suitcase? Are you sure?'

'Huh-uh. I think he was going to that lady's house. The one with the raspberry-coloured hair.'

'Bernadette?' On one occasion Lucy called to see her father and found this lady sitting at the kitchen table in Mum's place. She had made fresh sausage rolls. Lucy didn't cook. She stuck things in the microwave or under the grill.

'I don't know her name. They got into a car. A young man was driving. He had hair over one eye. I wondered if he could see the road properly.'

'Did my dad say where he was going?'

Terry shook his head. 'No. Are you his daughter? You have the same eyes.'

'We do?'

'Huh-uh. He didn't say where he was off to. Your dad doesn't speak much, does he?'

'Not really.' Lucy narrowed her eyes. The small brown bowl in Terry's hands moved. A head slid out and two eyes stared at her. 'Erm, are you carrying a tortoise?'

Terry nodded. 'It escapes from next door. It likes my lawn, though I don't know why. I like to keep it neatly trimmed. Not much food for this little guy. Each time he tries to escape I pick him up and give him back. He belongs to the two kids with red hair and bare feet. Do you know them?'

Lucy said she did not.

'Shall I tell your dad you were looking for him, if I see him?'

Lucy said that would be helpful and that she would phone him too. She wondered why her dad would have a suitcase and where he could possibly be going. It was difficult enough to persuade him to go to the village to buy milk. 'Maybe you should just let the tortoise wander around for a while. It might quench his thirst for adventure. Then he might be happy to stay in his pen, or whatever his home is.'

'I never thought about that.' Terry turned the tortoise to face him. 'What do you think about that idea then, buddy?'

'Thanks for your help,' Lucy shouted out absentmindedly over her shoulder as she crossed back over the road.

She made her way around to the back again and sat down on the edge of a large plant pot. She stabbed her dad's number on her mobile. It rang around twenty times as it usually did as he tried to remember where he had put it, or which button to press. Finally, he answered.

'Hello. This is Arthur Pepper speaking.'

'Dad. It's Lucy,' she said, relieved to hear his voice.

'Oh, hello, love.'

'I'm at your house, but you're not in.'

'I didn't know you were coming.'

'I . . . just kind of wanted to see you. Your neighbour, the one who loves his lawn, said he'd seen you with a suitcase.'

'He's right. I've decided to visit Graystock Manor. It's the place where the tigers live, in Bath.'

'I've heard of it. But, Dad . . . '

'Bernadette and her son Nathan were headed that way and asked me to join them.'

'And you wanted to go . . . ?'

'Well. Nathan is looking at universities. I'm, er . . . well, I thought it would be a change.'

Lucy closed her eyes. Her father wouldn't even have a cup of tea with her if it wasn't scheduled and now he had taken off with his flame-haired neighbour. He had been holed up in the house for a year. She sensed there was something not quite right about this sudden trip, that her father was keeping something from her. 'It's a long way to go on a whim.'

'It's got me out of the house.'

Lucy had worried that her father might be vulnerable living on his own. The newspapers were awash with stories about gullible pensioners. Now she didn't know what to think. Why had he agreed to go with Bernadette all the way to Bath when she couldn't get him to go to the garden centre for a potter around the bedding plants? She tried to control anxiety from coming through in her voice. 'When are you coming home?'

'I don't know what time I'll be back. I'm at a bed and breakfast now, and then off to

64

Graystock tomorrow. Anyway, I have to go now, darling. I'll give you a call when I get home, shall I?'

'Dad . . . *Dad.*' The line went dead. Lucy stared at her mobile.

She was about to ring him back, but then she started to think about his other strange habits; his strict routines. Whenever she saw him he wore that dreadful mustard tank top. He hadn't phoned her for weeks. He talked to his plant.

She'd never thought of her parents as old until Mum died. But she did now. If her dad could no longer cope on his own, she would have to start looking into home help or even old people's homes. She wondered how quickly his mind would go.

Her mouth went dry as she imagined helping him upstairs, feeding him, taking him to the toilet. Instead of a baby to look after, she would have her father.

She stood up and her knees wobbled as she walked toward the garden gate. On top of everything else that had gone wrong in her life, she now had to deal with her father succumbing to dementia.

Bed and Breakfast

The breakfast being served downstairs at the B and B smelled delicious. At home he and Miriam only ate cereal. If he had toast then it had to be with Flora margarine rather than Anchor or Lurpak butter. Miriam said that he had to look after his cholesterol, even though the doctor had tested it and told him that it was low. Arthur was used to waking and smelling only freshly washed cotton sheets rather than a full English fry-up. This was a treat. But he did feel guilty about his wife not being here to enjoy it too.

Despite having dropped off yesterday in the car on the way to the B and B, he had slept right through the night. It was the seagulls that had woken him that morning, cawing overhead and tap dancing on the roof.

After his phone call with Lucy last night, he had felt rather tired. He knocked on Bernadette's door and asked if she minded if he didn't join her and Nathan for dinner. An early night beckoned and he would see her the next morning. Bernadette nodded but gave him a look to show she was deeply disappointed in him.

He showered, dressed and shaved and made

his way to the breakfast room. It was rather jolly, with yellow wipe-clean tablecloths, silk daffodils and framed seaside postcards on the wall. Bernadette and Nathan were already seated at a table for four by the window.

'Morning,' he said brightly, joining them.

''Nin',' Nathan managed as he poked at the flowers with his knife.

'Good morning, Arthur,' Bernadette said. She reached out and lowered her son's hand. 'Did you sleep well?'

'Like a log actually. And you?'

'I didn't have a good night. I woke around three and then things started to wander around my mind. I couldn't stop them.'

Arthur was about to ask what she had been thinking about but a young waitress, who wore a smart black skirt and a yellow blouse, offered tea or coffee. He noticed that she had an anchor tattooed on one wrist and a rose on the other. This seemed to be a disturbing new trend for young people. He couldn't understand why such a pretty girl would want to resemble a sailor. Then, he scolded himself for being such a fuddy-duddy. Miriam had always encouraged him to be more liberal. 'I like your tattoos.' He smiled. 'Very nice.'

The waitress gave him a confused smile as if she knew the tattoos looked like they had been done by a toddler with access to a needle and pot of ink. Arthur ordered tea and requested a full English breakfast minus the grilled tomatoes.

He and Bernadette both stood at the same time and walked over to the sideboard on which sat mini boxes of cereal and a glass jug of milk. Arthur picked up Rice Krispies and carried them back. Bernadette picked two boxes of Frosties. 'They never give you enough in these little boxes,' she said.

The three of them ate in silence. Nathan looked as if he was about to fall asleep at the table, his head bowed and his hair almost dangling in his bowl.

After they had finished, the waitress took the bowls and brought over their cooked breakfasts.

'These sausages look really tasty,' Arthur said to Nathan, trying to make conversation.

'Are.'

'You mean, *they* are,' Bernadette corrected.

Nathan's face was blank. He speared a full sausage and ate it from his fork. Arthur was sorely tempted to give his foot a kick under the table. He was sure that Bernadette would have taught her son excellent table manners.

'We're going to look at the first university today. It looks promising,' Bernadette said. 'Are you coming with us, Arthur?'

'If you don't mind, I'm going to head off to Graystock. I'll take the train to Bristol and change for Bath there.'

'I'm sure it's only open on Fridays and Saturdays, and today is Tuesday.'

'It doesn't need to be open to the public. I can knock on the door.'

'I think maybe you should phone ahead . . . '

He wasn't in the mood to be told what to do. He was feeling rather single-minded and had made up his mind that he was going to pursue his mission. He cut into his bacon.

'And where shall we pick you up afterwards?'

'I can't ask you to do that. I'll make my own way home from the manor.'

Bernadette's face fell a little. 'You can't do that. It will take you ages. We've only booked in here for one night.'

'You've done enough for me already,' Arthur said firmly. 'I shall visit and then see what the day brings.'

'Well, don't be rash. Ring and let me know. You're welcome to travel back with us. But I do want to be back for my class.'

'Class?'

'Mum does belly dancing,' Nathan sniggered.

Arthur chewed. An unwelcome image of Bernadette wearing purple chiffon and shaking her hips popped into his head. 'I didn't know that. It sounds, er, energetic.'

'It gives me a bit of exercise.'

Nathan sniggered again.

Bernadette ignored him. 'How is your bacon, Arthur?' she asked.

'It's great,' Arthur said. He was glad that he was going to spend time alone today. Whatever he found out about Miriam should be private. He wanted to be on his own with his thoughts. 'I like my bacon nice and crispy. And don't you worry about me at all. I'll be just fine visiting the manor on my own.'

The Tiger

Bernadette and Nathan dropped Arthur off at Cheltenham train station. After arriving in Bath, he decided to walk the two miles to Graystock Manor.

It seemed a good idea at the time. The sun was out and the birds were singing. Arthur started off happily, tugging his case across the station forecourt, past the queue of black cabs. From a map he had sketched on a piece of paper, he headed across a small roundabout then onto a B road that led all the way to the manor house. He felt quite the adventurer, proud with himself that he had taken this decision. He strode forwards purposefully.

The pavement soon ran out and he found himself traversing nettles and thistles that prickled his ankles. The ground underfoot was uneven and he wished that he had worn his sturdy brogues rather than his grey suede moccasins. It was virtually impossible to wheel his suitcase across the stones and gravel that pocked the pathway. He alternated between dragging and carrying it along.

'Oi, Granddad.' A shiny red sports car whizzed by and he was sure that someone's backside hung out of the back window.

After half a mile or so, the pathway narrowed. He found himself wedged between a scratchy hedgerow and a wide, raised kerbstone. Unable to manhandle his case any further, he stopped and stood with his hands on his knees while he caught his breath. The furthest he had walked since Miriam died was to the post office. He was seriously out of condition.

There was a gap in the hedge and he stood and watched a bumble bee. Cows stood, placid and chewing. He admired a red tractor ploughing the field. He set off again but there was a pile of bricks and a wire shopping basket in his way. This was the last straw. He couldn't stand tugging the suitcase any longer. He picked it up and pushed it into the gap in the hedge then rearranged the foliage back around it.

Looking round, he made a mental note of his location. He was opposite a road sign for a car boot sale this Sunday and there was another sign that said 'Longsdale Farm 1 mile'. He would carry out his visit to Graystock and then pick up his case on the way back. It was made from sturdy nylon so a stay in the hedge should see it just fine.

He was lighter and quicker now. It was usually Miriam who planned what to take on their trips. The house would become overrun with small piles of things — underwear, his shaving stuff, biscuit two-packs and sun cream in every conceivable SPF. He doubted very much if she would be impressed by his stashing of his suitcase in a bush. However he felt rather pleased with himself. He was being resourceful, making

71

decisions and pushing on.

Graystock was still a way away and he pressed onwards, not stopping to admire the bursts of shepherd's purse that sprung from beneath the hedges or the fields of yellow rapeseed. He refused a lift from a couple of attractive blonde girls who pulled up alongside him in their silver convertible, and also informed a tractor driver that, thanks for asking, but he wasn't lost. People really were rather pleasant around here and he could forgive the bum-baring incident by the boys in the red car. The sun must have brought out their high jinks.

When he finally got to the gates of Graystock Manor he was met with a peeling wooden sign. Most of the letters had fallen off. It said: 'Welcome to Gray_____ Man____'.

They must have known I was coming, Arthur thought. Then he stared with dismay at the lengthy driveway that curved its way to the manor. He could see the building through the trees.

Graystock had once been magnificent. It now had a decayed glamour like it should feature in a moody 1980s pop video. The Doric pillars flanking its huge front doors were crumbling. The stone was the colour of the fluff picked up in Arthur's Dyson vacuum. A few of the upstairs windows were broken.

He stood with his hands on his hips for a while, aware that he was going to uncover another chapter of Miriam's life. He didn't know whether to feel excited or afraid.

By now he really needed to use the loo. He

72

looked around in the vague fantasy that a toilet block might suddenly sprout up from nowhere. His only option was to find a bush. Hoping that no tourists were around to see him, he headed into the undergrowth and did a wee. A grey squirrel bounded over, took a quick glance at him, and then ran up a tree. It sat on a branch, its whiskers twitching as he finished up. Thankfully he had a handy packet of wet wipes in his pocket and he cleaned his hands before carrying on his journey.

His breath came in short wheezes as he trekked toward the hall. Why hadn't he accepted Bernadette's offer of a lift? He could be a stubborn old git at times.

The manor was surrounded by tall black iron railings. The double gates were secured by a heavy brass padlock. Arthur pressed his face to the railings and peered through. The doors to the hall were shut. Why he had imagined he could simply stroll up to the manor and ring a doorbell he didn't know. His feet were sore and the wet wipe had made his hands sticky.

He stood there for at least ten minutes, feeling useless and not sure what his next move might be. But then he saw movement — a flash of blue behind the rose bushes in the gardens. Lord Graystock. Arthur stood on his tiptoes. The shape moved out of the bushes. The lord wore electric blue slacks and was stripped to the waist. His chest was boiled-lobster red.

'Hello,' Arthur called out. '*Hello*. Lord Graystock.'

The lord didn't hear, or did and ignored the

shout. It was then that Arthur spied a brass bell with a curled iron handle concealed by branches. He tugged on it but the sound was muffled by the trees. He jumped up to tug the branches and twigs away, but they sprang back into place. He gave the bell a final tug and rattled the gates, but it was no use. From a distance, he watched his target for a while. Lord Graystock stuck his hands into his pockets and strolled around his grounds. He stopped to sniff at roses or to pluck out weeds. His rounded red stomach wobbled over his waistband.

Was the man deaf? Arthur thought. How had he ever managed to attract a harem? Surely Miriam couldn't have been one of his girls.

Frustrated, he started to follow the railings around the grounds, trailing his fingers along them as he went. He stopped sporadically to raise himself onto tiptoes to peer into the gardens. The manor was like a fortress.

Then he discovered that in one place, around the back of the house and shielded by a huge oak tree, the railings no longer stretched to the ground, but instead were embedded in a low brick wall. He had an idea.

First looking around to make sure he was alone, he tried to lift his right leg high enough to climb up onto the wall. He could then peer over the top of the railings for a better view. But his knee locked when he tried to raise it, making a disconcerting crunching sound. He bent over, rubbed it, and then tried again. Cupping his hands behind his knee, he hoisted it up so he could place the sole of his foot flat on the wall.

He grabbed hold of the railings and then pulled with all his might to get his other leg off the ground. When he felt his second foot standing firmly on the wall he felt such a feeling of euphoria. Life in the old dog yet. He allowed himself a few deep breaths and pressed his face to the railings again.

There was a scuffling noise and an orange-eyed Jack Russell stared up at him. A lady wearing a silk patterned headscarf and a khaki Barbour jacket looked Arthur up and down. 'Can I help you?' she said.

'No. I'm fine, thank you.' He stood as nonchalantly as he could do with both hands clutching the railings.

The lady stood her ground. 'What are you trying to do?'

Arthur thought too quickly. 'I'm trying to find my dog. I think he might have gone over the railings.'

'Those railings are at least ten foot high.'

'Yes. Tsk.' He nodded. If he didn't speak and didn't explain then she might move away. He went into his National Trust statue mode.

The lady pursed her lips. 'I'm going to be ten minutes walking my dog. If you're here when I'm walking back, I'm going to call the police. Okay?'

'Okay.' Arthur shook his leg to release his trousers which had rolled up slightly over his sock during the climb. 'I assure you that I'm not a burglar.'

'I'm glad to hear it. I hope you find your dog. Ten minutes . . . ' she warned.

He waited until she had moved away. Today

had been a disaster. He should have stayed at home and read the *Daily Mail*. But then he saw a flash of electric-blue trouser. Damn it. He had to get the man's attention. He stood and rattled the railings but they didn't budge. So he began to wave. 'Lord Graystock. Lord Graystock. Lord Graystock,' he shouted. This felt idiotic, like he was at a rock concert. But it *had* to work. He had travelled for miles for this. He had gone against the voice in his own head that had told him to stay at home in his daily routine. There was no way he was going back without an answer.

The woman and her dog would return. If he was going to do this then he had to be quick. Without another thought, Arthur spotted a ridge of metal along the top of the railing. He used all his might to lift his leg up and wedge his foot on the ridge. With strength he didn't know he possessed, he managed to clamber up onto the top of the railing. He hung there for a moment then rallied himself. *Come on, Sir Edmund Hillary. Up and over, old son.* He steadied himself and flipped his leg over. He jumped. The iron fleur-de-lis on the top of the railing got fastened in the hem of his trouser leg. There was a loud tearing noise as he dropped onto the lawn. Looking down, he saw that his left trouser leg was torn to the thigh so it looked as if he was wearing a strange sarong. No matter. He was over. He stood and strode toward the manor house, his left leg exposed.

The grass was damp and squeaky. The buttery sun made it sparkle. It was a beautiful day. Arthur gave a sigh of relief. Birds twittered and a red admiral butterfly alighted on his shoulder for a few seconds. 'Hi there,' he said. 'I'm here to find out about my wife.' As he lifted his head to watch as it fluttered away, he didn't see the brick on the lawn.

He kicked it, then felt his ankle twist. He stumbled sideways, falling to the ground, and then rolled onto his back. Beetle-like, he tried to right himself, but his legs and arms flailed feebly in the air. He tried again and then groaned. The fall had winded him. His ankle throbbed. He had made it over the dizzying heights of the railings and then been foiled by a brick.

He lowered his legs and arms and looked up at the sky. It was Wedgwood-blue and a cloud shaped like a pterodactyl drifted by. An aeroplane left a vapour trail. Two cabbage whites flew higher and higher until he could no longer see them. The brick lay beside his ear. It was chipped around the edges as if it had been chewed.

He tried to right himself again by sucking in his stomach and attempting to sit up, but it was no use. *Idiot*, he sighed. He would have to do his statue thing for a while before he tried to move again. He wondered if he had ever come across a National Trust statue that lay prostrate. Hmmm, probably not. Lifting up his leg, he tried to rotate his twisted ankle. It circled and clicked. It wasn't as bad as he first thought. The manor was in striding distance. He was nearly there. A few more minutes and he'd roll onto his side and get up. He would crawl there if need be.

It took him a few seconds to realise that he

was no longer alone.

First of all he sensed movement beneath his fingertips as the grass rumbled. It was a strange feeling, not a thumping, or a buzzing but more of a padding sensation. Something brushed his right foot. A dog? A squirrel? He tried to move his head, to raise it, but a pain shot down his neck. Hell's bells. Ouch, that hurt.

The next thing he knew, his view of the sky was obliterated by something big. It was something with fur. It was something orange, black and white.

Oh, good God. *No*.

The tiger stood over him. Its face was so close that he could feel its meaty breath burning his cheek. There was an unmistakable tang of urine. Something heavy pressed down on his shoulder forcing it into the earth. A paw. A huge paw. Arthur wanted to screw his eyes shut but he couldn't help but stare, hypnotised by this great beast.

The tiger had black lips and whiskers the thickness of crochet needles. Its lips curled and a string of drool glooped down, down into Arthur's ear. He wanted to reach up and wipe it away, but he daren't move. This was it. He was a dead man. He turned his head slightly so the drool slid out onto the grass.

When he'd imagined his death (and he thought about it often now Miriam was gone) his preferred method was to fall asleep and not wake up — though he would want someone to find him straight away. It would be awful if he began to create a stink. And he wanted to look serene, not have his face screwed up in pain or anything. He supposed Lucy would find him so that wouldn't be nice for her. It would be most useful if he could have a premonition about his death and be prepared for it. If he could be sure that, say fifteen years on, say 8 March, he would go to sleep and not wake up, he could tip Terry off the day before. 'If you don't see me tomorrow morning, then feel free to break in. You'll find me in bed, dead. Don't be alarmed. I *know* it's going to happen.'

Or, he understood that cancer was very common amongst men his age. He'd seen a feature on daytime TV on how you should cup your testicles to check for lumps. It had been disconcerting seeing a hairy pair of balls on his television screen at that time in the morning. Afterwards he had felt around in his pants and decided that prostate cancer wasn't going to do him in.

What he hadn't ever pictured was being eaten by a tiger. He could see the headlines now:

Pensioner Mauled to Death by Tiger. Thigh Bone Found in Grounds of Graystock Manor.

This was not how he wanted to go.

The tiger moved its paw, this time further down his arm. Arthur could only lie there as he felt the dreadful sensation of claws dragging his skin. There was a sharp pain and he flicked his eyes to see four red stripes of blood appear on his forearm. Blood bobbled to the surface. He

79

seemed to float out of his body and watch the scene from above.

There was a painting once that he had seen in a book. It was a lion looming over a man. Was the artist Henri Rousseau? He was that man on the ground now. Did the man in the painting look terrified? Was there blood? As he lay there, paralysed with fear, he lost all sense of time. How long had he even been lying on the ground? He couldn't say if it was seconds, minutes or hours. The tiger watched him, staring and waiting. Its yellow eyes unblinking, unemotional. *Make a move*, it willed him. *Provoke me and let's see what happens.*

Arthur glanced at the tiger again. It seemed to be looking longingly at his exposed leg. He could hear Bernadette's voice in his head. 'You silly old bugger. Why did you climb the bloody fence?'

'Elsie. No.' A man's angry voice suddenly bellowed out. 'Get off. *Bad girl.*'

The tiger, or tigress, as Arthur now knew, turned her head to face the shout. Then she glared back at Arthur. They stared at each other and shared a moment. She was undecided. She could tear his head off at any time. Eating this white-haired old man would be a treat. A bit gristly maybe, but she could cope with that.

'Elsie.' There was a thud and a thick bloody steak landed on the grass a few inches from his ear. It must have been tastier than his head because the tigress gave him a haughty, *I'll let you go this time* glance and then sauntered off.

Arthur didn't like to swear but . . . *shit*. He released his breath as a loud whoosh.

He felt a strong arm push under his back, helping him to sit upright. He tried to assist all he could. His arm hung loosely by his side.

Beside him, squatting down, was Lord Graystock. He had put on a blue shirt and matching waistcoat adorned with small mirrors that glinted in the sun. It was the same hue as his blue trousers. 'What the bloody hell are you doing, man?'

'I just wanted to . . .'

'I should call the police. You're trespassing on private property. You could have been killed.'

'I know,' Arthur rasped. He looked down at his arm. It looked like he'd been paintballed with a splat of scarlet.

'That's just a scratch,' Graystock huffed. He rolled up his trouser leg to reveal a melted wax patch of skin reaching from his ankle to his knee. '*That* is a proper injury. You were lucky. Tigers aren't pets that you can come and stroke you know.'

'I didn't come to see the tigers.'

'No? Then why were you playing wrestling with Elsie?'

Arthur opened and closed his mouth. The accusation that he was playing was ridiculous. 'I came to see you.'

'Me? Hah! Can't you ring the doorbell like a normal person?'

'I've travelled a long way. I couldn't go without speaking to you.'

'At first I thought you were one of the local youngsters playing dare. A couple of times I've caught a poor teenage lad, hanging by his T-shirt from the railings, terrified and begging for help. You're lucky that Elsie just wanted to play with you.' He sat back on his heels. 'Don't you think you're too old for acrobatics?'

'Yes. Yes, I am.'

'You're not one of those animal rights activists?'

Arthur shook his head. 'I'm a retired locksmith.'

Graystock grunted. He helped Arthur to his feet. 'Let's get you inside and get you a bandage for your arm.'

'I think I may have twisted my ankle too.'

'Well, don't even think about trying to sue me. A journalist tried it once, when one of the tigers wanted to play and scratched his shoulder. I'll warn you now that I don't have a penny to my name.'

'I'm not going to sue you,' Arthur said. 'This is my own fault. I've been an idiot.'

★　★　★

The manor smelled of damp, furniture polish and decay. The entrance hall was all white marble and the walls were lined with portraits of Graystock's ancestors. The floor was paved with black and white chequered tiles, like a huge chessboard. An oak staircase swerved from the centre of the hallway. The manor was run down. Arthur couldn't imagine paying ten pounds to look around it, but that was the price displayed on a desk opposite the door as they walked in. The house had been grand once. But now paint peeled from the ceiling mural of swooping cherubs and swathes of red curtain.

Graystock led the way and Arthur limped a few paces behind. He wasn't sure which part of his body hurt the most.

'The house has been in my family for years. I only use a few rooms now,' Graystock said. 'I can't afford to live here but I don't want to move out. Come through.'

Arthur followed him into a dark room stuffed with leather armchairs and in which roared a real open fire. Over the stone mantelpiece was a pre-Raphaelite-like painting of a lady in a white flowing dress. She was sitting on the grass with her arms draped around a tiger that nuzzled under her chin. He peered more closely to make sure that it wasn't Miriam. It wasn't.

As he lowered himself into a comfy green leather chair next to the fireplace, Graystock poured brandy into a tumbler. 'No, I . . .' Arthur protested.

'You've stared death in the face, man. You need a drink.'

Arthur accepted it and took a sip.

Graystock sat cross-legged on the floor in front of the fire. He took a swig from the neck of the brandy bottle. 'So why are you here, prowling around my garden and upsetting my girls?'

'Girls?'

'My tigers, man. You got Elsie overly excited.'

'That wasn't my intention. I'm here to ask you about my wife.'

'Your wife?' Graystock frowned. 'Has she left you?'

'No.'

'Was she one of my harem?'

'You *really* had a harem?' He thought of Bernadette telling him about Graystock's life-style — of wild parties and orgies.

'Well, of course. I had money. I had good looks. What man wouldn't do the same in my circumstances?' He picked up a small brass bell off the hearth and rang it. 'Alas, I am a man of considerable age now. I have one woman and she is more than enough.'

After a few minutes a woman entered the room. She wore a flowing blue robe fastened with a silver chain belt. Her ink-black hair hung down to her waist. Arthur recognised her as the lady from the painting, though older now. She walked over to Graystock, leaned over and kissed him on the cheek. Then the two of them growled at each other.

Arthur sat in stunned silence. He imagined what Miriam's response might be if he had ever summoned her by bell. Or if he growled at her. He'd be the recipient of a pair of oven gloves batted around his head.

'This is Kate. She's been unfortunate enough to be my wife for thirty years and has lived with me for longer than that. Even when I squandered my fortune on drink and drugs, she stayed with me. She saved me.'

Kate shook her head. 'Silly. I didn't save you. I loved you.'

'Then love saved me.'

Kate turned to Arthur. 'Don't be perturbed by the bell. It's a simple way for us to communicate in the house. I have one too.'

'This man . . . ' Graystock pointed.

'Arthur.'

'Yes. Arthur is here to find out more about his wife. He clambered over our railings and I had to save him from Elsie.' He frowned as he tried to remember. 'What exactly do you want to find out?'

'My wife left this address in a letter. In 1963.'

'Hmmm. 1963.' The lord roared with laughter. 'I can hardly remember what I had for my tea last night, never mind that long ago.'

Arthur sat more upright in his chair. 'Her name was Miriam Pepper.'

'Never heard of her.'

'Miriam Kempster?'

'No.'

'I have this.' Arthur took the charm bracelet from his pocket.

'Aha,' the lord said. He leaned over and took the bracelet. 'Now that is something I can help you with.'

He weighed it in his hand then stood and walked over to a black and gold lacquered cupboard and opened the door. From inside he took out a glass bowl then handed it to Arthur. In it were a pile of gold charms, maybe fifty in total. All were tigers. All were identical.

'This is where your charm probably came from. I had a thousand made in the sixties. They were tokens of my . . . appreciation.'

'Appreciation?'

Graystock wagged his finger. 'I know what you are thinking, my man. Trinkets in return for sexual favours.' He laughed. 'In some instances, yes. But I also gave them to friends and associates, as well as lovers. They were my calling card.'

'He loves tigers,' Kate said. 'We both do. They're like the children we never had.'

Lord Graystock gave her a squeeze and planted a kiss on her forehead.

Arthur stared forlornly at the tigers in the bowl. He poked in his finger and gave them a swirl. He thought that the tiger on Miriam's charm bracelet might have a hidden relevance, as the elephant did. But the striped beast was just one of a thousand sisters. He wondered which of Graystock's categories Miriam fell into. Was she a friend, an associate or a lover? He knocked back the rest of his brandy in one. Kate took the bowl from him and placed it back in the cupboard.

'I'm sorry.' Graystock shrugged. 'Lots of people have stayed here over the years and I have the memory of a goldfish. I can't help you.'

Arthur nodded. He tried to stand but then a pain jerked in his ankle and he fell back into the chair.

'Don't try to move,' Kate said, her voice full of concern.

'Aarggh.'

'Where are you staying?'

'I've not made any plans.' He felt tired, shaken now. 'I stayed at a B and B last night. I didn't think it would take me so long to get here and I hadn't planned to be accosted by a tiger.' He really didn't want to call Bernadette to collect

86

him. She needed to focus on Nathan.

'Stay here with us for the night,' Kate urged. 'I can dress your wound properly. And you may need a tetanus jab when you get home.'

'I had one last year.' He thought back to when a snappy terrier had sunk its teeth into his hand as he had reached down for a roll of wrapping paper in the post office. Perhaps he was put on this earth for animals to attack.

'Even so. You should go to see a doctor. Now, where are your things?'

Arthur thought about his suitcase pushed into the bush at the side of the B road. He was too embarrassed to admit to it. 'I haven't got anything,' he said. 'I hadn't planned to stay.'

'That's no problem.' She left the room then returned carrying a small basket full of bandages and ointments. She knelt next to him and dabbed at his arm with an antiseptic-soaked cotton wool ball. She wound a bandage around and secured it with a small safety pin. Then she removed his shoes and socks and rubbed thick white cream into his ankle. 'We'll leave you in these trousers for now and I'll find some fresh ones in the morning.' She sat back on her heels. 'Now, I've just made some fresh pea and ham soup. Can I tempt you with a bowl?'

Arthur's stomach growled. 'Yes, please,' he said.

★   ★   ★

The Graystocks and Arthur ate the soup in huge bowls on their laps in front of the fire. His hosts sat on the floor on a pile of cushions and Arthur squashed himself into the corner of a large green leather armchair, trying to hide away. Even though the soup was delicious, with huge chunks of ham and served with wedges of bread and butter, he wished he could be at home eating sausage, egg and chips and watching a game show on TV.

It was the first night he had spent socially since Miriam died. He listened to Lord Graystock's stories of wild parties and flamboyant friends, and to Kate's gentle explanations that her husband tended to exaggerate. He wished that Miriam was here with him. She would have amusing anecdotes to tell; she'd know how to respond to the Graystocks' stories. Arthur didn't know how to interact, what to say.

Even though he protested, he was unable to prevent Lord Graystock from topping up his tumbler from an array of different-shaped bottles. He tried to put his hand on top of his glass but Lord Graystock just pushed it out of the way. To appear hospitable, and to numb the pain of his twisted ankle and scratched arm, Arthur drank each offering.

'This is a fine gin, made from my own juniper berries,' Lord Graystock announced. 'This is a vintage cognac given to me by Marlon Brando . . . You might find that brandy makes your ankle feel more pliant.'

The alcohol made Arthur's chest burn and throat wheeze, but it also numbed the disappointment from having reached a dead end with the tiger charm. There was nowhere for him to go next. He would have to go home and try to forget about the charm bracelet. His heart felt heavy from having to abandon his search. He accepted another glass of something golden.

'Steady on,' Kate laughed at her husband. Her cheeks were red from the drink and the fire. 'You're going to get poor Arthur drunk.'

'I am feeling rather woozy,' Arthur said.

'I'll get you a glass of water.' She stood up. 'It's lovely that you found us, Arthur. We don't have many visitors these days. We tend to enjoy our own company.'

Lord Graystock nodded. 'I'm sure my wife must get fed up of seeing my ugly mug day in and day out.'

'Never,' Kate laughed. 'How could I?'

She returned a few minutes later with the water and passed it to Arthur. He drank it in one and watched how the Graystocks sat holding hands. Sometimes he and Miriam would hold hands when they walked, but rarely in the house. He suddenly felt the need to tell his hosts something about his wife. He gave a small cough first, to ready himself. 'Me and Miriam liked the simple things in life too. We were rarely apart. We liked visiting stately homes together. She would have loved it here.'

'I'm just sorry I can't remember her.' Lord Graystock slurred a little.

'Yes.' Arthur shut his eyes and the room began to spin. He opened them again.

'Never mind, let's open another bottle of something, shall we. Whisky perhaps?' Lord Graystock stood and promptly stumbled over a cushion.

Kate stood up and pulled him close. 'I think that's enough for one night,' she said firmly. 'Our guest may want to go to bed.'

'I rather think I do,' Arthur said. 'It's been a lovely evening but I'm definitely ready to go to sleep.'

★　★　★

Arthur was glad that Kate placed his arm around her shoulders to show him upstairs. The alcohol had gone to his ankle; so he could hardly feel the twist as he made his way to the bedroom. The scratches on his arm stung but not massively so. His bandage looked pristine and so white. Pretty. And strangely, he felt like singing.

His room was painted orange with black stripes. But of course, Arthur thought as he flopped onto the bed. Tiger stripes — what else?

Kate brought him a mug of hot milk. 'I'll look through some old photos and see if I can find any reference to your wife, though it is such a long time ago.'

'I don't want to put you to any trouble . . . '

'It's no trouble at all. I was quite a photographer back in my day, before being Lady Graystock became a full-time role. I've not looked at our old photos for quite a while. Your search gives me a good reason to. I like a trip down memory lane.'

'Thank you. This might help.' Arthur took out his wallet. He handed Kate a black-and-white photo of Miriam. He had taken it on their honeymoon. It was battered around the edges and a diagonal crease ran through Miriam's hair, but he had always loved that photograph. His wife had one of those unique faces that you could never grow bored of looking at. She had a slight Roman nose and eyes that invited you to talk to her. Her walnut hair was brushed into a small beehive and she wore a smart white sheaf dress.

'I'll see what I can find. Graystock is a real hoarder. He doesn't throw anything away, so we might be lucky.'

Arthur lay awake and thought for a while of how Graystock and Kate had a closer relationship with their feline friends than he had with Dan and Lucy. He had always thought that cats were terribly sneaky, though perhaps that was just the ones who soiled his rockery. He snuggled down in the bed and wondered if Miriam had slept in this room and what had brought her to the manor. What did she do here?

As he drifted off to sleep, he pictured her running around the gardens barefoot, the tigers circling and keeping her safe.

The Photograph

The next morning there was a knock on his bedroom door. Arthur was awake but drowsing, wondering if the past twenty-four hours had been a strange dream. The paintings of tigers surrounding him, his orange bedclothes, his throbbing ankle, his scratched arm all added to the curiousness. He pulled up the blanket to his neck. 'Hello,' he called out.

Kate entered. She passed him a cup of tea. 'How is my patient?'

He pressed his arm. It stung, but it was a dull rather than a sharp pain. When he rotated his ankle, it felt stiff rather than sore. Kate's nursing skills had worked. 'Not bad,' he said.

Catching sight of a black lacquered clock topped with a brass tiger on his bedside table, he saw that it was already past ten. The time made him feel disorientated and rather grumpy. His routine had flown out the window again. He couldn't ever possibly catch up. He liked to plan and know what was lined up for the day, hour by hour, before it started. He was late for his breakfast. He was missing watering Frederica.

He also realised that he had left his mobile phone in his suitcase. Somewhere in the countryside a bush would play 'Greensleeves' if anyone rang him. He reached up and winced as he felt bristles poking through his chin. His teeth felt sticky from alcohol.

'I have washed most of the grass stains out of your shirt and brought a fresh pair of trousers for you. I couldn't repair yours. Graystock doesn't fit into these ones now. Come down to breakfast when you are ready. There is a bathroom next door so feel free to bathe.'

Arthur preferred a shower, but when he wallowed in the hot water for half an hour his ankle felt even better. He peeked under the bandage on his arm and saw that the stripes had scabbed over.

After getting dressed, he peered in the full-length bathroom mirror. He looked like a presentable pensioner from the waist up, but from the waist down . . . well! Graystock's electric-blue harem trousers were remarkably comfy — very soft and roomy — but made him look like a Scandinavian tourist.

Kate laid the table in the kitchen with fresh crusty bread and butter and a jug of orange juice. Again the walls of the large room were adorned with photos and paintings of her tigers. An open fire flickered, but the room was so large that the heat barely reached them. Outside, he could see that the sun hadn't yet warmed up the morning. Kate wore a tartan blanket wrapped over her shoulders and a long white cotton nightie underneath. 'We buy very little meat now, except for the tigers to eat. Graystock would prefer to feed the girls than to feed us,' she laughed as she sat on the bench next to him.

93

'How on earth did you end up living with the, er, girls?'

'My father was a showman. He travelled with circuses around Italy, France, America. All around the world. And he took me with him. I used to dress up as a little clown. My job was to run in the ring with a bucket of water to throw over the big clowns. It contained glitter really but always got a laugh from the audience. My father was a drinker. His temper would turn when he hit the bottle. He used to strike me too. One day, he was training a new tiger cub to perform. It was too young to learn, to understand properly what he wanted. He took up a crop and was about to strike the poor thing. I ran in and scooped up the cub. My father warned that he would beat me too unless I let it go. Or else I was to get out of his sight and never show my face again.

'Arthur, I hugged that cub to my chest and ran. I knew of Graystock through friends and I turned up on his doorstep. I was only eighteen. Both Graystock and the tigers needed looking after, protecting. The little cub I rescued was like our first child. We had many more after that.'

'So you didn't have children of your own?'

Kate shook her head. 'I never felt the need to reproduce. I had many friends with babies and I liked to cuddle and rock them to sleep, but it never happened for Graystock and me. I've never regretted it. The tigers are my family, though we just have the three adults now. There's Elsie, who you had the pleasure of meeting. Then there is Timeous and Theresa. Plus . . . come over here, Arthur.'

He stood and followed her to a corner of the kitchen, to the side of a huge black iron range cooker. There was a large, flat wicker basket full of crumpled blankets. In the middle, a tiger cub slept. Its beauty took his breath away. It didn't seem real, like a soft toy left there by a child. Except he saw its white chest rise and fall and the corner of its mouth twitch as if jerked by a piece of twine.

'Isn't he beautiful?'

Arthur nodded.

'He's been a little under the weather and Elsie is a bit grumpy at the moment, so I let him stay here last night. I kept a close eye on him while I was looking through the photographs for you.'

Now Arthur had never liked cats. To him they were demanding, crapping things that lay in wait then leaped and took great delight in digging up his rockery. But this little fellow was incredible. 'May I touch him?'

Kate nodded. 'Just a little. I don't want to wake him.'

Arthur tentatively reached out to touch the little tiger's chest. 'Wow,' he said. 'It's so soft.'

'He is three months old now. His name is Elijah.'

Arthur crouched beside the tiger. He could see now why Miriam would be attracted to this place.

Kate laid a friendly hand on his shoulder. 'Let's see if we can find anything out about your wife, shall we?' She pointed to several shoeboxes which sat on the table. 'I woke up early so started to browse through some old documents, photos and letters,' she said. 'I forgot that we had so many. My husband is so untidy but luckily I like to label things. All my photos have dates on the back.'

'Thank you.' Arthur eyed the pile and wondered where to start. 'Is Lord Graystock up yet?'

Kate shook her head. 'He's a late riser. I won't see him until past lunch, especially after all the drinking he did last night. He's not used to it these days.'

'I enjoyed the evening.'

'Me too. After breakfast, and after we've looked at the photos, I will give you a lift to where you want to go.' She handed him a handful of photographs. 'These are all dated 1963. I also included 1962 and 1964 to be certain. You have a browse and see what you can find.'

Arthur took the photos. They were lots of images of girls wearing flowing dresses, or with smooth beehives and wide kohl'd eyes, laughing, partying, posing. Part of him didn't want to discover that his wife had been part of Graystock's harem, another number, a gifter of something that had won her a tiger charm. 'Why did so many people come here?' he mused aloud.

'I was the Kate Moss of the day,' Kate said. 'Graystock was devastatingly handsome, albeit eccentric. Our house was open for artists, for performers, for dreamers, for travellers. Some were attracted by our glamour, others needed a retreat. Some loved the tigers. It went on for many years, until Graystock began to take too

96

many drugs. He became paranoid and aggressive. Slowly, people began to disappear from our lives. I'm the only one who stood by him. I loved him and so did the tigers. We fit together, somehow. It works.'

Arthur almost flicked past the photo of the handsome man wearing a black turtleneck jumper and tight black trousers. His hair was slicked back and he stood with confidence, with one hand on his hip, staring at the camera with smouldering intensity so at first Arthur didn't notice the petite lady stood to the side of him. Then he saw that it was Miriam. His wife was standing with this strutting peacock of a man and gazing at him, her eyes full of admiration.

A wave of nausea flooded over him at the sight of her with another man. He took a gulp of his orange juice to wash it away. He had no idea he was capable of such jealousy, but the thought of Miriam and this man curled up in bed together made him want to clench his hands into fists and punch something hard. He turned the photo to show Kate. 'Do you know who this is?'

Kate gave a short, sharp laugh that didn't suit her. 'That is François De Chauffant, aka the most arrogant man who ever lived. Graystock and he were friends in the sixties. He stayed here many times, with many different women. One night he and Graystock sat in the front room drinking too many brandies and Graystock told De Chauffant a family story that had been passed down through generations. A year later, De Chauffant published his new book — and it was Graystock's story. He called it *Stories We*

Tell. It should have been named *Lies I Tell*. He had the audacity to claim that it was his own family story. Tsk. After that, the men did not speak any longer. In my view, this was no loss.'

'He was a novelist?' Arthur took the charm bracelet from his pocket.

'Hah. So he said. He was a stealer of ideas. A pompous Frenchman who broke Graystock's heart.'

Arthur had felt uncomfortable yesterday, as he thought of how Miriam had acquired the tiger charm from Graystock. Since then he tried to convince himself the charm was just one of many that Graystock gave away willy-nilly. But now it was leading to his discovery of another chapter of Miriam's life, to what might be a love affair with this De Chauffant fellow.

Arthur thought back to the photos of himself at this time. He hadn't slicked back his hair, or worn tight trousers. He never wore black. It was too rebellious or dark. Just from this photo, François De Chauffant symbolised danger and anti-establishment. He looked exciting and tempestuous. How had Miriam gone from this man to Arthur? Had De Chauffant and his wife been lovers? It was a question that he didn't want to ask.

When he met Miriam she seemed so pure. They hadn't made love until their wedding night and he never imagined that there had been anyone else. But now he had to reassess. He tried to remember their dates but nothing had given him the impression that Miriam was experienced, that she'd had a passionate love affair

98

with a French writer. He felt as if someone had tied his intestines in a knot.

He tried to fathom out where such emotion had come from. He'd never had need to be jealous. His wife didn't flirt with other men. If he ever did see a man eyeing her with interest, as men did, then he felt rather proud.

Kate laid her hand on his shoulder.

'This is Miriam. I'm sure of it,' Arthur said.

'She is very pretty. I do not remember her though.'

They looked at the bracelet together. Kate touched the book charm. 'A book. De Chauffant was a writer. It could be . . . '

Arthur was thinking the same thing. He pinched the charm between his thumb and forefinger.

'Have you opened the book?' Kate asked.

Arthur frowned. 'Opened it?'

'There is a tiny clasp on the side.'

The more closely Arthur looked at the book, the more blurred it appeared. He wished he had brought his eyeglass. He hadn't spotted the tiny clasp. Kate bent and rummaged in a kitchen cupboard and produced a large magnifying glass. 'This should do the trick.'

They peered through it together and Kate unfastened the book. It fell open to reveal a single page, in gold not paper. On it was inscribed 'Ma Chérie'.

'It means my darling,' Kate said.

Arthur suspected as much. He stared again at the photo of his wife gazing adoringly at this other man.

'Take the photograph,' Kate insisted. 'Gray-stock wouldn't be happy that we had a photo of this intolerable man in the house.'

Arthur nodded. 'Do you have an envelope?' He didn't want the photo to press against his body. He needed some distance from it.

'Are you going to try and find him?'

Arthur swallowed. He could just go home. He could sit and watch TV with his leg raised on a pouffe, resting his ankle, taking it easy, applying Savlon to his arm. Bernadette would be around with pies and savouries each day, keeping an eye on him. Terry across the road would mow his lawn and the red-haired kids would pelt past his front door. Life could return to normal. He might even go back to Men in Caves and make something for the house, perhaps a wooden coaster for his mug of tea.

Except that everything wouldn't be normal again, because this search had stirred something inside him. This was no longer just about Miriam. It was about himself too.

He was experiencing emotions he didn't know existed. He had begun to discover people and animals that excited him. He wasn't ready to rot away in his armchair, mourning his wife and waiting for his children to call, and filling his days with plant-watering and TV.

And so even if the emotion he felt for this De Chauffant bloke was apprehension and jealousy, it made him feel alive. He needed a jolt to his system. Something to shake him out of the cosy prison he had created for himself. In a home where memories of Miriam were still fresh, he

100

needed something else. He would go home to see that Frederica was fine and watered and pick up some more clothes. Then he would continue his journey.

'Yes,' he said. 'I'm going to find him.'

★ ★ ★

In the car, Arthur didn't feel like speaking. Kate said that she had no idea if De Chauffant was even alive, and even if he was then she didn't care. She didn't bat an eyelid as Arthur asked to be dropped off next to a bush on the B road. 'I can run you to the station,' she said.

Arthur shook his head. 'This is fine.'

Really he had no idea how he was going to get back to the station. He could only hobble a short distance and his arm really stung. He was sure that he would get home though, somehow.

He stepped out onto the side of the road and said thank you to Kate. He shook her hand and assured her once more that he would not sue the Graystock estate. Pausing for a moment, he wondered whether to give her a kiss or to tell her how he was feeling, but instead he said, 'Cheerio then,' and gave her a wave.

If he concentrated on walking with his toes pointing out like a penguin instead of letting them turn in, as they usually did, then that helped his ankle. He traced his footsteps to the gap in the bush. The wind, which had been absent yesterday, whistled through his blue trousers giving him a draughty sensation around his nether regions. He tugged at his suitcase and

101

saw that the corner now had a large hole in it. The nylon was torn and frayed. Who on earth would vandalise an old man's suitcase? He looked out beyond into the field behind the bush. His toiletry bag lay covered in dew on the grass, a tube of toothpaste was trodden into the mud. In the distance a herd of goats stared at him. One of them seemed to be munching on a mustard piece of fabric. His bloody tank top.

Just then an electronic blast of 'Greensleeves' rang out. He stuck his hand into the hole in the suitcase and pulled out his mobile. He had twelve missed calls. Bernadette's name was listed on-screen for all of them except one from Lucy. In other circumstances, he might have pretended not to hear Bernadette's call, but his heart leaped as he pressed the green phone button. 'Hello, Arthur Pepper speaking. How may I help you?'

'Arthur. Thank God it's you. Where are you? You've not been answering your phone.'

He found her concern touching, that anyone could care for him. 'I'm fine,' he said. 'I lost my case with my phone inside. I'm just picking it up now.'

Bernadette explained that she and Nathan had stayed another night in the B and B. They were about to set off back home and would he like a lift?

There was nothing that Arthur had wanted more for a long time. 'Yes please,' he said. 'I'm on the B road leading to Graystock Manor. Look out for my electric-blue trousers.'

Lucy and Dan

The next lunchtime at school Lucy picked up her voice-mail on her mobile and found that her dad had left a rambling message about his visit to Graystock. She'd been out the day before with her two friends, Clara and Annie, who had talked continuously about their kids, so had missed his call. His message broke up constantly, his voice cutting in and out. She could hear road traffic and rock music. Also a woman's voice asking if anyone wanted to stop for sandwiches. Lucy stuck a finger in one ear and frowned as she tried to make out her father's words. At one point she thought he said that he'd been attacked by a tiger. She shook her head and tried to call him back but a snooty man told her that the phone was unavailable.

Attacked by a tiger? Lucy had a vision of her dad slumped on the ground, dead, as a huge cat chewed on his leg. Had she really heard correctly? Was he feeling okay?

Since they had spoken on the phone, when her dad said he'd gone off with Bernadette, she had been plagued with worries about his health. It was so unlike him to take off like that. And now he was leaving messages about tigers. Perhaps she might have to consider giving up her

103

teaching job at some stage in the future, to spend more time keeping an eye on him. She might have to move back into her old bedroom to care for him full-time.

Of course she would do it. She loved him. But the more she had to commit to looking after her dad, the further her dreams of starting her own family would fade. A woman who lived with her ageing dad would hardly be an attractive proposition if she posted a profile on Match.com.

She was sitting in the classroom, marking homework during her lunch break. Year Three was studying the Tudors. She had asked them to draw a scene from Tudor times and had been amazed that over half of the artwork was of executions and decapitated heads. Perhaps she should have asked for pictures of people who were alive instead.

'I'm so proud of you,' her mum said when Lucy qualified as a teacher. They'd gone out for lunch together and got a bit tiddly on a bottle of wine, before going to Debenhams and testing lots of perfumes. 'You'll look after those children as if they're your own.'

Lucy still loved her job. It's just that she sometimes felt she spent all her time looking after others. After hours of looking after kids, escorting them to the toilet, helping to cut up sausages, washing paint out of school skirts, helping to track down stray PE pumps, she now had her father to worry about too.

She'd once thought, in a darker moment, that out of both parents her dad would probably go first. She was sure that her mother would get by.

She was self-sufficient and sensible. Her dad on the other hand had a permanently bewildered air about him as if everything was a surprise. He was now acting in a way that she had never imagined.

'Look after Mum and Dad,' Dan had said as he kissed her on the cheek before he boarded his flight to start his new life in Australia. It seemed so easy for him to utter these five words and then disappear to construct his own happy family down under.

Relations between Dan and Dad were strained. Dad thought that Dan should stay in York, to keep the Pepper family where it had roots. That he shouldn't leave Mum behind or allow his kids to grow up without knowing their grandparents. Lucy phoned Dan to remind him whenever it was Mum's or Dad's birthday. She made excuses to Dad when Dan didn't call. She sometimes felt like the spider in the middle of the family web, trying to hold all the threads together.

When they were younger, Dan used to hang around with a group of lads from the estate. They all smoked and mooched around the street corners, the local shops, the park; wherever they could have a crafty fag and heckle girls who had the misfortune of passing by. When she was eleven Lucy had once seen Dan sitting on the top of the climbing frame. He had a cigarette dangling from his lips and was busy daubing graffiti on the red metal with a black marker pen. He hadn't seen his sister and her friend Eliza strolling past as he wrote the word *bollocks* in foot-high bubble letters.

'Is that your Dan?' Eliza asked. She was short and had long black plaits that swung like pendulums.

'I think so.' She had tried to act nonchalant, merely glancing in his direction.

'He is going to get in trouble for doing that.'

Lucy felt a strange mix of admiration and anger at her brother. He was older, in the last year of secondary school. He was hanging out, showing off — and that made him edgy. He had his own secret life away from Mum and Dad that she didn't have. She had to tell them where she was going and who with and what time she'd be back. Dan could mutter 'I'm going out,' and slam the front door without receiving the third degree.

'Do you know anything about Dan up to no good in the playground?' her dad asked.

'No,' Lucy lied. Her brother had charm and the ability to feign such innocence that if he hadn't become a motor mechanic, then he would surely have won an Oscar for his acting. What was the point of dropping him in it? 'I don't know anything.'

Afterwards she had chastised Dan, who had just laughed and told her not to be such a nerd.

Her brother had confidence and swagger, which Lucy yearned for. He left school and set up his own business, contacting the bank, securing premises and buying car parts on his own and without a doubt in his head. He seemed to be able to hone in on a goal and pursue it single-mindedly, without emotion or doubt getting in the way.

Lucy wished she could address her own life

and worries like that; that she could get a message from her father saying that he had been attacked by a tiger and think, Oh well, at least he's alive. These things happen. That's how Dan would tackle it.

Sometimes Lucy let the pressure get to her. Too tired to move after a day at school and full of reluctance to phone her father and hear how much he was missing Mum, she would unscrew the top off a bottle of red wine and not bother with a glass while she watched an American crime drama. She rather fancied one of the auburn-haired detectives because he never seemed to mind what life threw at him. He had the same attitude to life as her brother. A corpse in his own garage? No worries. A van full of illegal immigrants killed through an arson attack? He would find who did it.

She stood at the window watching the kids in the playground. Tapping her mobile phone against her chin she thought about her brother. *I bet Dan's sunbathing*, she thought. It would be so lovely to live near the beach with the waves crashing up to your front lawn. She'd not made it out to Australia yet but she saw his Facebook photos and always made sure she 'liked' them.

She didn't have a clue what time it was over there when she scrolled to find his number. All she knew was that she had to speak to him. She wanted to hear his take on the situation with their father. He would be practical and have an answer for everything.

A child with an Australian accent answered the phone.

Lucy's mind whirred. How old were Marina and Kyle now? Old enough to answer the phone anyway. She still thought of them as babies.

'Oh hi. Is that Kyle?'

'Yes.'

'Can I speak to Dan, I mean your dad?'

'Who is it?'

'It's Auntie Lucy, back in the UK. I don't know if you'll remember me . . . ' She tailed off her words when she realised that Kyle had already gone.

She heard Dan's voice before he picked up the phone. 'Who is it, mate?'

'Some lady. I don't know.'

The phone rattled. 'Pepper Car Mechanics.'

'Hello, Dan. It's me.'

'*Lucy?*'

'Yes.'

'Wow. It's good to hear from you. It's been a while.'

She resisted saying that it had been a while because he never phoned. 'I know. A couple of months now.'

'That long? Time flies out here.' Worry then crept into his voice. Lucy welcomed hearing it. 'Everything is okay, isn't it?' he said.

'Kind of. I just thought I'd phone. You know, seeing as it's a year since Mum passed on.'

'Yeah. I knew it was coming up. I decided to deal with it by keeping busy.'

'The anniversary was last week.'

'Oh. Right. I knew it was close. My plan worked then.'

Lucy felt a jolt of anger at his joke. Sometimes

108

he had the ability to make her feel eleven again. 'I'm worried about Dad,' she said more sharply than she meant to. 'He's been acting rather strangely recently.'

'Why, what's up with him?'

'Well, he never really leaves the house, only to go to the village. He's turned into a hermit. He wears the same clothes every day and has got a bit obsessed with this motley fern that Mum used to have. And then, without warning or explanation, he took off on a trip with his neighbour, Bernadette. I went round to the house and he wasn't here. He'd travelled down to Bath.'

'That doesn't sound too much to worry about. He probably forgot to tell you.'

'I don't think so. It sounded like there was something he *wasn't* telling me.'

'Well, that doesn't sound like him but I suppose it got him out of the house.'

'That's not all. While he was on his travels he says he went to a stately home to see a lord. And I *think* he said he was attacked by a tiger.'

Dan burst into laughter. 'A what?'

'A tiger.'

'Are there any tigers in the UK? Are they not in zoos?'

'I believe this Lord Graystock keeps them in his grounds.'

Dan didn't speak for a moment and Lucy wondered if he thought that she was the one going crazy. 'That sounds really very unlikely,' he said.

'It's true.'

'Well, that's great though, isn't it? You don't

want him to stay in the house and mope around day in and day out, do you? It shows that he's starting to enjoy life again.'

Lucy sighed. 'Perhaps he *shouldn't* be enjoying life again yet. It's only been twelve months since Mum died.'

'Twelve months is quite a long time. You don't want him to be miserable.'

'No, but . . . .'

'So, do you think he's beginning a relationship with this Bernadette lady?'

'No. I mean, I'd not thought about it.'

'I suppose, even if he did, it would be all holding hands in the park. It's not like it's going to be a hotbed of passion.'

'Dan!'

'It's true. The steamiest it will probably get is a cucumber sandwich and an ice cream with a flake in it. Dad's always been the quiet subdued type so I can't see him changing much now.'

Lucy blinked. *Her dad and Bernadette.* Was this why her father was acting cagey? 'I'm sure he's not ready for anything like that. He has the house to think about.'

'Woah, slow down. He goes out on a day trip and you're marrying him off and worrying about his state of mind. Let him get on with it. Concentrate on your own life.'

'I *am* letting him get on with it.'

'Lucy. He's on his own. It's great that he's got something going on in his life other than *Countdown*, murder mysteries and cups of tea. *Countdown* is still on over there, right?'

'Yes.' Lucy scratched her neck. She sat down

110

behind her desk. 'Anyway. Do you think you could come over soon, Dan? It's been over eighteen months. I thought you might have made it to Mum's funeral. I could do with a little support with Dad.'

'You know I couldn't come to the funeral,' Dan said quickly. 'Kelly was in the middle of her medical exams. Kyle had broken his arm. Marina had the measles. It was just the worst time. Besides, you didn't go either . . . '

'I'm not accusing you . . . '

'Well, just to say that you didn't go either.'

'I know . . . '

'Well . . . '

'Well . . . '

They had resorted back to being kids again.

'I'm just really worried about Dad, but you're on the other side of the world. You don't have to deal with the day-to-day stuff of making sure that he's eating, trying to cheer him up when he's depressed,' she said. Then unable to stop herself, she added, 'You always had it easy as a kid too.'

'Hey, where did that come from?'

'Sorry but . . . '

'Look, Lucy. You and Dad will always be my family but I have my own wife and kids now. They take priority. Maybe you should think about having your own family. There'll be a day when Dad isn't around any longer and you'll be on your own.'

Lucy felt like she had a boiled sweet stuck in her throat. She wanted a child more than anything. Dan didn't know about her miscarriage.

'Are you still there?'

She tried to swallow. 'Just about.'

'I'm sorry I shouted.'

'It's okay.'

'Do you mean that?'

'I don't know,' she sighed.

'There's nothing much I can do, Luce. Mum's gone and that's dreadfully sad. As for Dad, it sounds as if you're worrying over nothing. He must be okay for him to leave you a message. If he's been away with this Bernadette lady, then that sounds pretty normal too. When he starts to need real help, then we can talk. You can call me anytime.'

'Maybe he's starting to need real help now . . . '

'He sounds fine.'

'But, you're not *here*.'

'Don't say it like that. I left because it's a great life for me out here, not to escape anything in the UK. Okay?'

Feeling unable to carry on the conversation without getting more worked up, Lucy hung up.

Immediately her phone buzzed as Dan tried to call her back. She ignored it, pressing the red button to reject his call. He tried again and she rejected that too.

Needing time to think, she held her head in her hands. She didn't hear the school bell ring and stayed in that position until she felt a small hand on her shoulder.

'Are we okay to come into class now, miss?'

Mobile Technology

When Arthur, Bernadette and Nathan arrived back at Bernadette's house she insisted that Arthur come inside for a coffee. He just wanted to get home, to phone the doctor and get an appointment for a tetanus jab. He wanted to be in the inner, peaceful sanctum of his own house, to get away from the madness and unfamiliarity of the past few days. He longed to see beige walls and the pot pourri leaf in the hallway and to water Frederica. He wanted to call Lucy to tell her properly about his adventure; he was no good at leaving telephone messages.

As Bernadette sang a song he didn't recognise at the top of her voice in her kitchen, Arthur sat on the sofa. He reached up and pressed his forearm — it felt very tender, almost like a burn. But he smiled as he recalled Elijah the baby tiger curled up in his basket next to the range cooker. He thought about how bizarre he must look, with his holey suitcase sitting beside him, and his blue trousers.

He had never been inside Bernadette's home before. Everywhere she could add colour, she had done. The walls were daffodil yellow, the skirting boards and doors were painted a leaf green. The curtains were sumptuous velvet with large red and purple flowers. There were ornaments on every surface — small ceramic girls holding dogs, colourful glass vases with silk flowers, holiday souvenirs. It felt homely, lived in, compared to the clinical cleanliness of his own home. Miriam had been a tidier-upper too. Each time a newspaper might be put down or something was where it shouldn't be, it would be whisked away and put in its 'proper' place. 'Sit down and relax,' Arthur used to say when he got in from work and Miriam was ironing, tidying, cleaning.

'It won't do it itself,' she used to say. 'A tidy home is a tidy mind.'

So Arthur would sit as his wife maelstromed around him. When she died, he had picked up her mantle to carry on how she would have liked it.

Nathan entered the room. 'Hey, MC Hammer,' he said, nodding at Arthur's trousers. 'Can't touch this.' He threw himself into a chair and hung his arms over the back. His legs bent like sticks of liquorice. Sniffing every ten seconds or so, he occasionally wiped his nose with the back of his hand.

Arthur racked his brains for what to say. He had no idea who this MC Hammer person was, if it was a person. He recalled Bernadette's request for him to have a man-to-man chat with her son. Finally he settled on, 'How did your university search go?'

Nathan shrugged. 'S'awright.'

'Did you see anywhere you liked?'

Again the young man's shoulders did the talking.

Arthur looked at the line of photographs in frames on the mantelpiece. One proclaimed World's Best Mum. A much younger Nathan, Bernadette and Carl held up a large fish and smiled for the camera. A lone photo of Carl caught his eye. He was sunbathing and nursing a glass of red wine. 'What job did your dad do?'

Nathan shifted in his chair. 'He was an engineer. He mended lifts, I think. Y'know, the electrics and stuff.'

'Is that what you want to study at university?'

'Not really.'

'What do you want to study?'

'I'm looking at English courses. Mum thinks it will be a good option.'

'What do you think of that?'

'I dunno really.'

Struggling to spark any conversation that seemed to interest the boy, Arthur began to ramble. He found himself telling Nathan that when he was young it was natural to follow in your father's footsteps. His own father was a locksmith so that was the career path mapped out for him.

'We didn't call them careers then though. They were just jobs or trades. I had to do an apprenticeship. It meant working for two years shadowing a locksmith, just standing watching him a lot of the time, not being paid much. He was a good fellow was Stanley Shearing. He always took the time to explain things to me, show me how things worked. I'm not sure that young people have that these days, someone to take an interest in what they do. You seem to get set free in the world, to university and to make your own way in life. I suppose times change. We got married a lot younger in the old days too. By then I was established in my job so I could bring home quite decent money. We wouldn't have survived on my apprentice money or a student grant.'

All the time he spoke, Nathan stared at his phone. He wriggled both thumbs on the screen.

Bernadette brought three cups of coffee in. 'Are you boys having a nice chat? I'll make myself scarce then.'

Arthur stared after her helplessly as she left the room. What could he possibly have in common with this young man? He obviously didn't want to speak about work or university. In the end he said, 'Who on earth is MC Hammer?'

Nathan looked up. 'He's an American rap artist from the eighties. He wore baggy trousers with a low crotch like the ones that you're wearing. He's a preacher or holy man now.' He moved his fingers around his phone again then held up the screen.

Arthur looked at a photo of a black man wearing glasses and voluminous silver trousers. 'Aaah,' he said. 'So, do you like music?'

Nathan nodded. 'Mainly rock. But I like really old stuff too, like the Beatles.'

'I think I actually have an old Beatles album somewhere. You can have it if you like. It's a vinyl record though. You'd need a record player to listen to it.'

'Mum has one in the attic. What is it called?'

'*Rubber Soul*, I think.'

116

Nathan nodded. 'I have it as a download but it would be good to listen to vinyl. I didn't think you'd like the Beatles.'

'Miriam liked them more than I did. She was a John Lennon fan. I always appreciated Paul McCartney more.'

'That kind of figures. George Harrison was the coolest though.'

Arthur edged a couple of inches along the sofa. 'Can you look anything up on your phone? Is it like a library?'

'Kind of.'

'Can you look something up for me?'

'Sure.'

'I'm looking for a French novelist. His name is François De Chauffant. I want to know where he lives.'

Nathan tapped his phone screen. 'Simples,' he said.

Arthur took the phone from him. There was a small, square photo of a white stucco-fronted maisonette. It looked very grand. Underneath there was an address in London. 'Is this address current?'

Nathan tapped around a bit more. 'It's the only one for him, unless he's gone back to France. Well, actually he's from Belgium originally. His family moved to Nice when he was a small child.'

'Does it say all that on your phone?'

'I knew some of it. We studied De Chauffant in class. He's one of the most influential novelists of the sixties. His novel *Stories We Tell* is a classic. Have your heard of it?'

'I have actually.' Arthur thought of Kate's tale of how he had stolen it from Graystock and wondered what man would do such a thing.

Nathan took his phone back. 'Do you have your own mobile with you? I can Bluetooth you the link.'

'I'll just write it down,' Arthur said. He found a pen and scrap of paper in his suitcase. 'Can you read it out for me? My eyesight isn't very good.'

Nathan rolled his eyes but he read the address out in a flat voice. 'Did you really get attacked by a tiger?' he said as Arthur slipped the address into his back pocket.

Arthur nodded then unfastened the wrist button on his shirt and rolled up his sleeve. The padding that Kate had taped in place was just about hanging on. Blood had seeped through and dried leaving rust-coloured stripes. He saw Nathan's eyes widen but then the young man seemed to remember that it wasn't cool to show any interest. He shrugged and slumped back.

Bernadette appeared again, this time holding a plate of jam puffs. 'I've made these while you were chatting,' she said. 'You just roll out the puff pastry, cut it into squares and add a blob of jam in the centre of each. Then pop it in the oven and *voilà*! It's a very simple recipe. Now, eat them while they are still warm.'

Arthur and Nathan both reached out to take a jam puff at the same time. They sat and blew on them then ate.

'Nathan and I are thinking of visiting Manchester next week.' Bernadette settled on

118

the sofa beside Arthur. 'You are welcome to join us again, if you fancy another outing. I hear it's a vibrant city. The English course at the university is supposed to be superb.'

Arthur picked up his cup of coffee, which had now gone cold. 'Actually I was thinking of maybe trying London out next,' he said. 'There's a novelist's house that I'd like to visit. I think that my wife might have been connected to him in some way.'

He wasn't sure if under his thick black fringe Nathan raised an eyebrow, but Arthur thought that he might have done.

London

London was a surprise, a delight even. Arthur had expected to find a grey and impersonal city with buildings weighing down on him and blank Munch-like faces of disillusioned office workers. But it was vibrant, how he imagined a foreign land.

The weather was close and hot down here. Everything moved, a kaleidoscope of sounds and colours and shapes. Cabs honked their horns, bicycles whizzed by, pigeons strutted, people shouted. He heard more languages than he knew existed. He felt like he was at the centre of a carousel, motionless, unnoticed as the world whizzed around him.

Surprisingly he wasn't overwhelmed, even when strangers bumped into him without apologising. He wasn't part of this strange world. He was a visitor, transient and knowing he could return to the safety of his home. This made him feel braver, intrepid.

He'd got off the train at King's Cross and decided to walk as much as he could. The map he bought from the station made everything look close to hand.

He'd decided that his usual trousers were a bit too hot for a train journey and trip around the capital, so he'd washed, ironed and wore the blue trousers given to him by Kate Graystock. Bernadette had given him a voucher for a walking shop in Scarborough and he had ventured beyond the village and paid a visit. There, he purchased a navy nylon rucksack with lots of pockets, a flask and a compass, also a pair of walking sandals. They were sturdy but would keep his feet cool.

He strode ahead with his ankle strapped tightly with bandages. His blue trousers weren't anything out of the ordinary here, as he walked alongside a girl with pink hair and a man who had holes in his ears that could fit a CocaCola can through. He saw a poodle with a purple pompom tail and a man who rode down the pavement on a unicycle while talking on his mobile phone.

The sight of the man reminded him that he hadn't yet spoken to Lucy since he left a garbled message from the back of Bernadette's car. There had been just twenty-four hours between his return from Graystock Manor and setting off on the trip to London. He had called her twice but got her answer message. He wondered if she was avoiding him or was too busy to speak.

He carried on striding out, taking in the sights and sounds, but he found that the more he walked, the more feelings of embarrassment and regret began to set in.

When Miriam once suggested a week in London for their thirtieth wedding anniversary, catching a show and maybe a lunch in Covent Garden, he had laughed. *Laughed*. Why did she want to go to London? he'd said. It was dirty and smelly and too busy and too big. It was just a bigger version of Newcastle or Manchester. There were pickpockets and beggars on every corner. Eating out would cost a fortune.

'It was just a thought,' Miriam said lightly. She hadn't seemed too bothered that he had dismissed her suggestion out of hand.

He regretted it now. They should have visited new places together, had new experiences when the kids got older. They should have grasped the opportunity to do what they wanted to do and expand their horizons, especially now he knew that Miriam had lived a fuller, more exciting life before they met. He had stifled her. He had been so set in his ways.

The month after their conversation, Arthur booked them a mini-break in a spa hotel in Scarborough — much more civilised than London. He paid extra for an en suite room and there had been chocolate digestives on the bedside table. On the evening of their anniversary, he had taken Miriam to see an Alan Ayckbourn play, which she very much enjoyed. They bought chips afterwards and walked on the beach with their scarves wrapped around their heads to fend off the wind.

It had been idyllic. Well, to him anyway. He wondered now if it had been a comedown for his wife. Had she been thinking about De Chauffant when she had suggested the trip to London? Had she hoped for a glimpse of her ex-lover?

Jealousy wasn't an emotion that he was used to. He hated how it seemed to dig him in his side, made his stomach churn and sniggered at him. He had been wrong to laugh at Miriam. She was right. He was wrong.

He spent the day being a tourist, doing what he and Miriam should have done. He stood and gaped at the famous landmarks of London — the London Eye, the Houses of Parliament, Big Ben — and he loved the experience. He got on and off the red open-top tourist buses and walked where he could. Adrenaline coursed through his veins. He felt as if the city embraced him. He had expected it to be through fear of the unknown, but it was through exhilaration.

He bought a red bus fridge magnet and a pencil with a gold plastic Tower of London on top. He stopped for lunch at the Pearly Queen café, which had stainless steel tables that sat wonkily on the pavement. A man joined him without asking. He wore a grey pinstriped suit with a pink handkerchief poking out of the pocket. His face was red, as if he had been running or something had angered him. Sitting with his legs splayed open, his knees almost touched Arthur's. Arthur squeezed his out of the way and tried to look straight ahead. But when the man ordered a bacon and cheddar panini he made eye contact and nodded. 'All right?'

'Fine, thank you.'

'You married?'

'Yes.' He automatically reached out and twisted his wedding ring around his finger.

'How long for?'

'Over forty years.'

'Jesus. You get less for murder.' The man grinned.

123

Arthur did not smile. He hadn't wanted this man to join him. All he wanted was a quiet cup of tea and a bacon sandwich before he carried on his sightseeing, building himself up for going to find François De Chauffant's house. He looked over the man's shoulder to catch the eye of the waitress who had taken his order. He'd ordered his cup of tea ten minutes ago and it still hadn't arrived.

'Sorry mate,' the man said, his expression changed. 'Just my little joke. You don't hear of many long marriages these days. It must be nice, huh, having someone waiting at home for you?'

'It was nice, yes.'

'You said *was*?'

Arthur swallowed. 'My wife died a year ago.' He finally caught the waitress's attention with a wave. She immediately mouthed sorry and brought over his tea.

'Apologies, my darlink. I'm rushed off my feet,' she said. Her pink dress hung off her shoulder revealing a purple bra strap. 'I will bring you an extra-large sandwich.'

'The small one that I ordered is adequate.'

'But it will be the same price.' She had a Polish accent and long fingers like sticks of chalk.

'It is very kind of you.'

She nodded and gave a curtsy.

'I don't have a very big appetite,' Arthur said to the man. 'But I think she would have been offended if I had insisted on the small sandwich.'

The man's eyes followed the waitress as she went behind the counter and started to make a hot chocolate. 'She's a babe,' he said. 'Dark eyes, dark hair. I like that.'

Arthur poured milk into his tea and sipped it. He felt uncomfortable at the man's confidence, how his legs invaded his space, how he was eyeing up the waitress.

'Do you mind me asking you something, yeah?' the man said leaning forward. He didn't wait for Arthur to agree. 'I'm thinking of getting married too. You look like you'd be good at offering advice, yeah? You know, you've been around a while. You've done things, seen things . . . a man of the world.'

'I'll see what I can do,' Arthur said cautiously.

'Okay.' The man reached in his pocket and pulled out a small notebook. 'I've been writing stuff down and trying to clear my head, so that I can decide. I read my notes before I go to sleep.'

'It's a big decision to get married.'

'Tell me about it. How did you know that your wife was the one?'

'I met her and I knew she was the woman I wanted to marry.'

'Yeah? Go on . . . '

'When I was with her I didn't want to be with anyone else. I never considered if she was *the one* because there was no one else. I liked the simplicity of life with her. We met when I was twenty-six and she was a year younger. We held hands, we walked, we kissed. All the time I thought of just her. I never looked at anyone else. We got engaged and then got married less than two years after we met. It was like I was following an invisible path that had already been

125

laid out for me. There were other paths leading off it in different directions but I never wondered where they went. I just kept on heading forwards.'

'Hmmm. That sounds simple. I wish I had that.'

Arthur sipped his tea.

'Were you faithful?'

It was a fair question from someone who was thinking of committing himself to another for life. 'Yes, I was.'

'Did you ever wonder what it would be like with someone else? You know. Did you look at other women and wonder . . . ? I hope you don't think I'm being too obtrusive.'

Arthur thought that. Yes, the man was being very nosy; however he didn't detect any salaciousness, only curiosity in relation to his own situation. 'I did wonder, because that's human nature. But I had no desire to pursue anything. I might see another woman and think she was pretty or had a nice smile. But I knew what I could lose, so I just put thoughts out of my mind.'

'You're very sensible. I wish it was as easy as that. I wish I could compartmentalise my thoughts. I have two women, you see.'

'Oh.'

'I kind of love them both. I'm thirty-five. I want to get married soon and have kids.'

'By the time I was thirty-three we had the two kids.'

'I want to buy a house and do the family thing.' The man bent his head forward and drew a circle with his finger. 'I'm getting a bald spot. See it? It's time that I got a shed and went for walks in the country with my wife and kids. But I'm torn. May I tell you about both the girls? You'll be able to advise me. I can tell by your face.'

The waitress brought over their food. Arthur's bacon sandwich was the same size as the plate it sat on. 'Good, yes?' she said.

'Very good.' Arthur gave a thumbs-up.

The man bit into his panini. A string of cheese dribbled and stuck to his chin. 'One of them is my girlfriend. We've been together for three years. She's really lovely. I saw her sitting in the window of a teashop. And I walked past and went in to buy a cake just because I fancied her. I headed straight for her and asked her out, told her I'd take her to a flash restaurant. She said no at first. I liked that. She was a challenge. I worked at it though. I gave her my card when I left. I bought a bunch of flowers and waited outside for her. There was something about her that drew me to her, like you said about your wife. I wore her down. I made her friend laugh. Finally, she said yes and we went to see some Hugh Grant film at the flicks. It was a lovely night. We held hands like teenagers. And she didn't want a fancy restaurant afterwards, just a burger. Donna's a lovely girl, works really hard as a hairdresser.' He took out his wallet and showed Arthur a photograph. A girl with a heart-shaped face and a red scarf tied in her hair smiled back.

'She's a pretty girl.'

'The other one I see though, Manda . . . ' He blew on his fingers as if they were on fire and he was putting it out. 'She's hot stuff. She lets me do things to her, you know?'

Arthur didn't know, but he nodded.

'I met her in a massage parlour. She was the receptionist. I mean, if I was happy, if I was satisfied with Donna, I wouldn't have been in that type of place, would I? Donna was away at some hairdressing convention and Manda took me back to hers. I'd only known her an hour and . . . *wham.*' He clapped his hands together and grinned. 'Fireworks. That girl knew things I didn't know existed. The pair of us could hardly walk afterwards.'

'But what about Donna?'

'I don't ask her to do any of those things because if I did and she let me, I would lose respect for her. She's not that kind of girl and Manda is. It's a complicated situation.'

'Did you not feel guilty about cheating on your girlfriend?'

The man frowned. 'Kind of. Afterwards. I wish she hadn't gone to that damn convention and then I wouldn't have had to go looking for trouble.'

Arthur had lost his appetite. He cut his sandwich into quarters and then added brown sauce, but he didn't eat.

'So, who should I choose? Once I get married, that's it. I want to be faithful. I want to at least try. If I have kids then I'll be a family man, yeah? It should be Donna. She's the marrying kind, but I know what else is out there. It'll be very vanilla with her. I might miss the chocolate chips. But Manda's changing. She's started talking about doing other stuff outside the bedroom, y'know, like proper dating. We went to the theatre and she was all dressed up and we had a great night. I got even more confused.'

'But if you had the chocolate chips all the time, that would be sickly.' Arthur hated that he was comparing women to flavours of ice cream but it was a language that the pinstripe-suited man understood.

'So what would you do? Stay with the simple flavour or go for something more exciting?'

Arthur considered the man's predicament. He turned it over in his mind. It was obviously very important if the man went round asking strangers to help make decisions about his private life. 'The thing is, these days,' he said, 'there is too much choice. When I was younger, you were grateful with what you were given. You were lucky if you got socks at Christmas and now young people want everything. A phone is not enough; it has to be the best all-singing, all-dancing phone. They want computers, houses, cars, to go for meals and drinks. And not just any old food, it has to be at fancy restaurants and expensive beer in bottles.

'You say you wouldn't respect Donna if she let you do things, but you don't respect her now because you are seeing Manda too. Would you respect Donna if she married you? If she married you and *you* know that you're a cheat and don't really deserve her. And this other girl who is interested in certain things — how long will that appeal to you? Can you see yourself dusting and vacuuming the house together? Is she going to still want to let you do those things once she's a mother? Does she do those things with other men besides you? So, instead of thinking which woman is the most suitable to marry, perhaps the answer is that neither of them are. If I was Donna, I would look for someone who deserved me and treated me with respect. If I was Manda then I wouldn't want to be with a man who cheated on his girlfriend. Therefore I don't think you should ask either of them to marry you, just in case one of them says yes.'

The man sat for a while, his eyebrows knitted, his hands clasped on his lap. He shook his head. 'It's not an option I'd thought of. You have just fucked with my mind.'

'Sorry. It's best to tell the truth.'

'I appreciate it. You're brutal though. That's a third option thrown into the mix. You mean I should dump them both and find someone else?'

'Maybe someone who is vanilla with a few chocolate chips.'

'Brutal. Let me pay for your lunch, yeah?'

'It's fine. I can manage it.'

'I don't think I'll ask anyone else's opinion.' The man stood and shook his head again. He threw a twenty-pound note on the table. 'I need to work this out for myself.'

'Sorry if I've confused you.'

'Nah. I asked for your advice and you gave it. Fair and square.'

Arthur hesitated. He saw how the man had changed. His shoulders were rounded, his eyes searching for the truth. He swallowed before he spoke. Perhaps he himself needed the brutal truth too. 'Before you go,' he said, 'can I ask you something? It's unlikely we'll meet again and you can give me your thoughts.'

'Sure. What is it?'

'If you met a girl and there'd been other men before you and she'd lived in different parts of the world and had done lots of things, but she didn't tell you about it, would it bother you?'

The man cocked his head on one side as he considered. 'Nah. It would make her who she was. I mean there might be reasons that she didn't tell me. Some people live for the day and don't look back. Why look back at the past if you're happy with the present?'

Arthur took time to think. He took a serviette and wrapped his bacon sandwich in it and put it in his pocket. 'And do you ever buy jewellery for Manda and Donna?'

'Sure. Donna likes glittery cheap stuff. She has drawers full of it. Manda likes the expensive shit. Diamonds and platinum, to show how much I like her. Costs me a fortune.'

'Do you give a great deal of thought to what you buy them?' Arthur asked, thinking of the singular engraved page in the book charm and how enamoured De Chauffant might have been with Miriam.

'Not really. I leave it to them. They point out stuff they like, or buy it themselves. Or I might pick up a little something off friends I know who get nice stuff cheap. I'd make an effort with a wedding ring, though. That's for ever.'

'Thank you. That is helpful.' Arthur stood up and faced the man. 'You asked if I made a good choice with my wife. I absolutely did. But I'm not sure whether I was a good choice for her.'

The man reached out and punched Arthur's shoulder. 'Nah, you seem like a kind man. I think you probably were a good choice.'

'Do you think so?' He suddenly felt like he needed affirmation, even from this cheating, brash stranger.

'You were faithful. You're kind. You listen. You're thoughtful. You offer good advice. You're not a bad-looking fellow. I'm sure she made a good choice with you, yeah.'

'Thank you,' Arthur said quietly. He paid his bill and left a two-pound tip. The waitress saw him and waved.

'She sure is a babe,' the man said as they walked away together. 'Do you think that . . . ?'

'No,' Arthur said firmly. 'No, I do not.'

The Book

François De Chauffant's house was larger than Arthur had expected. It was extravagant, opulent, like it should be a five-star hotel with a man wearing a grey top hat standing at the door. Its white frontage gleamed in the sunshine. Arthur felt suddenly embarrassed by his own three-bedroom red-brick semi-detached. He had never aspired to own anything grander. He and Miriam had once discussed moving to be a little closer to Dan and Lucy's school, but he had never judged himself or others by the size of their home. Home is where the heart is, his mother used to say. Should he have worked his way up the career ladder so he could have afforded something grander for his family? Should he have strived to be more successful? These were questions that he had never considered until he had started this journey.

As he stood before the house and surveyed the swooping crescent, the poplar trees, the neatly trimmed square, he imagined De Chauffant and Miriam strolling hand in hand, she all in white and he dressed all in black, drawing admiring glances from neighbours and passers-by. In his imagination they stepped in unison and giggled, heads bowed and touching. Then they kissed on the threshold before disappearing into the house.

Arthur dug his hands in his pockets and surveyed his ridiculous blue trousers, his sturdy walking sandals, his nylon rucksack with a compass. Glamorous he was not. If Miriam had stayed with the French writer she could have lived a life of luxury and creativity, rather than plumping for domesticity with a boring lock-smith. Her kids could have been privately educated and wanted for nothing. Arthur had often refused to buy toys for Dan and Lucy because they were too expensive.

But not once had his wife made him feel like he wasn't good enough. He was doing that to himself.

His knees shook as he ascended the stairs. He took hold of the black iron door knocker, which was the shape of a lion's head. Straightening his back, he stood in readiness for the door to be opened by an ageing, raven-haired French love-god.

He had already decided that De Chauffant would still be wearing his tight black trousers and turtleneck jumper. It was his trademark, Arthur was sure. He would be barefoot and have a pencil tucked behind his ear. How would he answer the door — with a flourish, or with a sigh because his latest masterpiece had been disturbed?

Arthur rapped as assertively as he could. He waited for a few minutes then knocked again. He felt nauseous, as if he had just stepped off a train after a long journey. His head told him to about turn, to leave and forget about this silly mission. His heart told him to stay, that he had to carry on.

There was a rattle behind the door, the sound of chains being removed. The door opened by a few centimetres. He saw a flash of pink clothing. An eye pressed to the gap.

'Yes?'

He couldn't tell if the voice belonged to a man or a woman. It wasn't the voice he had granted to his love rival.

'I'm here to see François De Chauffant.'

'Who are you?'

'My name is Arthur Pepper. I believe that my wife was a friend of Mr Chauffant.' The door remained ajar so he added, 'She died a year ago and I am trying to trace her friends.'

The door opened slowly. A young man, in his mid- to late twenties, stood there. He was very thin and wore jeans that hung off his hips. Led Zeppelin, his T-shirt said. It was short enough to display his navel, which was pierced with a red glittery stone. Hollow navy eyes blinked through his spiky, powder-pink hair.

'He won't recognise her, your wife.' His accent was soft, Eastern European.

'I have a photograph.'

The man shook his head. 'He is not good at recognising anyone.'

'I have reason to believe that he and my wife were close. It was a long time ago. In the sixties . . . '

'He has Alzheimer's.'

'Oh.' This was unexpected. Arthur's vision of a cocky beatnik dressed in black vanished, not replaced by anything else.

The young man looked as if he was going to

close the door, but then he said, 'Would you like to come inside? You look like you could do with a sit down.'

It was only when he said this that Arthur realised that his ankle was threatening to lock up. He had been walking since he had met the man with two girlfriends at the café. 'That would be most kind.'

'My name is Sebastian,' the young man said over his shoulder. His feet made a sucking noise as he padded across the mosaic tiles in the hallway leaving prints that vanished after a few seconds. 'Please. Make yourself at home.' He waved toward a door. 'Would you like tea? I don't like to make it for just myself.' His eyes were wide, full of longing.

'I would love tea.'

Arthur opened the door and went into the room. Each wall had floor-to-ceiling shelves stacked with books. A long stepladder was propped against a wall. The furniture was made from heavy dark wood with worn velvet-padded seats and cushions in shades of ruby, sapphire, gold and emerald. The ceiling was painted indigo blue and specked with silver stars. Wow, Arthur thought. He stood on the spot and turned. The room was like a film set. He didn't want to sit down. He wanted to circle this room and reach out to touch the books. There was a large oak roll-top desk positioned in the bay window, looking out into the street. On it sat an old typewriter with a piece of paper, ready for De Chauffant to conjure up another masterpiece, or plagiarise. Arthur moved closer to see if there were any words on the crisp white sheet. There were not. He felt a brief wave of disappointment. He wasn't artistic or creative himself, so it intrigued him that people could earn a living through painting or writing.

It was only after a while that he noticed that the sideboard was coated in dust. Mugs were dotted around the parquet floor. Chocolate-bar wrappers poked out from behind the cushions on the sofa. All was not as glossy as it first seemed. Arthur selected a chair upholstered in chartreuse velvet and sat down.

Sebastian came back into the room. He carried a red and white polka-dotted plastic tray upon which sat two chintzy teacups and a matching teapot. He set the tray on a coffee table, pushing a pile of magazines onto the floor. Arthur reached out, picked them up and put them on another chair.

Sebastian didn't acknowledge this, as if it was normal to create a mess as he went along. 'Here we are,' he said. 'Shall I be Mother, and pour? That is how you say it, yes?'

'Yes.' Arthur smiled. He stopped himself from reaching out to help when he saw the young man's hand trembling.

'So.' Sebastian handed Arthur his cup and saucer. He pointed his finger in turn at chairs dotted around the room then picked the largest one, which had stuffing poking out from the corner of the faded teal upholstery. He tucked up his feet. 'Tell me about your wife. Why are you here?'

Arthur explained about the bracelet and how

137

he was tracing the story behind the charms, so he could learn more about Miriam before they met. 'I am learning more about myself too,' he admitted. 'With each person I encounter, with each story I hear, I feel as if I am changing and growing. And maybe others benefit a little from meeting me also. It's a strange feeling.'

'It must be exciting.'

'It is, but I feel guilty too. I am living but my wife isn't.'

Sebastian gave a small nod as if he understood. 'I felt alive once too. I was here, I was there, I was excited. Now I am here. Trapped.'

'You're not really trapped, are you? I mean, you can leave here when you want?'

Sebastian waved his hand dismissively. 'Let me tell you about my life, Arthur. While you are discovering yours, mine is dying. This may sound dramatic, but it is how I feel. François and I were together for a couple of years before he forgot who he was. It started with small things — he forgot to turn off the lights, he lost his spectacles. Everyone does these things, yes? It is easy to put the breakfast cereal in the coffee cup cupboard, or lose your shoes under the bed. You come upstairs and forget why, or buy a bottle of milk when you have some in the fridge. Except François nearly burned the house down.' His eyes grew watery with emotion. 'He went upstairs for his afternoon nap — always between two and four. I leave him alone during these times, so he can regain his strength before he starts to write again. I came into the bedroom to wake him and the bed was on fire. Flames, reaching almost as high as the ceiling. François just sat looking out of the window. He didn't even notice that he was in danger. I ran like a gazelle, took a blanket into the bathroom and ran the shower to dampen it. Then I used it to smother the flames. The mattress was black, smoking. And still François he said nothing. I took his shoulders. *Are you okay?* I asked. But he stared at me blankly. It was then that I knew his mind was gone. He would never be brilliant again.'

A strange feeling crept over Arthur; an awareness that Sebastian wasn't talking about De Chauffant as an assistant would. 'How did you meet him?'

'I came to London four years ago and worked at a nightclub, behind the bar. My employers spoke to me badly and cut my wages if I broke a glass. I was too young to stand up for myself. François came in one night with friends and we chatted, about this and that. He started to come in most nights. We talked each time for three weeks and he offered me a job. He said it would be part housekeeping, part admin tasks and part keeping him company. I found him fascinating. I was flattered that a famous writer was interested in me. I moved in to help and our relationship developed from there.'

Arthur sipped his tea, pondering on the word *relationship*.

'I hope you do not mind me talking to you, Arthur,' Sebastian said. 'My words run away with me. I have kept them inside for a long time.

So many people hate him. His friends and family don't care any longer. He changed agents and the new one did not care, only for making money. There is only me left. I can't walk out. So I stay and care for him. I cannot leave. I am twenty-eight and stuck.'

'Are you his . . . carer?'

'I am now, for there is nothing else between us. Not like there was. When we met he was magnificent. He was free. That is what I liked about him. I helped him to type up his words, with day-to-day chores, helped with his diary. He said that I reminded him of a poodle, so pretty and eager. I laughed at this and he liked that I wasn't offended. He could say nasty things, be grumpy and awkward, but he gave me a home. He gave me confidence. I had money to send back to my family. I feel I owe it to stay and care for him. If I go, who will look after him? I have all these . . . worries.' He spun his hands around at the side of his head.

'There must be others who can help out?' Arthur asked.

Sebastian shook his head. 'Not for me.'

'Do you have someone to talk to?'

'I have a couple of friends, but they are not close. It has helped to talk to you, Arthur. To get my words out of my head. I needed to speak and I feel a little better now. I know that I will have to leave one day . . . or else I will go crazy.'

'I feel better for leaving my home and meeting people,' Arthur admitted. 'I never thought I would.'

Sebastian nodded. 'Thank you for listening to me.'

They finished their tea and Sebastian gathered the cups. He put them on top of a sideboard with four others. 'Do you think that François and your wife were lovers?' he asked.

It was a direct question, but one that Arthur had been mulling in his head since Kate Graystock had shown him the photograph. 'I think they might have been,' he said.

'And this makes you feel sad, yes?'

'Not so much sad, but confused. I didn't know that she had lived with a man before me. I'm not sure how I could live up to a man with such a voracious reputation.'

'Hmmm,' Sebastian said thoughtfully. Then, 'You do know that François is a homosexual?'

Arthur shook his head. 'No. How can he . . . ' He had guessed that Sebastian was gay, but De Chauffant? Kate had depicted him as a promiscuous playboy.

'He and your wife might have been lovers. In the sixties, the seventies, he could not, how you say, keep it in his trousers. But he liked men too. But to say so then would have ruined his work, his reputation. He liked to think of himself as a legend, so there were lots of girls and women. Too many. I do not think he was with anyone long enough to break their heart; only if that person was very needy.' He said it as though it were a question.

'Miriam was a strong woman.'

'Then I doubt he would have left her broken-hearted . . . if that helps you at all . . . '

It did not. 'Do you think I could meet him?'

'I can tell him that you are here . . . He

141

doesn't get many visitors. He might be pleased.'

Arthur wanted to see for himself this man who had lied to women, to his wife, who had stolen Lord Graystock's idea. This enigma. 'Yes.' He stood. 'I want to see him.'

He followed Sebastian up two flights of stairs. When they reached a door at the top of the house, he found that he was clenching his fists. But he had to confront this part of his wife's past, this man who was the antithesis of everything he himself was. Had this wild, reckless genius stolen Miriam's heart?

Sebastian pushed the door open. He stepped inside first. 'He is awake,' he said. 'Do not stay long though. He tires easily and I will be the first in the firing line.' He made a gun with his finger and then fired it at his own temple.

Arthur nodded. He hesitated outside the room for a moment and then walked inside.

Although he knew about De Chauffant's illness, it hadn't prepared him for the sight of the man who sat hunched in an armchair in the corner of the room. He was small with white straggly hair and overlong eyebrows. His hands were clawed, his face distorted. His eyes were staring and hollow — a mere echo of the swaggering young man in the photograph given to him by Kate Graystock. He didn't acknowledge Arthur or Sebastian's presence.

The room smelled of piss and disinfectant, poorly masked by rose air freshener. There was a single bed with grey woollen blankets and a used ceramic chamber pot at the side. A bedside table was piled with books and a baby monitor. The red light was on. He can still read, Arthur thought, relieved that this poor creature had at least this pleasure left.

He stepped forwards and Sebastian backed away and out of the room. 'I will return in five minutes.'

Arthur nodded then turned back. 'Mr De Chauffant. I am Arthur Pepper. I believe that you knew my wife.' His hand shook as he presented the photograph. 'I'm afraid this is from rather a long time ago. Nineteen sixty-three. She is stood here with you. Can you see? When I saw this I grew rather jealous at how intently she is looking at you.' He gently tapped the top of Miriam's head in the photograph. He waited to see if De Chauffant responded. Arthur studied his wizened face for the flicker of a smile or the widening of his pupils. There was nothing.

He took the bracelet from his pocket. 'I'm here to see if you gave her this charm on her bracelet. It's a book. Inside is an inscription. It says '*Ma Chérie*'.' All the time he spoke he knew that his words were lost. The old man didn't show any realisation that someone was there talking to him. Arthur stood there for a while but then sighed and turned away.

Sebastian stood in the doorway, his arms folded. For the first time Arthur saw the bluey-grey bruises that punctuated his arms. He walked over. 'Did *he* do this to you?' he whispered.

'A few, when I have to move him around and he gets confused. Last night, though, I was lonely. I called an old . . . friend. He came over.

Things got out of hand. He shook me.'

'Did you call the police?'

Sebastian shook his head. 'It is my own fault. I know what he is like. But still. I needed someone to hold. Do you understand what it is like, to be so lonely, Arthur?'

'Yes. Yes, I do.'

Sebastian made his way downstairs and Arthur followed.

'I will have to move him downstairs soon. I am not strong though.'

'You need help. You shouldn't be doing this alone.'

'I will work things out for myself.'

In the hallway Arthur held out the charm bracelet. He could not let his journey here end with the sight of De Chauffant curled like a dead leaf in his chair. 'Inside this book charm, it says '*Ma Chérie*'. Can you tell me anything about it?'

Sebastian touched the charm, and then he nodded. 'Yes,' he said. 'I think I can.' In the front room he bent down and opened up a cupboard. Then he handed a book to Arthur. 'I know François's work inside out. I've read all his novels and poems and musings, in between cleaning and changing his clothes. There is a poem in here. It's called '*Ma Chérie*'. It is a coincidence, yes?'

'Yes. Maybe.'

Sebastian flicked to the page. 'It was written in 1963. This was the same year you think François and your wife were friends?'

Arthur nodded. He didn't want to read the words, to see if they uncovered what had gone on between the novelist and his wife, but he knew he had to look, to know.

'Keep it. He has a good ten copies. He always was a fan of his own work. I do not like his work. It is so . . . overwrought. So dramatic. I love him because I remember what he was, but I hate him because he keeps me here. I am like a bird in a gilded cage.'

'You should contact social services.'

'I am illegal. I do not exist. I cannot give my name. I do not have a number. I am invisible and must remain so. I am a non-person. I have only two choices in my life — to stay or to go. If I go, where will this be?' He threw up his hands. 'I have nowhere. I do not know what I am without him.'

Arthur suddenly felt full of responsibility for this young pink-haired man whose life was on hold because of an old man who had always been selfish. 'You must find out. You are young. You have your full life in front of you. You are missing out on adventure and experiences and love. Leave a note, send a letter, make an anonymous phone call, but you must live your own life. You will find someone. Do not settle for anyone who hurts you. Find someone who loves you, who is perhaps your own age.' He wondered where his words came from. The last time he tried to advise Dan on his science homework, his son had snatched the workbook away. ('Don't tell me what to do. That's Mum's job. You're never around.')

Arthur had stared at him, stunned at the outburst. He wasn't around as much as Miriam, but he could still support his children. After that he kept his mouth firmly shut and left homework to the rest of the family. Miriam was the empathetic one, the one who 'understood'. He knew his place, which was to go out to work and provide.

'Thank you, Arthur.' Sebastian leaned forward and gave him a kiss on the cheek. 'I hope that I have helped you.'

'Yes. Thank you.' Arthur had never been kissed by a man before, except toddler kisses by his son. If felt strange, unwelcome really. But at least he felt useful.

It had been a long day. He hadn't found what he expected. He wondered if Miriam had felt trapped in their marriage as Sebastian was here. He took hold of Sebastian's arm, gently below the bruising. 'If you want to go, go now,' he whispered. 'I will stay here. I will make the arrangements for Mr De Chauffant. He will be fine.'

Sebastian froze, considering Arthur's offer. He shook his head. 'I cannot ask that of you. I can't leave him. Not yet anyway. But I will think about your words. You are a kind man. Your wife was lucky, I think.'

'I was the lucky one.'

'I hope you find what you are looking for in the book.'

'I hope that things work out well for you.'

The sky was sapphire blue when Arthur left the house. Lights were on in each of the houses in the crescent giving a glimpse of the people's lives inside. As he walked away from De Chauffant s house, he saw a girl with a black bob taking a piano lesson, two teenage boys stood on the windowsill in the front room flicking the 'V' sign at passers-by and a woman with blonde hair and black roots wrestling one baby carrier into her house, then another. 'Twins,' she shouted to him. 'Double the trouble.'

Arthur wondered if the neighbours knew what was going on at number fifty-six: that a young immigrant boy was looking after his ill, elderly former partner, who was once a prominent writer. He could not tell anyone, he could not compromise Sebastian's situation. It wasn't his business.

He found a bench opposite a square where a couple and their English bull terrier were enjoying a picnic in the dark. They drank from the neck of a bottle of Prosecco.

The bench was well illuminated by a street lamp and when Arthur sat and opened the book, the pages glowed orange. Running his finger down the index, he found the poem 'Ma Chérie'.

Ma Chérie

Your laugh tinkles, your eyes twinkle
How can I ever be alone without you?
You help me live, you hear me cry
Yet your lips do not spill, they do not lie

A lithe body, chestnut hair
India, and to me
Yet you say you do not see
And that matters greatly to me

A brief romance but so vital
Our fingers touch and you know

147

Your importance to me, your glow
Togetherness

Ma Chérie

Arthur shut the book. He felt sick. There was no doubt the poem was about his wife, even if De Chauffant preferred men. The references to her hair and where she had lived before were obvious.

It was evident to him that this had been a major love affair — one full of passion and which compelled De Chauffant to pen a poem. Arthur had never written letters to his wife let alone a poem.

If you don't want to find woodlice, don't go looking under wood. His mother had said that to him once. The memory flooded back. He screwed his eyes shut and tried to remember when and where, but all other details evaded him. He wished that he could be with her now, a small boy again with no worries or responsibilities. But when he opened his eyes he saw his own wrinkled hands grasping the book.

So, now he knew about the book charm, and the elephant and the tiger. There was still the paint palette, the ring, the flower, the thimble and the heart.

He was an old man, sitting on a bench in London. He had a sore ankle and an aching feeling of emptiness from leaving Sebastian behind in his book-lined prison, but he had to carry on his quest.

He closed the book of poetry and left it on the

bench. As he walked away, he couldn't help but wonder which little charm he'd find out about next.

Lucy the Second

Arthur didn't have a plan. He hadn't thought beyond finding De Chauffant. He had a few toiletries in his rucksack but hadn't booked into a hotel for the night, half-expecting to travel back home that evening. It was late now, gone ten. He had jotted down the train times to return home to York, but he didn't fancy getting on board a night bus to take him to King's Cross station, or tackling the tube for the first time.

He walked the streets until he no longer had any inkling where he was, or even who he was. Images and snippets of conversations ran through his head. Sebastian's eye peeping through the door was juxtaposed with watching Miriam in bed as she slept on their honeymoon. In his mind, he wiped away a tear as he dropped Dan off at school for the first time, but then he saw the man at the Pearly Queen café trying to decide which of his two lovers to marry.

He was once Arthur Pepper, beloved husband of Miriam and devoted dad to Dan and Lucy. It was so simple. But now he said that to himself, it sounded like a bog-standard obituary. What was he now? Miriam's widower? No. There had to be more to him than that. He couldn't be defined by his wife's death. Where would he go to next?

What would his next clue be?

He was too tired to think, annoyed at the things whirring around in his mind. *Please stop*, he thought as he trudged around yet another corner. He found himself on a lively street. A group of kids were hanging around outside a fast food place, eating stringy pizza from a cardboard box and pushing one another into the road. A black cab slammed on its brakes and honked its horn. The kids jeered. Tables of tourist merchandise still lined the streets. Pashminas, two for £10, phone chargers, T-shirts, guidebooks.

The sounds and sights filled Arthur's head even more. He wanted to lie down somewhere quiet and let his brain process the events of the day, to think what to do next.

Along the street there was a small sign on a door. Hostel. Without thinking he walked inside.

A young Australian woman on reception wore a white vest, which showed off the blue tribal tattoo that covered her right shoulder. She informed him that it was thirty-five pounds for a room for the night and there was only one bed left. She gave Arthur a rolled-up grey blanket and floppy pillow and directed him down a corridor to the room at the end.

Arthur had expected that he might have to share a twin room, but he stepped inside the room to find three bunk beds and five German girls sitting on the floor. They all wore denim shorts and too-tight checked shirts over coloured bras. They were sharing a crusty loaf, a slab of Edam cheese and cans of cider.

Masking his surprise, Arthur bid them a

cheery 'hello' then located the bed in the room that wasn't piled high with clothes and rucksacks. He didn't want to make a fool of himself by climbing into his bunk and finding that his knees seized up halfway up, so he excused himself to reception where he read a three-day-old newspaper until the girls filed out of the room. He watched as they gave each other donkey rides as they headed out for the night.

He thought about how exuberant he himself used to feel as he got ready to meet Miriam when they first started courting. Butterflies flew in his stomach as he washed, shaved, slicked back his hair with a comb and smear of Brylcreem. He made sure that his suit and shirt were pressed, his shoes were buffed. He would put his comb in his pocket and whistle as he walked to meet her. There was an ice-cream parlour where they would sit in the window and drink lemonade with a blob of vanilla floating on top, or they sometimes went to the cinema. At that time a trainee, he didn't have much money so he would save up all week just in case Miriam wanted to go for a nice meal, but she was happy to go for a walk with him and with their simple dates. He didn't know at that time that she'd lived with tigers, and had a poem written about her by a famous French writer.

A group of girls passed by the hostel window. One wore a bridal veil and an L-sign; the others sported red devil horns, red tutus and fishnet stockings. They sang a song at the top of their voices. 'Like a virgin,' were the words he heard.

They waved to him and he waved back. For

Miriam's hen night she had gone for a meal with her mother and two friends to a Berni Inn. It had been the height of sophistication. The night before his wedding, Arthur and his friend Bill (now deceased) had been to a football match and enjoyed two pints of shandy afterwards. All his senses had been heightened by the excitement of marrying Miriam the next day. The lemonade in the shandy had been sweet, the football chants made his ears throb. He could feel the label in his shirt rubbing his neck. Every inch of him had been ready to make Miriam his wife.

Their wedding day had whirled by like the confetti that swirled down on them as they left the church. The reception was for thirty people in a community hall. Miriam's stern-faced mother made the sandwiches and pork pies as their wedding present. Arthur's parents paid for them to go on honeymoon for two nights to a farm. They set off that night with tin cans jangling and a cardboard 'Just Married' sign taped to the back of Arthur's Morris Minor.

The farmhouse had been teeth-chatteringly cold. The sheep bayed all night and the landlady looked as if she had swallowed a wasp. But Arthur loved it. Miriam got ready for bed behind a wooden screen in the bedroom and Arthur in the toilet shed outside. He had to tuck his pyjamas into his boots and carry his clothes across a muddy field.

Miriam looked beautiful in her floor-length cotton nightdress with pink embroidered roses around the neck. He had tried not to groan with desire as he touched her waist and she shuffled toward him. They had got into bed and made love for the first time. And afterwards they had lain in each other's arms and talked about where they were going to live and the children they were going to have. And, even now, that day was the best of his life because it was so full of tenderness and relief and desire. Even though they had many wonderful days after that — the births of Dan and Lucy, family holidays — that time with Miriam, when they were spending their first hours as husband and wife, was the greatest. He hoped that the girl with the L-sign would experience the same feelings on her wedding day.

The thing was, when you got to his age, it was unlikely that there would be more wonderful days to come. Ones where you stopped and thought, *I will remember this day for ever*. He had held Kyle and Marina when they were babies and smelled their sweet baby-milk breath and wriggly bodies. He wondered what there was now to look forward to.

He wished that he was no longer in London but tucked up in bed with his customary hot chocolate and newspaper. Instead he was here, alone, perturbed.

Recognising his melancholic mood, he told himself that the best thing he could do was to go to bed. He returned to his room and climbed into his bunk at just gone midnight with his ankle throbbing. He snuggled under his blankets fully clothed and tried to think about his honeymoon. Buses rumbled past the window and there was a lot of shouting and he finally drifted to sleep to the sound of an ambulance siren.

He was awoken at three in the morning when the girls returned. They were drunk and singing in German. One had brought a man back to the room. He climbed with her into the bunk below Arthur. There was giggling and much swishing of bedclothes.

Luckily, the creaking and rocking of the bed that ensued only lasted a few minutes. The other girls giggled and whispered. Arthur tugged his own itchy blankets over his head though his eyes were wide. At first he told himself that they couldn't possibly be having sex. Who would go out, meet someone and then fornicate in a room full of others? But it was obvious from the panting and sighing that this was the type of activity going on beneath him. He thought about how much things had changed and that he sometimes didn't like this new modern world very much.

The chattering slowly died out and the couple in the bottom bunk kissed noisily for a while. He heard the zip of a bag, a packet of tissues being opened, and then there was quiet.

Lying there, he thought about how this was the first night in a year that he hadn't been alone. He hadn't imagined that he would ever spend a night sleeping in the company of others. Strangely, he found that the gentle breathing and snores that began to ripple around the room comforted him as he went back to sleep.

In the morning, he climbed down out of bed

while the girls were all still asleep. As he slipped on his sandals, the man from the bunk below sat on the floor fastening his trainers. He wore dusky pink jeans rolled up at the ankle. They clashed with his wiry copper hair. 'Shh.' He held his finger up to his lips. 'Let's sneak out of here, man,' he said in an American accent, as if Arthur was part of his plan.

Arthur wanted to explain that he was a lone traveller, that he hadn't been part of last night's antics. He wasn't with the German girls in any respect, but he just nodded.

'Do you know which way it is to King's Cross?' he asked as they stood on the doorstep blinking at the early morning light. The hostel breakfast was a brown paper bag left at reception with his name on it. Someone had written 'Arthur Peeper'. The American man had helped himself to a bag with the name 'Anna' written on it.

'Er, head left and you'll come to a Tube station. You can get to King's Cross from there.' The man looked in his bag and wrinkled his nose. 'An apple, flapjack and carton of orange. Jeez, is that it?'

Arthur thought that he was being rather ungrateful, seeing as he had enjoyed sex, got a bed for the night and stolen himself a free breakfast.

The man put the flapjack into one pocket and the orange juice carton into the other. Then he jammed the apple between his teeth, crumpled up the paper bag and threw it onto the floor in the doorway of the hostel. 'See ya,' he said and then broke into a sprint as if he had to be somewhere else.

Arthur walked to the Tube station and down into the underpass. There was music from a man playing the flute and, further along, a woman strummed a guitar with an upturned trilby hat at her feet. He dropped a fifty pence in front of each of them and followed the stream of people heading into the depths of the station.

He fed coins into a shiny machine, which spat out a ticket. He felt lost, not just because he had never been on an underground Tube train before. He thought that he'd find clear answers in London, but there were yet more layers. Did he want to keep peeling them away, like a giant onion, or should he leave them alone?

The map on the tiled wall in front of him couldn't have been any bigger. It was clear, with strong black letters, but he just couldn't fathom it out. He'd watched an engineer once open up a telephone box on the street. Inside was an inexplicable (to Arthur anyway) tangle of coloured wires. This map looked similar, though even more complicated. He wanted to reach out and trace his finger around the lines to find where he was going because his eye kept following a line and then getting lost. Everyone around him seemed to know what they were doing and where they were going. They glanced at the map, nodded and then strode off with purpose and confidence. He in turn felt very small and insignificant.

He tried to follow the route to King's Cross again, but he couldn't work out where to change.

157

By now he wondered if he should just jump on some random tube train and see where he ended up, or go back outside and wait at a bus stop.

But then, 'Hello,' a friendly voice said in his left ear. 'Having a bit of trouble?'

He turned to find a young man standing beside him, shoulder to shoulder. He had his hands dug deep into the pockets of his low-slung baggy jeans. A good few inches of his red underpants were on display over his waistband. His T-shirt might be black and white and have 'The Killers' emblazoned on it, but his smile was wide and friendly.

'Ah, yes. I'm afraid I've never been on the Underground before.'

'First time in London then?'

'Yes. I'm not used to finding my way around. I need to get to King's Cross to get a train home.'

'Do you live far?'

'Near York.'

'Lovely. Well, King's Cross? It's not a difficult journey, just a couple of changes from here. Do you have a Tube ticket?'

'Yes.'

'Let me have a look then.'

Grateful for the young man's kindness, Arthur took his wallet from his back pocket. He was about to flip it open to retrieve his ticket when it vanished from his hands. Poof. The man was running away at full pelt and was immediately swallowed up by a sea of people.

In what seemed like slow motion, Arthur stared at his empty hands then after the man in disbelief. He had been robbed. He was a bloody idiot. Newspapers loved telling stories about the type of person he was: a gullible pensioner. His shoulders drooped involuntarily, defeated.

However his sense of foolishness was soon overtaken by a surge of anger. There was a photograph of Miriam in his wallet. She was smiling and had her arms wrapped around the kids when they were little. He didn't have a copy. How dare this man take advantage of him. The anger rumbled in his stomach and then careered up his chest and burst out of his mouth as words. '*Stop. Thief!*' Arthur yelled as mightily as he could, surprised by how loud it was. He shouted again.

He began to run.

Now Arthur couldn't remember the last time he had asked his legs to work in this way. It was probably two years since he had broken into a sprint for a bus, but that hadn't mattered if he missed it or not. Before that, he had no idea. Maybe tearing after the kids on a beach? He was a plodder not a runner. But it was as if his legs had a mind of their own. They were not going to let the thief get away with it.

Any thought that his legs might wobble or could give way flew out of his head as he picked up pace after the man. He shouted out polite 'Excuse me's and 'Coming through's.

He negotiated his way around office workers carrying papers and briefcases, past Japanese tourists sporting saucer-size sunglasses and peering out from behind huge maps. He passed a girl with violet hair whose friend had green hair and several studs through her eyebrows. All of them showed little or no interest, as if they witnessed an elderly man running after a thief every day.

'That man has stolen my wallet,' Arthur shouted to no one in particular, pointing at the man. He sped on. His heart thumped in his chest and his knees jolted with each stride. The grey walls of the Tube station, plastered with posters for the theatre and opera, went by in a blur. Weaving and stumbling a little as his legs tired, he continued his pursuit.

But suddenly the passageway out of the Tube station surged with people. His target had seemingly gone. This is no good, Arthur told himself as he stopped for a moment to catch his breath. *Just let it go.*

He was about to stop, to give up, when he saw a flash of red underpants — a good tracking device. He willed his legs to continue. *Go on, Arthur. Keep going.*

He had a flashback to when Lucy and Dan were young. They were on holiday and Miriam stood at an ice cream van buying cones. The children were playing tig, slapping each other on the arm or back and then pelting away. Lucy ran with her hand outstretched to whack Dan on the leg but he swerved out of the way. He moved backward in small jumps, each time jerking out of the way of Lucy's swipes. Further and further until he was at the edge of the pavement, then in the road. Lucy continued toward him, focused, oblivious to anything but her annoying brother and trying to tag him. A car drove past then another, perilously close. An articulated lorry began to rumble toward them. Arthur stood rooted, unable to move as the events unfolded so quickly. He was twenty-five feet away. He shouted for Miriam but she didn't hear. She was licking raspberry sauce from around the rim of a cone. Arthur found an inner strength, almost a superpower that he hadn't thought possible. Without knowing how he got there, he found himself yanking on Dan's and Lucy's arms, tugging them from danger. Superman. Dan glared, indignant. Lucy gave her brother a triumphant slap as Arthur all but threw the two of them back onto the pavement. A tear ran down his cheek. Unaware, Miriam bustled up and offered them each an ice cream. Only he knew what dreadful thing could have happened.

Tapping into that experience now, he pushed his way out into the sunlight. Blinking against the brightness of the sun, he stumbled forwards. The white light faded so he could make out a red double-decker bus, trees and a crocodile of schoolchildren wearing yellow high-vis jackets. 'Stop, thief,' he cried out again.

The man was making good ground now; his strides were long. The space between them widened. Still Arthur ran. His heart and feet pounded. Uneven flags, upturned chip shop trays, empty crisp packets, feet, passed by. Then a pain hit him in his chest. *Oh God, no.* He stumbled and came to a standstill. His heart felt as if someone was grasping it in their fist. Miriam's voice was in his head. 'Just let him go. It's not worth it.' He knew when he was done. He tried to think what was in his wallet — his

Visa card, ten or twenty pounds in notes, photos. He was lucky he hadn't been stabbed.

As he stood panting, another young man loped toward him. He was dressed similarly to the thief in baggy jeans. He wore a green hooded top with a hole in the shoulder. His nose was freckled and his hair was the colour of rusty nails. 'Has he stolen something from you?'

Arthur nodded. 'My wallet.'

'Right. Stay here.' The second man pressed something into Arthur's hand and then was gone. Looking down, he found that he was holding a frayed pink strip of material, used as a makeshift leash and tied in a loose bow around a dog's neck.

The dog was small and dithery. It had black wiry fur and stared up at him with bemused orange eyes. 'I don't think your master is going to be long,' Arthur said. 'Don't worry.' He reached down and scratched the dog's head. It wasn't wearing a proper collar and didn't have a name tag. There was a tweed cap on the ground beside them, which the man must have tossed down there.

Arthur and the dog stood in the sunlight. There was nothing else to do. There was a jangle of money as a lady wearing a woollen purple cape gave the dog's head a ruffle and then threw a handful of change into the cap. Oh dear, she thought he was a beggar. Now he thought about it, he supposed he did have the look of a down and out about him. He hadn't shaved for two days and his blue trousers were a bit grubby.

'Is this your job, then?' he said to the dog. 'Do

162

you sit here and wait for people to pay you?' The dog blinked.

Arthur now longed to sit down. *What on earth have you done to me?* his body said.

Another ten minutes passed. He began to formulate plans in his head for if the man didn't return. He would have to take the dog to the nearest police station and drop it off. He couldn't take it on the train back home. Were dogs even allowed on the Tube?

Finally, the man reappeared. He held out Arthur's wallet. Arthur stared at it in disbelief. 'You got it back?'

'Uh-huh.' The man was out of breath. He bent over and rested his hands on his knees. 'I've seen that bastard thieving here before. He picks on helpless old people or foreigners. Scum of the earth. I managed to catch up with him. I stuck my leg out and he flew right over it.' He gave himself a congratulatory chuckle. 'That taught him a lesson. Next time, keep a firm grip of your wallet.'

Arthur's immediate reaction was to insist that he was neither old nor helpless, but that wasn't true. 'I will do,' he said meekly. 'I feel rather foolish.' He felt his knees buckle. The need to sit down overwhelmed him.

The young man picked up his hat then shot his arm out. He wrapped it around Arthur's back to steady him. 'There's a bench over here. Come on.'

Arthur let the man guide him. He sank down on the bench. The dog pushed its way between his legs and sat on the pavement resting its head against his leg.

'Ah, look at that. She likes you. That's pretty rare. She's usually a timid beast; scared of her own tail.'

'She's lovely.'

Bernadette had tried a few times to persuade him to get a dog, telling him that it would give him purpose to his life. But he had resisted. It was hard enough to look after himself, let alone something with four legs. In the past few years Miriam had mentioned getting a pet, but he had said, 'It will just outlive us.' So they hadn't bothered.

'What's her name?'

'It's Lucy.'

'Ha,' Arthur said.

The man raised an eyebrow.

'Lucy is my daughter's name.'

'Oh. Sorry. An ex-girlfriend chose it.'

'Don't be. It suits her. They have the same demeanour. My daughter is quiet and thoughtful too.'

'I think that this small dog worries about me more than I worry about her. I opened my front door one day and she was sitting there like she was a guardian angel or something. I said to her, 'You can do better than me. Go find someone half decent with a job.' I showed her out of the building. But the next time I opened up, she was there again. She trotted inside my apartment and sat down and we've been together ever since. She can see something in me that I can't.'

Arthur closed his eyes. The sun felt warm on his lids.

'I'll get you a coffee,' the man said. 'I bet you

164

need a drink after that incident. You should think about reporting it to the police.'

'It's all my fault. I doubt they'd even be interested.'

'I know what you mean. I've had my run-ins with the coppers. Always moving us on. Me and Lucy are just trying to make a living.'

It was now that Arthur saw the flute sticking out of the man's pocket. 'A lady threw some money in your cap,' he said.

'Great. Well, I mean it's good someone bothered. Not going to make me a millionaire though.' He shrugged.

'I'll buy the coffees. I owe you a big thanks.'

'Whatevs.' The man held out his hand. 'I'm Mike. I take it black with three sugars.'

'Arthur. Arthur Pepper.'

'Do me a favour, Arthur. Take Lucy with you. She could do with a piddle. I don't like her doing it near the Tube entrance.'

Lucy seemed happy to trot after Arthur. Her claws made a lilting tapping sound on the pavement as they walked on. There was a van selling coffees and hot food just across the road. Arthur asked for two coffees and then added two sausage sandwiches to the order. As he paid, he batted away the thought that Miriam used to hate people eating food in the street. Mike looked like he might not have eaten for a while.

Arthur followed flute music until he found Mike sitting cross-legged on the grass with his cap at his feet. He put down his flute as Arthur approached. 'Thought I may as well earn some cash while you were gone. Here.' He felt around in the cap and took out a two-pound coin. 'For my coffee.'

'Don't be silly. It's on me. I got you a sausage sandwich too.'

Mike's eyes lit up. 'With ketchup?'

'Of course.'

There was nowhere else to sit so Arthur sat on the grass too. He tore off a piece of bread and threw it to a one-legged pigeon. He was immediately surrounded by a further fifty of them. One pecked at his shoelaces.

'You shouldn't feed them. They're pests. Flying rats. They have to clear tons of pigeon shit off Nelson's Column each year. Did you know that?'

Arthur said that he did not.

They sat and ate together. If Miriam could see him now, sitting in the sunlight with a young man and his dog, basking and eating sausages in bread, she would certainly disapprove. *Sorry, Miriam*.

'So, what's your story, Arthur?' Mike batted a wasp from his copper hair.

'Story?'

'Huh-uh. Those do not look like your trousers. You've obviously never been to London before, yet you're here wandering around on your own without a map, waving your wallet around. There must be more to you than meets the eye.'

At first Arthur thought about spinning a loose yarn about being in London for a spot of sightseeing but it seemed wrong to he to this young man who had just put himself in danger. So Arthur told Mike a brief version of his actual true story, about Miriam and the bracelet, about Bernadette and the man with the tigers and the man with the books. Then he asked Mike about himself, but Mike just shook his head.

'I have nothing to tell you as interesting as *that*,' he said. 'I'm just a simple man trying to earn a living. Though I do know someone who knows about gold bracelets. He's got a shop not far from here. We could take your bracelet to him, if you like. He might be able to tell you something about it.'

Arthur was really not in the mood for trying to catch a train again yet. There was no rush to get back. He was at a dead end with leads for the remaining charms. 'Why not?' he said. 'It's a lovely day for a walk.'

It was only when they reached yet another side street with polystyrene fast food cartons trodden underfoot and dubious smells that he began to doubt his own trusting nature. Could it even be that Mike was in cahoots with the mugger? That this was some kind of set-up, for them to get more than just a wallet out of a foolish old man. They seemed to have been walking for ages and he had lost all sense of where he was. After turning a corner, all the people who had been milling around them dried up. It was just Arthur, Mike and Lucy heading down a gloomy, cobbled street. Brick buildings bore down on them either side. The sun dipped behind a cloud. Arthur slowed his pace.

'Am I walking too fast for you? We're nearly there now.'

Images from the musical *Oliver!* popped into

167

Arthur's head. Young dirty boys pickpocketing, Fagin and the dog with the black eye. What was his name? Oh, yes, Bullseye. Preying on unsuspecting folk in Victorian England. He steeled himself, waiting for a hand to shoot out of a doorway and batter him on the head with a truncheon. He had always wanted to believe the best in people. Now he was going to be mugged again for his trouble.

But then, his hopes lifted. At the end of the passageway, there was a market. The street teemed with shoppers and stallholders selling mangos, e-cigarettes, earmuffs, colourful skirts flapping in the breeze. Shops and cafés lined the road.

'Here it is.' Mike stopped and pushed open the doorway of a tiny shop. It had dark windows emblazoned with gold lettering. *Gold. Bought and Sold. New and Old*. A bell jangled overhead. Arthur could smell meat pies and polish. 'Jeff,' Mike hollered into the shop. 'Jeff. Are you in here, mate?'

There was a creak and a rustle from behind a beaded curtain and a man with a face as beaten and brown as an old handbag pushed through. His shoulders were so wide it looked as if he was wearing a yoke under his red tartan shirt. 'Mike, mate. How ya doin'?'

'Good. Good. I've brought my friend Arthur to see you. He has a bracelet for you to look at. A nice gold piece.'

Jeff scratched his head. His fingernails and knuckles were black. 'Okay. Let's have a gander. Not like you to bring me nice stuff, Mike.'

168

Arthur reached into his pocket and his fingers curled round the bracelet. Mike and Jeff stood waiting for him. They were an intimidating presence. If he was in trouble here there was no escape. Still, it was too late now. He placed it on the counter.

Jeff gave a low whistle through his teeth. 'That's a real beauty. Very nice indeed.' He picked up the bracelet, handling it with great respect. Reaching into a drawer he took out an eyeglass. 'There, I can see it even better now. This is very fine craftsmanship. Very fine indeed. How much are you looking for it, Arthur?'

'I don't want to sell. I'm just looking for some information about it. It belonged to my wife.'

'Righto. Well the bracelet itself is eighteen-carat gold. Heavy-duty stuff. Probably European, maybe English. I'd have to look up the mark. The charms though, they vary in quality and age. They're all good but some are better than others. The elephant one: that's a top-class emerald in there.

'I'd say the bracelet is Victorian, but most of the charms are newer. The heart looks like a modern piece, it's new. See, it hasn't even been soldered in place properly, just the jump ring pinched together. Did your wife buy that one recently?'

Arthur shook his head. 'I don't think so . . . '

'Well, that one looks like it was added hastily,' Jeff continued. 'The tiger is nice but mass produced, I would say, probably in the fifties or sixties. The thimble and book are lovely quality, but the elephant is exquisite.'

'I think it's Indian.'

'I wouldn't argue with you there, Arthur.' Jeff peered more closely. 'Hmmm, the flower charm could be acrostic.'

'Is that when you're not sure of higher powers?' Mike said.

Jeff laughed. 'No. That's 'agnostic'. 'Acrostic' was popular in Victorian times. It's jewellery set with gemstones that spell out a name or message. It's usually given by a relative or loved one as a sentimental gift. Here.' He took a gold ring out of a cabinet. 'Can you see the stones are set in a line? The first letter of each of the gemstones spells out the word 'dearest'. Diamond, emerald, amethyst, ruby, emerald, sapphire and topaz.'

'So you think the flower spells something?' Arthur said.

'Well, let's see. It's probably 1920s — it's art nouveau style. I think it was originally a pendant rather than a charm as the link is very dainty. There's an emerald, an amethyst, a ruby, a lapis lazuli and a peridot.'

Arthur rearranged the initials in his head several times. 'The outer stones could spell *Pearl*. And is that a tiny pearl set in the middle?'

Jeff nodded. 'It sure is. Impressive stuff, Arthur. Do you know anyone called Pearl?'

Arthur frowned. 'I think it might have been Miriam's mother's name.' He had always called her Mrs Kempster, even after he and Miriam had married. She died before Dan was born.

When Miriam had first invited him for tea, her mother's first observation was that he had big

170

feet. He had looked down at his size tens and didn't think they were unduly large, but from then on he had become conscious of them.

Mrs Kempster had been a still, stiff kind of woman with a square jawline and a steely-eyed stare. Miriam always called her 'Mother' and never 'Mum'.

'Well, there you go then. Does that date ring true then — 1920s?' Jeff said.

'She would have been born around then.'

'Maybe a christening present.' Jeff shrugged. 'Then she might have given it to your wife.'

Arthur nodded. It sounded entirely plausible.

'I like the look of this paint palette too. It's a nice item. It's got tiny initials engraved on it. S. Y. It's not a mark I'm familiar with.' He slid the bracelet back over to Arthur. 'You have yourself a beautiful piece of jewellery. I reckon you'd be looking at a grand, or more, to replace it. I'd happily take it off your hands for that.'

'Really. That much?'

'Charm bracelets are special to people. The charms usually mean something significant and important. It's like wearing memories on your wrist. Looking at these charms, it seems like your wife had an exciting and varied life. I bet she could tell a few tales, eh?'

Arthur looked at the floor.

Mike noticed. 'Well, cheers, Jeff mate,' he said.

Back outside, Arthur felt the weight of the bracelet back in his pocket. The visit had left him even more confused. The heart charm couldn't be new, could it? And he still wasn't quite sure if Miriam's mother had been called Pearl. He hadn't noticed the initials S. Y. before.

'Were you tempted to sell?'

'I don't know.' He felt a little shaken to learn so much from a stranger, to uncover more clues when he'd thought his search had come to a pause. 'I suppose I'd better go.'

'Go where? Do you have a train ticket home?'

Arthur said that he didn't. He looked around him blankly.

'Do you have anywhere to stay tonight?'

'I hadn't thought that far ahead. I suppose I'll find a hotel.' He couldn't bear the thought of shacking up in a hostel again.

'Well.' Mike mused for a moment. 'You'd better stay at mine then. It's not much, but it's home. Hotels can cost a pretty packet around here.'

This silly adventure of his was muddling Arthur's mind. He had messed up the head of the man in the café and now he was doing the same to himself. He didn't want to sleep in a stranger's house, but his whole body felt rigid, as if he was turning to stone. The thought of venturing back into the Tube station filled him with dread.

He nodded and took hold of Lucy's leash.

Mike's Apartment

Mike's apartment was sparsely furnished. At the end of a concrete corridor the bottle-green wooden door had a hole where it looked as if someone had kicked it in. Inside all the furniture was well worn and old-fashioned. A 1970s coffee table, coated in orange varnish, had a blue and white tiled mosaic top. A sofa with wooden legs was covered with a floral sheet. The floorboards were scuffed and spattered with paint.

Arthur found himself staring at the bookcase. It was six feet tall and fully stocked. There were thrillers, biographies, a Bible and *Star Wars* annuals. 'You have a lot of books,' he said.

'Er, yes I *can* read,' Mike said. His voice was prickly.

'Sorry. I didn't mean anything by that . . . '

'Oh. Okay.' Mike delved his hands into his pocket. 'Sorry. I snapped a little then. You know, when you make a living on the streets, some people automatically think you have no brain-power. I've been on the receiving end of a lot of snotty remarks. I get a bit touchy. I'll make us a drink. Is coffee okay? I've run out of tea.'

Arthur nodded and sat down on the sofa. Lucy leaped up and settled on his lap. He stroked her head and she looked up at him with her orange eyes.

'Where's next on your travels?' Mike said, as he placed two steaming mugs on the table. 'What's the next charm you're trying to trace?'

'I don't know. I'm intrigued by the paint palette. And I haven't thought about my mother-in-law for years. Or perhaps I should just stop searching. It makes my head hurt.'

'You should never give up,' Mike said. 'Those charms on your bracelet could be lucky.'

Arthur shook his head. After what he had been through, he doubted it. 'Lucky?'

'You know. Lucky charms. Lucy is like my lucky charm.'

'I don't think so . . . '

'How old are you, Arthur?'

'Sixty-nine.'

'Well, that's kind of elderly, but not decrepit. You could have twenty years of life left. Are you really going to waste it planting hyacinths and drinking tea? Is that what your wife would have wanted you to do?'

'I'm not sure,' Arthur sighed. 'Before I found the bracelet, I'd be doing just that and thinking it's what Miriam would have wanted for me. But now I don't know. I thought I knew her so well, and now I'm finding out all these things that she didn't tell me, that she didn't want me to know. And if she kept these kinds of secrets from me, what else did she not tell me? Was she faithful to me, did I bore her, did I stop her from doing the kinds of things that she loved to do?' He looked down at the multi-coloured rag rug on the floor.

'You can't stop people doing what they want to do if they really want to do it. Perhaps she thought that her life before you was no longer relevant. Sometimes when you've lived a chapter of your life, you don't want to look back. I lost five years of my life through drugs. All I remember is waking up feeling like shit, or roaming the streets looking to score, or the delirium after I'd shot up. I don't ever want to look back at that. I want to get back on my feet, get a proper job, maybe find a girl who's good for me.'

Arthur nodded. He understood what Mike was saying, but it wasn't the same. 'Tell me about your books,' he said. 'I'd like to hear about them.'

'I just like them. I still remember one from when I was a child. It was about a bear trying to get into a jar of honey. He never gave up. I thought about that when I was trying to get clean. I had to just keep on trying to open that honey jar.'

'I liked to read to my kids when they were young. My son much preferred my wife to do it, but when I got to do it, it felt really special. I liked the stories too.'

'Everyone has a good story to tell, Arthur. If you'd have told me last night that I'd have an adventurous old bloke kipping at my house for the night, I'd think I was going mad. But here you are. You're all right, Arthur, for a posh pensioner,' he teased.

'And so are you, for a bit of a scruffbag.'

The two men laughed.

'I am rather tired now,' Arthur said. 'Do you mind if I go to sleep?'

'Not at all, mate. The bathroom is at the end of the hallway. You have my bed and I'll sleep on the sofa.'

'I won't hear of it. I'm absolutely fine on here and it looks as though Lucy will be joining me.' The little dog had curled up beside him and gone to sleep.

Mike left the room and returned with a green woollen blanket that smelled a bit musty. 'This will keep you warm.'

'It certainly will.' Arthur laid it over his legs.

'Goodnight then, Arthur.'

'Goodnight.'

Before he went to sleep he tried to phone Lucy again to tell her where he was and about her little furry namesake. But there was no reply. He stuffed his mobile under the cushion on the sofa. He laid down and his eyes began to close straight away. The last thing he saw was the paint palette charm glinting, catching the light from the street lamp outside.

★　★　★

When Arthur woke the next morning, Lucy was gone. He yawned and glanced around Mike's sitting room. His eyes slowly fell upon the coffee table. There was nothing on it. The charm bracelet was no longer there. It no longer glinted in the light.

His eyes widened and he sat bolt upright. A wave of nausea hit him in the back of his throat.

Where was it? He was sure he had left it there. Standing, he nearly fell back over. His knees had locked and his back was curved. He slowly eased himself upright. Mike couldn't have taken the bracelet. He trusted him. This was his flat. But then he wondered if it really was. There were no personal possessions. He remembered how Mike had tensed when he had mentioned the books.

'Lucy?' he called out. His voice sounded hollow and he listened for the sound of her nails clipping on the floorboards. All he could hear was a couple shouting in the flat next door. He called her a lazy git. She called him a fat loser.

He dropped the green blanket to the floor then stood and walked around the flat. Again, all the furniture was functional. There were no photo frames or ornaments. In the bathroom there was an empty tube of Colgate on the sink. He opened the fridge and there was only half a pint of milk inside. He was alone. There was nothing here.

He sank back onto the sofa and held his head in his hands. He pulled out his phone from under the cushion and saw that Lucy hadn't returned his call. He should never have started on this journey. His boring life felt like a luxurious comfort now compared to this rollercoaster ride of emotions and events. Then he remembered his backpack. Had that disap-peared too? He had put his wallet in the front pocket. How the hell could he get across London with no money? He didn't even know where he was. 'I've been an absolute pillock, Miriam,' he said aloud. He would have to do whatever he

177

could to get out of here and get back home.

It wasn't possible for his heart to feel any heavier when he heard a key in the front door. His heart leaped. 'Mike?' he called out. 'Mike. Is that you?'

'That's my name. Don't wear it out.' The front door slammed shut. Lucy scampered toward him. She leaped up at his legs and he rubbed her neck.

Mike dumped a carrier bag on the sofa. 'I've been out to get a few supplies. I can't afford much but I got bread and some butter for toast. I couldn't afford milk and the stuff in the fridge is off, so black coffee only.'

Arthur couldn't help himself. He stepped over and hugged Mike. The young man's body stiffened. 'Er, is everything okay?'

'Yes.' Arthur nodded with relief. His eyes flicked to the coffee table.

'Ah. You're wondering where your bracelet is. You woke up and saw it was gone and I was gone. You thought I'd done a runner.'

'I'm sorry. It crossed my mind. I'm not very trusting at the moment.'

'I can understand that.' Mike walked over to the bookshelf and slid out a dictionary. He took out the bracelet. 'I got robbed last month. I don't leave anything valuable hanging about; not that I have anything any longer.'

'Did you lose something important?'

'My dad's watch. It was a gold Rolex. Jeff offered me a fortune for it, but I couldn't let it go. I'd prefer to starve than to sell that watch. It was the only thing of his I had left. I sold the other stuff to pay for drugs. I really regret it now. He died when I was three.'

'I'm sorry.'

'The thing is, I reckon I know who it was. Those bastards next door. They know when I go out and come back. I kept the watch in a box in my kitchen cupboard. One day I got back from my pitch and the door had been forced. I knocked on next door and the bloke acted too friendly. He'd never had the time of day for me before but this time he offered me a cup of tea. I asked him about the watch and all the time his eyes were moving about, sly-like. I'm sure he's got it. It had my dad's name engraved on the back. Gerald.'

Arthur could offer little comfort. He knew how much an item of jewellery could be invested with emotions and memories. 'I'm sorry to hear that. You must let me give you some money for letting me stay.'

'I don't want it.' Mike lifted a cushion and then let it fall again. 'I'm not a charity case. Where is my bleedin' flute?'

'It's on the bookshelf.'

'Oh. Right. Ta.' He shoved it into his pocket and picked up Lucy's leash off the coffee table. He fastened it in a bow around her neck. She shook her head and then looked at Arthur.

'I'm not coming with you today.' He stroked her chin. 'Just you and Mike.'

They had a quick brew and slice of toast and then they left the apartment together. The atmosphere had changed. Arthur felt like he might have offended the young man and didn't

179

want to make it worse.

Mike locked up and they made their way down the concrete stairs.

'All right, Arthur,' Mike said distractedly when they reached the bottom. 'I'll leave you to it. There's a bus stop opposite. The 87a will take you to King's Cross Station.'

'Thanks. Are you sure I can't give you anything?'

Mike shook his head. 'Nah. It was a pleasure. See you then.' He turned and began to walk away.

Arthur stared after him. The two of them had shared an experience. There should be more to their goodbye than this. His friend had restored his trust and faith in people a little. He stepped forwards. 'Mike,' he called after him.

His saviour turned, his brow furrowed. 'Yeah?'

'Thanks for everything.'

'No probs. Now don't get lost. No talking to strange men. And don't forget to look on the bright side. Those charms might bring you luck.'

The Flower

Arthur got the bus and travelled to King's Cross following Mike's instructions. He boarded the train and slept all the way back home. He was awoken by a bony hand gripping his shoulder. 'We've arrived in York,' an old man with eyebrows like white feathers said. 'Do you need to get off here?'

Arthur nodded thanks. At the station he bought a bottle of water from a vending machine. He squirted the water into his palms and splashed his face. Although he was still tired, there was a yearning sensation in his stomach.

He left the station and stood on the forecourt watching the taxis and people running for trains and those greeting relatives, loved ones and friends. He was glad to be back on home turf and recognised all the accents around him.

There was part of him that wanted to return to his house, to see Frederica and make a nice cup of tea. Yet there was also a part that wasn't ready to settle back home. Not just yet. He wanted to find out more about Miriam's mother.

As he walked, he took a bit of a detour, through the centre of Thornapple. There was a more direct route home but he needed a bit of thinking space. The events of the past few days jumbled around in his mind and he wanted to reflect on them.

He had found out where Miriam had lived during her adventures, who she had known. But he didn't know why she had left. It was unusual for anyone from Thornapple to do anything other than marry, have kids and stay in the village.

Had she been excited to live in a manor with tigers, or was it an inconvenience until she found something else? Did she know that François De Chauffant was gay, or had he been the love of her life? Had her cold mother smiled when she handed over the little flower pendant? Had mother and daughter shared a tender moment? He supposed he would never find out.

What he had discovered were things about himself. He hadn't expected to act so bravely while being mauled by a tiger. He had taken it in his stride. Really he thought he would have screamed and freaked out. And he had survived a night in the strange manor, without his own toothpaste and pyjamas. The day before that, the thought that his routine might have gone out of sync was enough to bring beads of perspiration to his forehead.

He offered relationship advice to a stranger in a café, and when he spoke he hadn't sounded like the silly old man he told himself he was. He confronted a past love rival, when he could have walked away, and he tried to help Sebastian. His openness and acceptance of a young man with a drug problem and his dog had surprised him. These were qualities that he didn't know he possessed. He was stronger and had more depth than he knew and he liked these new discoveries about himself.

What these people and events had stirred in him was *desire*. Not in the sense of lust or longing, but a reaction to others. When they had shown a need, he found a desire to help. When the tiger attacked he felt a desire to live. As the orange beast stood above him, he thought of the future and not the past.

This was at odds with all that he had felt over the months since Miriam died, when he wanted to go to bed at night and not wake up. When he planned to send his letter to Terry across the road to come and find him dead in his bed.

He had never paused to consider how other people lived their lives. To him, the whole nation might live in houses identical to his own, with the same layout. They would all rise at the same time in the morning and carry out their daily routines, as he did. He was forever reading in the newspaper about reality TV, following people in their everyday lives. How boring, he would think, not realising that people's lives varied wildly from his own.

Now he had uncovered difference and variety. People had their own gilded cages, like Sebastian waiting hand and foot on a man he had loved for mere months and who then became a stranger. He thought about Lord and Lady Graystock summoning each other by bell. They made his own life seem as grey as the cardigans in Miriam's wardrobe.

Once he had looked back and viewed

everything in Technicolor — the sky, the sand, his wife's clothes. With each discovery the colour of his memories was fading to a murky mingling together of hues. He wanted to stop, to turn back the clock, to put Miriam's brown suede boots into the charity bag without first slipping his hand inside. Then he would be oblivious. He could be a widower in peace, looking back at his life with his wife through rose-tinted spectacles. Thinking that everything had been perfect.

Except it hadn't been. He knew that really. He had two children who had drifted away from him. He heard the worry and love in Lucy's voice when they spoke, but she kept her distance a lot. He hadn't felt able to tell her about the charm bracelet yet. She was keeping things from him too, he could sense it. When he sporadically called Dan there was always noise and the busyness of family life. They hadn't managed to find the rhythm of being a family without Miriam.

He needed to bring back some control. Just as he was taking charge of the charm bracelet, not letting its mysteries remain uncovered, he had to do the same with his family. He had to find out the roots of the reason they were no longer tight knit and pull them back together again.

He felt as though he was a seed that had been thrown away into a field onto fallow land. But against all odds there was a root emerging, pushing into the hard soil. A green shoot was peeping through. He wanted to carry on growing. Frederica's leaves had once been withered and tinged with brown. He had nurtured her

184

with water and attention and he was doing the same for himself.

He felt brave.

He decided that he should thank Mike for his troubles and found himself nearing the post office. He would risk going behind enemy lines to purchase a thank-you card.

When he arrived at the little red post office the sign said 'Closed for Lunch'. It would reopen at one-thirty. He knew that Vera stood by the door and took great relish in turning over the 'closed' sign at precisely 12.25. Latecomers might rattle the handle, but they were not coming in.

With fifteen minutes to go, Arthur paced up and down on the uneven pavement outside. Many a pensioner had gone sprawling on the flagstones.

He looked down the road with its identical tiny stone cottages. Miriam used to live in the one with the red door. There was a young family who lived there now, two women and their children. Rumour had it (as he had overheard from Vera) that they had left their husbands for each other.

Miriam had been an only child. Her mother had been very protective. Arthur had tried to win Mrs Kempster round by making sure his shoes were highly polished, by bringing cake and listening for hours about the story of how she got her finger trapped in the machinery at the cotton mill. He and Miriam stole knowing smiles whenever she chirped up, 'Did I ever tell you about my accident?'

Their wedding photos showed the smiling

newly-weds, faces pressed cheek to cheek and grinning about what their future held. Mrs Kempster looked as if she belonged in a different photo. She clutched her giant brown leather handbag to her chest and her lips were pursed as if she had eaten sour sherbet.

When they cleared her house, her belongings had fitted into the back of a small Transit van. She had been most frugal. He wondered if the charm had been passed onto Miriam at this time, though again he couldn't remember his wife telling him about it.

He paced some more and found himself standing outside number forty-eight when the door opened. One of the women came outside. 'All right there?' she asked cheerily. She wore a purple scarf tied around her hair and a green vest top with no bra. Her hair was coiled in black springs and her skin was the colour of coffee. She wrung out a dishcloth onto the front step then shook it out.

'Yes. Righto.' Arthur raised his hand.

'Are you looking for something?'

'Nope. Well, kind of. My wife used to live in this house you see, when she was young. I always have a little think when I walk past.'

'Ah right. When did she leave?'

'We got married in '69. But it would have been '70 or '71 when her mother died.'

The woman jerked her head. 'Come in and have a little look, if you want.'

'Oh no. There's no need. I'm sorry to have troubled you.'

'Not at all. Feel free to have a nosey. You'll

have to clamber over the kids' stuff mind you.'

He had been about to protest again, but then reconsidered. Why the heck not? It might spark a memory. 'Thank you,' he said. 'That is most kind.'

The house was unrecognisable. It was colourful and bright and cluttered. It felt happy. He pictured himself and Miriam sitting primly in chairs at opposite sides of the fireplace. Mrs Kempster sitting in the middle, clicking her knitting needles and proudly displaying her gnarly finger. The walls had been brown, the carpet frayed. He could still smell the coal fire and the dog that sat so close to the flames that its fur smoked.

'Does it look familiar?' the woman asked.

'Not really. I mean it's the same layout, but everything is different. It seems happier now. Modern.'

'Well, we're trying our best on not much money. The view's not bad, though the woman at the post office disapproves. I live with my partner, you see. Even worse, in her eyes, that we're both mixed race.'

'Vera isn't very diverse. She likes to gossip.'

'Tell me about it. What that woman doesn't know, isn't worth knowing.'

Arthur walked into the kitchen. It had shiny white units and a yellow dining table. Mrs Kempster's kitchen had been dark and unwel- coming, with a creaky floor and an arctic-like draught that whistled through the back door. Nothing looked familiar.

He then went upstairs. Standing on the

landing, he peered through the door into the bedroom that was once his wife's. The walls were painted bright red. There were bunk beds, lots of teddies and a brightly coloured map on the wall. He stared at it for a moment then his eyes widened. A memory began to creep back.

Mrs Kempster had only allowed him upstairs once, to fix the leg on her bed. She liked to keep him and Miriam in her sights, to make sure they didn't get up to anything untoward. Whenever Arthur needed the bathroom he had to use the one in the backyard.

He had carried up a screwdriver, screws and a can of oil to carry out the repair. At the top of the stairs, he hadn't been able to resist taking a quick peek inside Miriam's room. Her bed was covered with a patchwork quilt. There was a doll sat on a wooden chair. On her wall was a map of the world, in a similar position to the one here now. It was smaller, faded and the edges curled.

At the time Arthur thought that the presence of the map was strange. Miriam had never talked of travelling or wanting to explore. He remembered that there were three red-topped pins stuck in the map. He had walked into the room for a closer look. The colour of the pins had stood out against the pale green of the continents. As he reached out to touch them, he assumed that his wife had an interest in geography or that the map wasn't hers. There was a pin in the UK, one in India and one in France.

He screwed the leg of the bed firmly in place and sat on it to test it wasn't going to collapse with Mrs Kempster in it. When he was satisfied, he gathered up his tools and went downstairs.

He never mentioned the map to his wife, not wanting to appear as if he had been prying. It was something of insignificance that he had buried in his mind, until now.

Arthur knew Miriam had been to London and had lived in India. And now he began to wonder if she had been to France too.

As he took a quick look into the master bedroom, he thought a voice might pop into his head, to tell him that Miriam's mother had definitely been called Pearl. But it didn't come. When Miriam had sorted through her mother's belongings there had been no birth certificate and only a few family photos.

There was only one person who might be able to help him with the name. A person who knew about everyone and everything in Thornapple: Post Office Vera.

He went downstairs and thanked the lady, then walked back over to the post office.

The door was heavy. He heard Vera's sharp intake of breath as he entered. He hadn't set foot inside since he had snapped at her for asking him about Bernadette.

Walking around, he built up his nerve. He picked up a mini roll of Sellotape, then a tube of Polo mints, a pack of luggage tags and a thank-you card with a dog wearing a party hat on it for Mike, and one with a cat on for the Graystocks. He could sense Vera's eyes boring into his back. Soon his hands were full and he couldn't fit anything else into his grasp. He

189

tipped the items onto the counter. Vera flipped up the glass partition. She took each of the items in turn and made a great show of finding the price and tapping her calculator.

'It's, er, a lovely day,' Arthur said to kick-start the conversation.

Vera grunted. She gave a slow blink to show that she was not impressed.

He swallowed. 'I popped into my wife's old house. Number forty-eight. The lady there was saying how knowledgeable you are about local people.'

Vera tapped some more.

'Yes. I didn't recognise the place. Years have flown since Miriam was a young girl, living there.'

He could see Vera's lips twitch, as if they wanted to join in the conversation. However she marched off to check the price of the Sellotape on the shelf. She brought back an orange sticky label and pressed it to her desk.

'You must have seen some comings and goings over the years. It must be a privilege to own the post office and be an important part of the community. I'm afraid that I was rather snappy when I was last here. I'm still at sixes and sevens trying to get back on my feet, after Miriam, you know . . . ' He looked at his feet. This was hopeless. Vera didn't want to speak to him. He had blown it.

'She was a lovely woman, your wife.'

He lifted his head. Vera's lips were still set in a straight line. 'Yes, she was.'

'And her mother before her.'

'So, you knew her?'

'She was a friend of my mother's.'

'You can probably help me then. I'm trying to remember Mrs Kempster's first name. Was it Pearl?'

'Aye, it was. I remember my mother sitting me down when I was a girl and telling me that two important things had happened. One, that Marilyn Monroe had been found dead and two, that Pearl Kempster had moved her fancy man into the house when her divorce hadn't yet come through.'

'So, Marilyn Monroe died in 1962?'

'Yes, that's right.'

'You have a good memory.'

'Thank you, Arthur. I like to keep the old grey matter busy. Pearl's new man though, eeh he was a bad 'un, but she couldn't see it. No wonder poor Miriam took off like she did.'

'You know about that?'

'Well, yes. A young woman sees her parents split up, and then her mother gets a rough new boyfriend. I presume that's why Miriam followed that doctor chap she worked for when he moved back to India. Why else would you go somewhere so very foreign?'

Arthur blinked. Understanding washed over him. No wonder Mrs Kempster had been so sour-faced with him. She'd gone through a divorce, her daughter flitting abroad and an errant lover. She was a survivor.

'Thank you, Vera. That is most helpful.'

'That's fine. Any time.' She pushed her tortoiseshell glasses up her nose. 'I suppose you think I stand here gossiping all day?'

'I, er . . . '

'Well, that's not true. I talk to people about what they know, what they're familiar with. The post office is a community hub. It's important to village life.'

'I understand. Thanks again.' He felt a bit humbled at how obliging she had been.

Turning to leave, he found a small semicircle of pensioners around him. They had their heads cocked at various angles as they listened in to the conversation. For a moment he remembered a zombie film he had watched late one night on TV where the undead honed in on their victims, ready to eat their brains. But he was being unkind. They were probably just lonely, like him. 'Hello.' He raised his hand. 'Nice to see you all. I was just having a lovely chat to Vera. Can I just squeeze through? Thank you. Thanks.'

He walked back outside and the sun had come out. He had solved another charm. There was nothing untoward about this one. Perhaps the others might be the same, throwing up no other lovers, or questions, or unease. Yes, he felt better now.

'Oh, hello, Arthur.' Across the road Bernadette spotted him and waved. She ushered Nathan across. 'Well, just look at you. You go to Graystock and then there's no stopping you on your travels again. You're like Michael Palin all of a sudden.'

Arthur smiled.

'I called round today with a pie for you. That nice man opposite with the lawnmower said that you'd gone out. I gave the pie to Mrs Monton instead.'

'Sorry about that. I should have told you.'

'You don't need to explain to me, Arthur. I'm not your keeper. It's nice to see you out and about, that's all.'

'How is the university search going?' Arthur said to Nathan.

The young man shrugged. ''S okay.'

'The uni in Manchester looked interesting,' Bernadette said. 'Very contemporary.'

'Good.'

'You have a rucksack,' she said.

'Yes. And sandals.'

'You do look like a real traveller.'

'I've been to London.'

Nathan looked up, his face full of anticipation. Arthur didn't elaborate. He didn't want to talk about De Chauffant.

'Are you doing anything tomorrow?' Bernadette asked. 'I'm doing rag puddings. I cook them in white cotton handkerchiefs.'

Arthur's mouth began to water, but he had already thought of a plan. 'I've decided that I'm going to visit my daughter,' he said. 'It's been too long since we saw each other.' He didn't want to risk Lucy disappearing out of his life as Miriam had moved away from Pearl.

'Lovely. Well, it was nice to see you. Perhaps another time?'

'Yes, definitely. Cheerio then.'

Arthur took out his mobile phone and rang his daughter. When she didn't answer, he hung up. But then he dialled again and left a message.

'Lucy. It's Dad. I've been in London. I'm just phoning to see if we can start over. I, er, I miss you and think we should be a family again. I need to talk to you about something to do with your mother. I'm going to call round to yours at ten-thirty tomorrow morning. I hope to see you then.'

He then stuffed his post office purchases into his rucksack and walked back toward his house. Now he knew why Miriam had set off on her travels. But why hadn't she told him anything about them?

Green Shoots

Something had changed when Arthur woke up the next morning. For one thing, he had overslept. His alarm clock had stopped, the digits frozen at three in the morning. He knew it wasn't that early because outside the sky was tissue white and he could hear Terry's lawnmower. His watch showed it was nine o'clock. Usually this would have thrown him into a state of panic. He was already an hour late for breakfast. But now he lay back on his pillow and thought of nothing except going to Lucy's house.

When he got up, he didn't lay his clothes out on the bed. He went downstairs in his pyjamas. He decided that he would eat breakfast with his cereal bowl on his knee in front of the TV rather than sit alone at the too-big kitchen table. He enjoyed ignoring his routine.

He left his house at nine forty-five giving him plenty of time to walk. Terry gave him a wave as he went past. 'Arthur. You're back. Your daughter was looking for you the other day.'

'I believe so.'

'Uh-huh. I think she was worried. I mean, you don't really go out much.'

'No, I don't suppose I do.' Arthur stood poised with one foot in front of the other, ready to be on his way. Instead he reconsidered and crossed over to speak to his neighbour. 'I went to Graystock Manor in Bath and then I went to London. You know, sightseeing and things.'

'I think that's great.' Terry leaned on his mower. 'I really do. When my mum died, well my dad went to pieces. He kind of retreated into himself and gave up. It's good that you're getting out and about . . . making the most of things.'

'Thanks.'

'You're always welcome to pop round to mine for a cup of sugar or a chat. It's just me so I'd welcome the company. It's not the nicest thing being on your own, is it?'

'No. It isn't.'

'And it would be nice to see you at *Men in Caves* again.'

'Is Bobby still barking commands?'

'Oh yes. And my woodwork is still as appalling. I still make tortoises that look like cars.'

Arthur raised himself up onto his toes. 'Speaking of which . . . ' He narrowed his eyes as he saw movement in Terry's ornamental grasses.

Terry gave an exaggerated sigh. 'Not again.' He strode over and stooped to pick up the escaped tortoise once more. 'What is it about my garden that is so attractive to reptiles?'

'Maybe it's you it likes.'

'Maybe. Or perhaps he just has a sense of adventure. He doesn't like to stay put this one.'

★   ★   ★

196

As Arthur walked to Lucy's, he took in the sights and sounds around him that he didn't usually notice, stopping occasionally to admire what a beautiful place he lived in. The fields in the distance were a patchwork of greens. He noticed bursts of daisies sprouting from the cracks in the pavement. He was aware of each step he took, from the soreness of his ankle to the thrilling feeling that he was moving closer to his daughter.

The top of York Minster gleamed gold in the sun and Arthur really couldn't remember the last time he had visited and gone inside. He'd never had a to-do list, taking each day as it came, doing whatever Miriam and the kids wanted to do, but he thought that he might start one.

He arrived at Lucy's in the realisation that he hadn't been there for months. Lucy always came to them, at Christmas, for birthdays, for her usual weekly visits — before they petered out after Miriam's death. He wasn't even sure if she had picked up his message.

The door was freshly painted in scarlet and the window frames were white and bright. When Lucy opened the door, he had an urge to leap forward and hug her, as he had done with Mike, but he held back, unsure of what her reaction would be. He wasn't certain of her feelings toward him any longer.

'Come in,' she said and opened the door. She was wearing a white apron and green rubber gardening gloves. A smudge of soil ran from her eye to her chin. She turned and for a moment she looked just like her mother. Arthur stopped

197

still. The resemblance was uncanny. They shared the same tilted nose and aquamarine eyes and the same air of serenity. 'Dad?' she said. 'Are you okay?'

'Oh yes. I . . . well . . . you reminded me of your mum then. Just for a moment.'

Lucy looked away quickly. 'Come in,' she repeated. 'We can go through to the garden. It's too nice to stay indoors.'

Arthur recalled that there used to be beige carpet in the dining room and now there were stripped-back floorboards. A pair of men's Wellington boots stood at the door. Were they Anthony's old ones or did they belong to a new man? He didn't even know if Lucy had met anyone else, or if she was still mourning her marriage.

As if she could read his mind, Lucy followed his gaze. 'They're too big but I wear them for gardening. I'm not giving them back to Anthony but they're too good to give away. A few pairs of thick socks and they fit me just fine.'

'Good. They look nice and sturdy. I need to get some new boots. Mine have a hole in them.'

'These ones are size ten.'

'Oh. I used to be a ten. I'm eight and a half now.'

'You should take them.'

'No. I can't. You use them . . . '

'They're too big.' She picked them up and thrust them into his arms. 'Please have them.'

He was about to protest but then he saw the determination in her eyes. The hurt. So he relented. 'Thanks. They're just the ticket. Maybe your mother has some that will fit you.'

'She was a four and I'm a six.'

'Oh.'

They chatted and agreed that it had been a good year for carrots but not so great for potatoes. They listed the different dishes that you could make with rhubarb and the merits of using wooden lollipop sticks to mark the rows of vegetables. They agreed that there had been a lot of sun that year so far but not enough rain. Lucy asked what kind of savouries Bernadette was making at the moment and Arthur said that he particularly enjoyed her sausage rolls but he wished that she wouldn't bring marzipan cake, as he didn't like the taste but didn't want to offend her by not eating it. Lucy agreed that marzipan was by far the worst food she could imagine and wasn't it strange that it was made from almonds and she liked those. They both thought that Christmas cake would be much better with just a layer of icing.

It was a hot day. Arthur wore his slacks and a shirt with a stiff collar. He wondered how he had ever felt comfortable wearing these clothes day in and day out. He decided that he had never really liked them. Miriam had laid them out for him each day and they became a uniform.

Sweat dribbled down his neck and gathered in a small pool beneath his collar. He found the belt on his trousers cut into his waist as he bent over. 'I owe you an explanation about my travels,' he said.

Lucy dug in the trowel, scooped and then flung weeds, not watching where they landed.

'Well, yes you do. You took off to Graystock Manor then left me a garbled message to say you'd been attacked by a tiger.'

'I went to London too.' He had decided that he needed to tell her the truth. He wanted her to know about the bracelet and the stories it held.

Lucy clenched her teeth, which made dimples appear in her cheeks. She focused intently on each weed, staring then jabbing. 'I'm really worried about you.'

'There's no need.'

'Of course there's need. You're acting very oddly. What on earth are you doing travelling around the country?'

Arthur looked at his shoes. The toes were flecked with soil from Lucy's digging. 'I need to tell you something. It will explain what I've been up to. It's about your mother . . . '

Lucy didn't look up. 'Go on then.'

Arthur wished that she would meet his eyes, but she was intent on attacking the lawn. It looked as if moles had been on a rampage. He spoke anyway. 'I was clearing out your mother's wardrobe, you see, one year after she . . . you know. I was most surprised to find a gold charm bracelet stuffed inside her boot. I'd never seen it before. It had all sorts of charms on it — an elephant, a heart, a flower. Do you know anything about it?'

Lucy shook her head. 'No. Mum didn't wear stuff like that. A charm bracelet? Are you sure it was hers?'

'Well, it was in her boot. And Mr Mehra in India said that he gave her the elephant.'

'An *elephant*?'

'Well, a charm one. Apparently your mother was Mr Mehra's child minder in Goa, when he was a boy.'

'*Dad*.' Lucy sat back on her heels. Her cheeks reddened. 'You're not making sense. Mum never went to India.'

'That's what I thought too. But she did, Lucy. She lived there. Mr Mehra told me and I believe him. I know it sounds awfully strange. I'm trying to find out where else she lived, what she did before we married. That's why I went to Graystock, why I went to London.'

'I don't understand what's going on here. What are you talking about?'

Arthur slowed down his words. 'I found a number engraved on one of the charms on the bracelet. It was a phone number. I spoke to a wonderful man in India who said that Miriam used to look after him. I'm finding out things about your mother that I never knew.'

'Mum *never* went to India,' Lucy insisted.

'I know. It's difficult to believe.'

'There must be some kind of mix-up.'

'Mr Mehra is a doctor. He described your mother's laugh perfectly, and her bag of marbles. I believe he's telling the truth.'

Lucy started to stab the soil again. She stopped briefly to scoop up a worm with the tip of her trowel and deposit it a plant pot, then used her trowel like a dagger again. All the while she muttered under her breath.

Arthur didn't know how to handle other people's emotions. When Lucy's teenage hormones reared their ugly head when she turned thirteen, he found the best way to deal with it was to study the newspaper and to leave it all to Miriam. It was she who dealt with tears over boys, a brief dabble with blue-streaked hair, the slamming of doors and the occasional thrown coffee cup. She told Dan to quieten down when he was high-spirited and regularly said to him, 'Don't speak to your father like that.'

Arthur felt if he ignored moods maybe they would go away. But now he could see that his daughter was consumed by something. It was as if she had swallowed a swarm of bees that were bursting to get out. He couldn't stand it any longer. 'Lucy. Are you okay?' He placed his hand on her arm. 'I'm sorry I didn't tell you this before.'

She squinted against the sun, her forehead rippling. 'Yes, I'm fine.'

He paused for a moment wondering whether to leave things alone, like he had done so many times over the years. But he kept his hand in place. 'No, you're not. I can tell.'

Lucy stood up straight. She dropped the trowel to the ground. 'I don't think I can handle all this.'

'All what?'

'You, on your mad travels and telling me strange stories about Mum. Trying to cope without Anthony. Having lost the . . . ' She ran her hand through her hair then shook her head. 'Oh, look, it doesn't matter.'

'Yes it does. Of course it does. I didn't mean to worry you. Sit down with me and talk. I promise to try to listen. Tell me what's wrong.'

For a few seconds she gazed off into the distance. Her lip curled up to the left as she seemed to consider his offer. 'Okay,' she said finally.

She wrestled two deckchairs out of the shed and set them on the grass next to each other, batting off the dust and soil with a gardening glove. She and her father sat down, their faces tilted toward the sun, squinting so that whatever they said to each other was done without looking into each other's eyes. It brought a kind of anonymity to what they had to say.

'What is it?' he said.

Lucy took a deep breath. 'I want to tell you why I didn't go to Mum's funeral. You need to know.'

'It's in the past. You were poorly. You said goodbye in your own way.' He spoke the words, forgiving her already even though it agonised him that she hadn't been there. He longed with every bone in his body to know how his daughter had done such a thing.

'I was ill, but there was something else. I am so sorry . . . '

It was then that she let out a cry. Arthur's eyes widened. But his daughter wasn't a little girl any longer. Should he scoop her into his arms? He followed his instincts and got out of his deckchair. He stood, his body in silhouette against the sun, and then dropped to his knees. Circling his arms around her, he held her tight, like he should have done so many times when she was growing up. For a moment she resisted, her body stiff and unresponsive. But then it was as if she was a puppet and someone let go of her strings. She crumpled into his arms. She tucked her head under his chin and they stayed there for a while, holding on for dear life.

'Whatever is the matter?'

She stifled a sob but then let it go and a noise came out of her like nothing Arthur had heard before, from deep within her chest. It was a strangled mewl. Swallowing, she wiped away a trail of spittle from her chin. 'I had a miscarriage, Dad. I was fifteen weeks gone. I had the scan and everything was fine. I was going to tell you and Mum face to face. It seemed too exciting a thing to announce over the phone. It was my big story. I'd arranged to come over for tea, remember? I was going to tell you that I was pregnant.' She gave a sigh full of regret. 'I had bad stomach cramps the day after the scan. I curled into a ball on the bathroom floor and the baby started to come too early. Anthony called for an ambulance. It arrived within minutes, but they couldn't do anything.' She shook her head. 'Sorry, I don't want to think about it.

'We'd been drifting apart before I found I was pregnant. And then Mum died. I tried to get back on my feet. I forced myself to get out of bed and get washed and dressed, but on the day of Mum's funeral, I broke down. I couldn't bear to be in the church with the coffin and prayers and the crying. It was where me and Anthony got married. I'm really sorry, Dad.'

Arthur was silent as he took in her story. Everything made sense now, her distance from him. He tried to block out the thought of her curled on the bathroom floor alone. 'You've been very brave. Your mum would understand. I wish I had known though . . . '

'You had to sort out her funeral. You were grieving.'

'We should have been together as a family. There was so much to do, certificates to sign, doctors to speak to, arrangements, flowers. It helped to keep my mind busy. I didn't notice anything wrong when I spoke to you.'

Lucy nodded. 'We started to drift apart, didn't we? When I got wrapped up with trying to save my marriage . . . with Dan moving away.'

Arthur reached out and brushed away a tear from her cheek. 'We're here now.'

Lucy gave a weak smile then glanced around the lawn. 'I've made a terrible mess of my garden.'

'It's only grass.'

She flopped back onto the chair and supported her head with one hand. 'Do you think about Mum a lot?'

'All the time.'

'Me too. I pick up the phone to give her a call for a chat. But then I remember that she's not here any more. I pretend that she is though. I imagine that the two of you are at your house together, and that she's bustling around dusting, or writing her letters. If I didn't think like that then it would be too much to bear.'

Arthur nodded. He pulled up a daisy and twirled it around in his fingers. 'I'm glad I came over.'

'Me too. I have to phone Dan though, to tell him that everything is okay.'

'Okay?'

'When you took off with Bernadette and then left a message about a tiger attack, I phoned Dan. I thought that maybe . . . '

'What?'

'That you might be starting with dementia or something.'

'Oh, Lucy, I'm sorry. I think I'm as right as rain. It's just the bracelet triggered something in me: a need to find out about your mum. I didn't mean to cause you any alarm.'

Lucy studied her father's face. He had the same kindly eyes, the same red nose as usual. She believed that he was fine. 'I'm just glad that you're okay.' She sighed with relief. 'And is it really true about the bracelet? About the charms and India?'

'Yes.' He took the bracelet from his pocket and passed it to her.

Lucy studied each of the charms. She shook her head. 'This doesn't look like something Mum would own.'

'It was hers. I know it was.'

'Then I want to hear more about it. Tell me about your adventures.'

Arthur nodded. He explained how he found the bracelet. He told Lucy about the tiger, rolling up his sleeve to his shoulder to display his wound. He expressed his concern for Sebastian coping with the elderly De Chauffant and how Mike's dog was called Lucy. He told her of his visit to see Post Office Vera.

Lucy spun the emerald in the elephant charm. 'I can't believe this is what you've been up to.'

'I should have told you, but it all seemed so unlikely.'

'I know now though.' She handed the bracelet back to him. 'Where next then?'

Arthur shrugged. 'I'm not sure. There are initials on the paint palette. S. Y. The jewellery shop owner didn't know what they were.'

'You have got to carry on your search.'

'But what if I find out more things that should remain undiscovered? The more I find out, the more questions it raises.'

'Isn't it better to know? Do you remember that Mum gave me her pink and white striped box before she died? It has lots of photos in there. I've not been able to bring myself to look through it. I could get it now . . . ' She let the comment hang in the air.

Arthur had forgotten about the candy-striped box that Miriam kept in the cupboard over the bed. She had asked Arthur if he minded her giving it to Lucy and he said that he didn't. He remembered people and things and times in his head and wasn't sentimental for taking snaps, or keeping train tickets or postcards or holiday souvenirs. Arthur stared up at the sky and then the soil-studded grass. 'It's up to you,' he said.

Lucy went to get the box and they sat at the kitchen table. When she took off the lid, Arthur could smell old paper, ink and lavender perfume.

He watched as Lucy took out a chunk of photos and browsed through them one at a time. She turned them this way and that and smiled.

She held one up and Arthur saw it was of his wedding day. His brown hair curled and flopped over his right eyebrow. The sleeves of his suit were too long, almost covering his knuckles. Miriam wore her mother's wedding dress. It had been passed down through the family. Her grandmother had worn it too. It was a little too big on the waist. 'Are you sure you don't want to look?' she said.

Arthur shook his head. He didn't want to view pictures of his past.

When Lucy had finished, she peered inside the box. 'There's something wedged in the corner,' she said. She picked at it with her thumb and forefinger.

'Let me try,' Arthur said. He managed to pinch out a piece of crumpled paper. He handed it to Lucy and she smoothed it out. It was grey with faded lettering.

'I think it's the top of a compliments slip or an old receipt.' She peered more closely. 'The name says *Le Dé à Coudre D'or*. There's also some writing but it's been torn off. Numbers, I think.'

They looked at each other blankly.

'It means nothing to me.' Arthur shrugged.

'I think *d'or* means *gold* in French,' Lucy said. 'I'll check on my phone.'

Arthur took the paper. 'I think the numbers say '1969'. That's the year me and your mum got married.'

Lucy tapped a few buttons searching for a translation. She frowned and tried again. 'I think I've found something,' she said. '*Le Dé à Coudre D'or*. It means *The Gold Thimble*. There's a wedding boutique in Paris with that name.'

'Paris?' Arthur said. He thought of the pins in the map on Miriam's bedroom wall. UK, India . . . and France. He couldn't remember if the pin had been stuck in Paris.

Lucy turned the screen to show him. A photograph showed a charming shop with a tasteful white sheath dress in the window.

Arthur felt as if his heart stopped beating for a second. This couldn't be coincidence. A gold thimble on Miriam's charm bracelet and a piece of paper with the name of a shop called The Gold Thimble from their wedding year. There *had* to be a connection. But was he ready to find out even more about his wife? Would it only lead to bewilderment and hurt, especially as the thimble charm might be about to lead him to Paris?

'Do you think we should we go?' Lucy asked softly.

Arthur mused the same thing. 'It looks like a good lead . . . '

'Mum once gave me some money, when she took her pension. She told me to spend it on something frivolous, but I never did. 'Spend it on yourself. Choose something special. I forbid you to spend it on household appliances or bills.' I remember her exact words,' Lucy said. 'I thought I might spend it on something nice when I had a baby, except it wasn't to be . . . I still have the money in a jam jar in my wardrobe.'

'You should spend it on yourself. Like Mum said, get something nice.'

'Well, I've decided I'm going to treat both of

us. How do you fancy a trip over to France? We could stop by at the wedding boutique.'

Arthur only took a moment to consider this. Even if he found out nothing further about the bracelet then he would get to spend some lovely time with his daughter. 'That sounds wonderful. Let's go,' he said.

The Thimble

If Arthur had ever been asked to describe how he imagined Paris, he would say that actually he had never given much thought to the place. He had seen the Eiffel Tower on the placemats that Miriam had bought for half price in the Sainsbury's sale and once watched a programme about a cruise boat that took tourists up and down the Seine, sailed by a captain who was both seasick and allergic to helping people. Arthur thought that the water looked rather murky and that if he had to sail anywhere it would be on one of those sleek white cruise ships with swimming pools onboard, hopping off around the Mediterranean. Paris just wasn't one of those places that appealed to him.

Miriam however had a preoccupation with all things French. When it was on offer, she subscribed to a magazine called *Viva!!*, which featured lots of photos of chic women dancing through puddles while holding umbrellas, sipping tiny cups of coffee or carrying small dogs in the basket on the front of their bicycles.

As far as he could remember she had never expressed a strong desire to visit Paris. She had said that the prices in shops were very expensive. He thought she knew this through reading her magazine. He himself had pictured a cliché: lots of people wearing striped tops, with strings of garlic and baguettes of bread poking out of their baskets.

His views were challenged yet again. It was as if everything he thought he knew, or even thought, was being rewritten. Paris was beautiful.

He stood at the side of the street and took in a picture postcard scene. A skinny black cat slinked across the pavement in front of him. The white dome of the Sacré-Coeur shone like an iced cake in the sunshine. The sound of a violin drifted from the louvred windows of an apartment over a coffee shop.

A man on a bicycle rode past whistling something melodic and beautiful. He could smell freshly baked bread from the patisserie, and his mouth began to water as he saw the flamingo-pink macaroons and meringues piled high on a cake stand.

Blossoms drifted from the trees as Arthur crossed the road to the boutique. Lucy didn't want to come into the little Parisian wedding dress shop fearing it would bring back bad memories of her wedding to Anthony. 'I'll get a coffee and croissant at the café across the road and wait for you there,' she said. Then she added, 'Good luck.'

In the window, one wedding dress lay draped over a white iron garden chair. A birdcage hung from the ceiling in which sat a feathered papier-mâché dove. The dress was oyster white with a bodice intricately adorned with tiny pearls in the shape of a clamshell. The skirt was embroidered with wave-like swirls. A dress fit for a mermaid. The sign read:

Le Dé à Coudre D'or

In smaller letters underneath it said:

Propriétaire: Sylvie Bourdin

As he reached up to twist the large brass doorknob, he caught sight of the back of his hand. His skin was translucent with blue motorway map-like veins. His nails were thick and yellowing. In the glass of the door, the young man who had married Miriam had vanished and in his place was an old man with too-thick white hair and wrinkles like a walnut. Time had gone so quickly. Sometimes he barely knew himself. He gave a wry smile and at least recognised his front teeth, which had always been slightly crooked.

A chain of small bells tinkled as he stepped inside. The shop was so cool that he shivered. The white marble floor glittered beneath a chandelier the size of a tractor tyre. A row of wedding dresses hung on a rail down one side of the shop. There was a gold throne covered in blue velvet on which sat a Pomeranian dog. It wore a blue studded collar, the same colour as the chair seat.

A lady appeared through an archway. She wore an immaculately cut cobalt-blue suit and a wristful of gold bangles. He estimated that she

213

was a similar age to himself, though a good skincare regime, lashings of black mascara and scarlet lips made her look fifteen years younger. Her hair was platinum and coiffed into a high bun and she had the lithe body of a dancer. '*Bonjour, monsieur*,' her voice lilted. '*Comment puis-je vous aider?*'

Arthur felt like he was back in French class stumbling for words. He had never been any good at languages, telling himself that it was unlikely he was going to venture far enough away from York to put them to any use. '*Bonjour*,' he said, but then any French words whatsoever evaded him. He smiled to make up for his ignorance. 'I am, er, looking for Madame Bourdin, the owner of the boutique.'

'I am she, *monsieur*.'

'Oh good.' He sighed with relief. 'You speak English.'

'I try. *Comme ci, comme ça*.' Her laugh tinkled around the shop like the silver bells hung over the door. 'Sometimes though, my words are not so good. Are you looking for a wedding dress, sir?' She waved her hand as if waving a wand over his clothes.

Arthur looked down half expecting to now be dressed like Prince Charming. 'Oh no,' he said. 'Not for me. Well, obviously not for me. But I came to see you. I think.'

'*Moi?*' She held her hands to her heart. 'How lovely. Take a seat.' She led the way to a white desk and waved him to the chair opposite — another throne with a blue cushion. 'How can I assist you?'

Arthur took a photograph out of his pocket and placed in on the desk. It was one of Miriam and the children on the beach at Scarborough. 'Have you owned the shop long?'

'Ah *oui*. Many many years now. I am the original owner.'

'Then I think you may have known my wife.'

She raised one eyebrow but then picked up the photograph. For a moment she studied it. She looked up at Arthur. Her eyes widened. 'Oh my. This is Miriam, *non*?'

Arthur nodded.

She peered back at the photograph. 'Could you be . . . you are Arthur?'

'Yes.' His heart did a small flip. 'You know of me?'

'A long time ago, Miriam wrote to me. Not very often, but then I wasn't very good at keeping in touch either. I am a good dress designer, but at letters, not so good. She told me that she was getting married to a lovely man named Arthur. I was invited to your wedding but unfortunately I had to stay in Paris to look after my mother. I offered Miriam a dress from the boutique but she wore her mother's dress, yes? So I sent her a present instead. It was a little charm that I found in an antiques shop: a gold thimble. It is the name of my shop.'

'My daughter and I found a slip of paper with the name on it.'

'I enclosed a small note when I sent Miriam the charm.'

Arthur took the charm bracelet from his pocket and held it out for her.

215

'But, this is the charm!' Madame Bourdin exclaimed. 'Miriam used to wear this bracelet all the time. That is why, when I saw the charm I had to buy it to send to her.'

'I am trying to find out the stories behind this charm and the others, *madame*.'

'*Madame*. Tsk. You must call me Sylvie. You are asking me the stories, but can Miriam herself not tell you?' Her voice rose an octave with anticipation. 'Is she here with you? It has been too many years.'

Arthur lowered his eyes. 'I'm afraid she passed away, a year ago.'

'Ah *non*! I am so very sorry, Arthur. *C'est terrible*. Many times I thought of her over the years. Many times I said that I must find her and get in touch. But then I am so busy with the shop and something else would pop into my head other than Miriam. But there are always some people that you keep in your heart, yes? That you never forget.'

'How did you know each other?'

'We met through a man. He was named François.'

'De Chauffant?'

'*Yes*. You know of him?'

'A little.'

'I was one of his girlfriends when Miriam worked for him. He did not treat either of us well. When I came to my senses and decided to return to Paris, I suggested to Miriam that she join me. So we escaped together! We had no plan, no money. It was an adventure.' She hesitated. 'What happened to her?'

'She died from pneumonia. It was a huge shock.'

Sylvie shook her head. 'She was good person. When we met I spoke only a little English and she spoke only a little French, but we connected. Did you know that she helped me to set up this shop? I had always wanted to own a little wedding boutique. Me and Miriam used to sit on the benches at the side of the Seine and feed the swans with seed and bread. We talked about our dreams, or rather I did. I was always, how do you say it? A dreamer?'

Arthur nodded.

'One day we walked past a wholesaler's shop. It was closing down. They were selling off the wedding dresses very cheaply, by the box. A van was parked on the road and two men were carrying the boxes and putting them in the back. We stood and watched. When it drove off, one of the men — the owner — noticed that we were interested and asked if we would like to buy the rest of the dresses. Miriam did not understand much of what he was saying so I translated. The dresses were a good price but not cheap enough for me. I was very poor, surviving only on bread and cheese. But Miriam told me not to take no for an answer. She told me what to say to the man and I did as she said. I said that I was a young woman looking for an opportunity to sell wedding dresses; that he could help to change my life. Together, we charmed him.

'In the end I bought twenty dresses for half of what the man asked originally. So, now I had all these dresses and nowhere to sell them. I had no

217

shop and my apartment was on the third floor over a launderette. Miriam shook her head and said, 'Of course we have somewhere!' We hung them from a blossom tree and sold them in the street. They looked beautiful hanging there in the sunshine like exotic birds. There were many chic ladies passing by and, even if they weren't getting married themselves, they told their friends. Word was passed on from lady to lady. At the end of the day there were only two dresses left. That is how my business started. Or I could say *bloomed*. We went back to the wholesaler and bought another box and did the same thing for the next three days. When we had finished I had enough money to put down three months' rent on this shop. Over the years the shop has grown. I have extended. I create my own dresses now, but it all started with me and your wife hanging twenty dresses from a tree.'

'That's a lovely story.' Arthur hadn't heard it before but he could picture Miriam and Sylvie as young women laughing and climbing in the blossom tree.

'When she travelled back to England, we wrote to each other for a while. I had the shop and then Miriam had her children. Time moves so quickly.'

As she spoke, memories began to develop in Arthur's head. Miriam had mentioned a friend who owned a dress shop. He couldn't recall her saying if it was in France or not. So, she hadn't kept this part of her life secret. Occasionally, she would use a French word — *pourquoi* or *merci*. Now he cursed himself for not paying more attention. It had been difficult to concentrate on anything other than his tea when he got in from work. When the kids were in bed, he had enjoyed time with his wife. They chatted about their day rather than about their past. He wished he had taken more of an interest.

'You must join me for a glass of champagne and a little something to eat in Miriam's memory,' Sylvie said. 'I will tell you more about how we met and what fun we had. We only knew each other for a few months, but they are memories that last for ever. And you can tell me too. Tell me about your life together and your children. I want to know more about my friend.'

★   ★   ★

It was over an hour later that Arthur went to meet Lucy at the coffee shop.

'I thought that you might be staying in there for the day,' she laughed.

He looked at his watch. 'Gosh, I didn't realise I'd been so long. Have you been here all this time?'

'I've loved it. Anthony would only ever go to Starbucks!'

'*Madame?*' A waiter appeared before them. He wore black trousers and shirt and had a white and blue striped apron tied casually around his waist. His nose had a slight hump, which made him look like he should be in a 1920s silent movie.

'I'd like another café crème, please,' Lucy said.

'For you, *monsieur?*'

Arthur stared blankly.

'A coffee, perhaps? Something to eat?'

'A coffee, yes. Just the ticket.' He turned to Lucy. 'Do you want lunch?'

She patted her stomach. 'I've already had two chocolate croissants, so I'll give it a miss. The French onion soup looks delicious though. I've seen a few bowls go by.'

'Then that's what I'll have.'

The waiter nodded.

Arthur put his napkin on his lap. 'Sylvie confirmed that she bought and sent the thimble as a wedding gift. Your mother lived here for a while.'

'How interesting that she lived in Paris but didn't tell us about it. Do you have any idea why not?'

Arthur shook his head. 'But I now know the story behind another charm.'

Their drinks and Arthur's soup arrived minutes later. He peered into the brown earthenware bowl. The soup had a thick Gruyère crouton on top. 'I think that waiter likes you,' he said as he blew on his spoon. 'I saw him watching you as I crossed the road.'

'He just wants me to leave a big tip.' Lucy blushed.

'That is probably not the case.'

'I'm not sure why else he would be looking at me.'

Arthur lifted his eyes. His daughter looked so pretty, with her pinkened collarbone and freckles. It was as though a veil had been lifted from her face, taking her strain and upset with it.

He wondered for a moment if he should tell her as much, but he couldn't form the right words. Instead he looked back into his bowl. 'This soup really is fine,' he said. 'I don't know how they get the onions to go so soft.'

They sat in silence while he finished. Lucy picked up a newspaper left behind by an old man with a black poodle from the table beside them and browsed through it.

Arthur tilted his bowl to ensure he got the very last spoonful of soup. The warmness in his belly and the sun streaking through the trees made him feel calm and relaxed. His shoulders didn't feel as tight. Being here with Lucy had given him time to reflect on the past couple of weeks. He looked back over to the boutique. 'You know, through my travels and meeting people who were part of Miriam's life, I'm learning that it's the things you say and do that people remember you for. She is no longer here but she lives on in people's hearts and minds.'

'That's a nice thought.'

'I'm not sure if anyone will remember me so kindly.'

'Don't be silly, Dad.'

'I'm not being. The more I find out about your mother's remarkable life before me, the more it emphasises that I've never done anything adventurous, or travelled, or met anyone that I might have had an impact on.'

'But you are doing that now. It's not too late.'

Arthur hitched his shoulders.

Lucy shook her head. 'You're feeling emotional, Dad. It's bound to be the case. It's been a long journey here and you're hearing stories about Mum that you've never heard before. But, I assure you, you will always be part of my life. You'll always be special to me.'

Arthur gave a small nod, grateful for her sensible words. 'Thanks.' He felt he should say something in return. He wanted to tell Lucy how he loved her from the minute she was born. He had listened to Miriam say it over and over again with such ease. But the words had never come easily to him. When Lucy was a child and asleep then he could kiss her forehead and whisper 'I love you,' but here, in public, in a café, well he couldn't respond. 'I, er . . . well. Ditto.'

'Oh, Dad.'

He felt Lucy suddenly wrap her arms around his neck. 'Are you okay? Whatever's the matter?'

Lucy sniffed. 'I just miss Mum, that's all. It would be lovely if she was here with us.'

'I know.' He patted her back not knowing what to say that could change things.

Lucy broke away first. She felt around in her bag for a tissue.

'*Madame?*' The waiter appeared at her side. He raised one of his eyebrows. 'Are you okay?' He shot a glance at Arthur as if accusing him of upsetting his young companion.

'Yes. I am fine. This is my father. We are happy.'

'You are 'appy?'

'Yes. Very. Thank you for asking. I just need a tissue,' Lucy said.

The waiter vanished and then reappeared, sliding a box of tissues onto the table. 'For you.'

'*Merci.* You are very kind.'

'Claude,' the waiter said. 'My name is Claude.'

'This is my treat,' Lucy insisted when she had dabbed her eyes and blown her nose. 'It's my money to spend on what I want. Remember?'

'Yes, darling.' Arthur smiled, making out that he was hen-pecked.

He went to the bathroom and when he came out saw that Claude was talking to his daughter. The waiter had a tray tucked under his arm and Lucy was smiling and twirling a strand of hair in her hand. Arthur bent down to retie his shoelaces and, when he saw they were still chatting, he checked how many euros he had in his wallet. When Claude moved away from the table, Arthur walked back. 'Okay?' he asked.

'Yes. Good,' Lucy said. Her cheeks were flushed.

'I saw you talking to the waiter.'

'Ah, yes. He, er . . . ' She cleared her throat. 'He asked me if I wanted to go for a walk with him this evening. It was a little unexpected.'

'That's a coincidence because Sylvie asked me to join her for dinner.'

They both looked at each other and laughed.

'I hope you said yes,' Arthur said.

Paris Match

Arthur lathered his chin with shaving foam and took hold of his razor. He paused in front of the hotel bathroom mirror and studied his reflection. It felt strange to be making an effort with his appearance. He was meeting a stranger for dinner, on a Friday night in Paris. He was surprised that someone as lovely as Sylvie had nothing else planned for her evening.

His fingers tingled. He didn't want to think too deeply about this in case he tried to talk himself out of it. Friday night was when he and Miriam used to have their chippy tea in front of the TV. But he told himself that he and Sylvie were going out to talk about Miriam, to share their memories and stories. It was something he should want to do, not shy away from.

One thing he was trying not to worry about was *what* they might eat. Did all French restaurants serve frogs' legs and cook everything in garlic? He hoped not. For a moment he had a longing for one of Bernadette's pies. He was missing her home cooking and also her company. He hoped that Sylvie would be gentle on him.

After lunch in the little café across the road from the bridal boutique, he and Lucy had been out shopping. He rarely went shopping with

Miriam. If they did then he would end up loitering outside changing rooms, looking at his watch. Miriam would hold up shirts and trousers against him, then she would either nod and put them in the basket or whisk them away to hang back on the rail. The clothes would then appear as if by magic in his wardrobe, with the shop creases ironed out and the labels snipped off, ready for him to wear. Likewise, when he had a birthday in the family or at Christmas, well-chosen presents would appear on the kitchen worktop neatly wrapped in brightly coloured paper, with ribbon bows and gift tags signed 'From Miriam and Arthur'. He actually liked the idea of shopping for his family, to pick something out that he thought they might like, but gift buying was Miriam's domain. She took to it with relish.

This time he found the experience joyous. He and Lucy strolled around the streets in no hurry. They tried different French cheeses and sampled olive oils together. They found a clothes shop with a closing down sale and Lucy insisted that he buy five new shirts, two jumpers and a new pair of trousers. As he stood in the changing room and looked at his reflection in the new clothes, even he had to admit that he looked younger.

He bought a small bunch of freesias for Sylvie and an enamelled black cat brooch for Lucy when she wasn't looking. In the window of an antiques shop he saw a simple string of pearls and pointed them out. 'I think your mother would have loved those,' he said.

Lucy agreed. 'You knew her so well,' she said.

* * *

Arthur wore his new clothes as he stood outside
the bridal shop once more, waiting for Sylvie.
The lights inside were switched off and, for a
brief moment, he half hoped she'd had a change
of heart; that she had reconsidered. He walked
up and down outside the shop trying not to grip
the little bunch of freesias too tightly.

Friday night seemed to be couples night in
Paris. An array of well-dressed, gorgeous couples
of all ages sashayed past him. They smiled as
they saw him waiting. Don't worry, they seemed
to be thinking, she will be here for you soon.

Ten minutes later, he heard the shop door
rattle and Sylvie appeared. 'My apologies,
Arthur. I was ready to leave when I took a phone
call. A young bride was panicking about her
dress. She has been starving herself for her
wedding and has lost too much weight so that
her bosom no longer fills the dress so well. I told
her not to worry and that she should come and
see me tomorrow. Her wedding is in three weeks'
time so she may put weight back on. I do not
think alterations are the answer. Maybe a little
more padding in her bra . . . Anyway.' She
brushed her hair with her hand. 'What am I
telling you all this for? I am sorry to keep you
waiting, that is what I am trying to say.'

She smiled as she took the flowers. She bent
her head to smell them, took them inside the
shop and then locked the door. He noticed that
she was wearing the same suit as when he met
her earlier, but she had added a sparkly

turquoise necklace and a cream crocheted shawl. He felt less nervous now, that she hadn't changed especially for dinner.

They walked together down the cobbled streets, winding down toward the river. At one point Sylvie lost her footing and he held out the crook of his elbow so she could steady herself. As they walked, her hand remained there, linking him. Arthur felt his arm stiffen. They were walking along arm in arm. It was more familiar than he was comfortable with. He wondered if anyone passing would think they were together and this made him feel self-conscious. He hoped Sylvie didn't think their outing was anything more than friendly. This is just the French way, he told himself. Being tactile and friendly is the norm.

He glanced at her. She smiled and had a dance in her step as she pointed out a dove on a telephone wire, a mural of a girl being pulled into the air by the bunch of balloons she was carrying. Sylvie reached out to pluck a couple of olives from a bowl outside a shop. She waved to the shopkeeper inside then passed one to Arthur. He took it and the oil dribbled down his hand. He retrieved his handkerchief from his pocket. Then he kept his arm pinned to his side.

They walked to a tiny bistro with just eight tables. *Chez Rupert*. Sylvie explained that she was a friend of the owner. 'I have told them to bring us whatever dishes they feel we will enjoy. I have explained that you are an Englishman with simple tastes,' she laughed. 'We can try a little of everything.'

'A bit like tapas?' Arthur said. He and Miriam had once gone to Spanish night at the local village hall in aid of raising funds for the church roof. They had each received a glass of sangria piled high with chunks of apple and orange. 'It's kind of like a boozy fruit salad,' he said after taking a sip. Each table then received around six small terracotta dishes with different foods in each. He and Miriam had peered at each of them in turn. There were things that he didn't recognise, but they had eaten the whole lot. It had been an enjoyable evening, even if they had to call at the chippy on the way home because they were still hungry.

'Yes. Like tapas,' Sylvie agreed.

While they waited for their food, they finished a nice bottle of Merlot with ease and ordered another. Arthur's head felt lighter, as if any worries he had were drifting away.

He surprised himself by trying mussels cooked in garlic butter and a thick French fish soup called bouillabaisse. He ate veal and a mushroom stew and quaffed more red wine. And he tried not to think about why he hadn't been open about trying new things in the past.

When a passing musician stepped into the bar and played the accordion, Sylvie insisted that they stand and dance. Even though the people around them laughed at the pathetic dancing efforts of this Englishman, Arthur bowed and laughed with them.

After dinner, Sylvie took his arm again and this time it felt more natural. They walked alongside the Seine. The sunset was spectacular, making the sky look like it was on fire. Arthur found her charming company but he couldn't help wishing that it was his wife he was with, was laughing with, was admiring the sunset with. He felt the need to speak her name, to remind himself that he was here because of her. 'Miriam would love it here,' he said.

'She did love it here,' Sylvie said. 'We came here a few times to walk and talk and plan our futures. We were full of youthful confidence. I was going to be the best wedding dress designer in the world. All the celebrities and film stars would want to wear a Sylvie Bourdin dress. But then, as the weeks and months and years pass, you become more sensible. You recognise that dreams are just that.'

'But you have your shop. You've done amazingly well. You help to make dreams come true.'

'Did Miriam's dreams come true? She talked of meeting a man and having lots of children and living in the country with a big garden.'

'She said those things? Nothing about tigers and being swept off her feet by a rich novelist?'

'You are teasing me, yes?'

'A little.' They stopped and watched a rowing boat sail past, cutting through the water that looked like mercury in the fading light. 'We had a small house, two children and lived on the outskirts of the city. I worry that her life with me didn't match up to her dreams.'

'I think that out of the two of us, she is the one who got it right. I didn't have children, you see. I was always too busy with work. I have a beautiful shop instead of babies. The ladies who come to see me are like my daughters. I have many, many daughters,' Sylvie laughed. 'Hopefully some remember me after their big day. I sometimes wish my dreams had been simpler or that I had time for both a family and my shop.'

They found a small bar that rang with laughter and sat at a black wrought-iron table on the pavement. 'Even I do not know this place,' Sylvie exclaimed. 'You are making an explorer out of me, Arthur.'

It was past two in the morning by the time they returned to the wedding boutique. It was with some guilt that Arthur realised they hadn't talked very much about Miriam. They chatted about York and about Lucy and Dan. He told Sylvie about Bernadette and Frederica and more of the stories behind the charms. In turn, Sylvie told him of her lovers over the years and how she had nearly left Paris to live in a rural watermill with a penniless artist but had come to her senses before she walked down the aisle. 'I own a bridal shop but have never been a bride myself,' she said.

As they neared the boutique, Arthur's pulse quickened. What was the etiquette in these matters — a kiss to the cheek? Both cheeks? A hug? He wasn't sure. He grew silent as they stood in front of the bay window.

'I have had a lovely time, Arthur. I have not laughed so much in a long time.'

'Me neither.' He felt he didn't have to try too hard with Sylvie. There was a natural ease between them that he hadn't felt with anyone other than with his wife. She was connected to his wife and that made him want to be close to her. He wanted to touch the lines around her eyes, to stroke her cheek. Sylvie moved a little nearer. He could feel her breath on his neck, see how the ends of her eyelashes curled up and the small furrow between her eyebrows.

He wanted to kiss her.

Kiss her?

Where had this thought come from? He should only want to kiss his wife.

Sylvie smiled at him, as if she could read his thoughts.

He felt his own hand slip around her waist. Should he pull away before it was too late?

While he was still thinking about it, their lips met.

It felt strange to be kissing someone else. It was something that he wanted to stop and reflect upon before he continued, but he could not pull away. He needed human contact, to feel wanted again. Her lips were soft and warm. Time slipped away.

Sylvie pulled away first. 'It is getting cold now.' She shivered, pulling her shawl tighter around her shoulders. 'Would you like to come up for a coffee?'

It was a question that he hadn't expected. But it was a natural end to the evening, to sit and talk some more. He could ask her more questions, the ones he had forgotten to ask already. But it would be dangerous too. Might she be thinking of more than just coffee?

'I really must get back to the hotel,' he said.

'Lucy may wonder where I am.' This sounded silly as soon as he said it. Of course they had separate rooms. He wouldn't see her until breakfast.

'But Lucy met with her waiter friend?'

'Yes. Claude.'

'I am sure that your daughter is a big girl now.'

'Yes, but I will always worry about her.'

'I am sure that Claude will make sure she gets home safely. And she has a mobile phone, yes?'

'Yes.' Arthur took his own phone from his pocket. 'Oh look. She has left a message.' He opened it up. Lucy had sent it twenty-five minutes ago. It told him not to worry, that she was on her way back to the hotel and would see him in the breakfast room at nine in the morning. 'Ah, that's good.' He smiled.

'So you would like coffee, yes?'

Arthur put his phone back into his pocket. He let his hand linger there. 'I . . . ' he started.

Sylvie interjected. She lifted her chin proudly. 'The thing is Arthur, I am lonely sometimes. I feel that time is passing me by. I would very much like you to join me for coffee and perhaps spend the night. I meet men who are young and who are bridegrooms, I meet fathers of the bride who sometimes propose to me what they shouldn't propose. I am professional and I say no. I do not meet many people whom I like, who I feel something for.'

Arthur felt longing ache within his belly. He hadn't expected to feel like this about anyone ever again. It was delicious but also made him feel sick with guilt. This wasn't lusting over a film

232

star or someone unobtainable, which might be acceptable in a marriage. Sylvie was flesh and blood. She was beautiful and she was here, asking him to go to her room.

It felt as if he would be being unfaithful to his wife.

The thought struck him. Of course he could justify to himself that Miriam was no longer here, so how could he be cheating? But he knew that he would feel as if he had done. Sylvie was his wife's friend. Maybe from a very long time ago, but he could not betray Miriam.

He let his arms fall by his sides. 'I am so sorry, Sylvie. I would like a coffee with you very much, but . . . ' He looked down.

Sylvie stood still. She gave a small nod. 'I think I understand.'

'I hope you do. Because I think you are wonderful. You are beautiful and graceful and bright and clever. But . . . '

'But you are still in love with someone else?'

Arthur nodded. 'With my wife. Always, I think. If there ever is anyone else, and I really can't think about that, then I need to take things slowly. I am only here for another night and that isn't enough for me. If I met someone, I would need to think that Miriam would understand.'

'I think she would want you to be happy.' Sylvie took the keys from her purse.

'I'm not sure if I would be happy afterwards. And I want to be. I'd want it to be wonderful; I'd want to feel that it had been right.'

She touched her necklace. 'You may not believe this, but there was once a time when I never had to ask. Men would wait for me, they would follow me.'

'I can completely understand that. You are *très magnifique*.' They both laughed at his attempt at French. 'But — ' he reached in his pocket and held out the bracelet ' — until I know all the stories I cannot move on. I'm not ready for any woman other than my wife.'

'You are honourable.' Sylvie pursed her lips. 'Though if you continue on your search you may find out things that you do not like to hear.'

'I already have done.'

'There may be more.'

Arthur detected how her tone had cooled. He took hold of her hand. 'Is there something you know, Sylvie?'

He saw a flicker in her eyes as she denied it. '*Non*. It was just a thought . . . '

'If you know something, please tell me.'

'As I said, Miriam wrote to me a few times.'

'What is it?'

Sylvie held her breath. Then she said, 'If you want to find out more, you should try to find her friend, Sonny.'

'Sonny?' Arthur asked.

'If I recall correctly, she made jewellery.'

Arthur thought of the bracelet. 'Do you know her surname?'

'Hmmm. I think it began with a Y. Ah yes, Yardley. I remember it because I have a cousin who married a man with that surname. I have a good memory, yes?'

'Yes. Excellent. Sonny Yardley. The initials S. Y. are on the paint palette charm. It sounds as if there could be a connection. Do you know where I can find her?'

'No.'

'Can you think of anything else at all, to do with her?'

Sylvie frowned. 'I think her brother may have been an artist, but other than that, no.'

'I will try to find her.'

'If you do, she may be able to tell you what you do, or do not, want to know.'

'What do you mean?'

Sylvie shrugged. 'You will find out for yourself.'

Arthur could tell that Sylvie wanted to get inside. He had wounded her pride. All conversation had come back to his wife. He kissed her on the cheek, thanked her for her hospitality, and then walked back to his hotel. He felt regret, heavy in his stomach, but he had done the right thing.

The night sky was already streaked with powder blue in preparation for the next day, the stars fading. He wrapped his fingers around the bracelet and held it tight until he reached the hotel. Before he used the revolving door, he paused to straighten his collar. As he did, he caught sight of movement from the corner of his eye. Turning, he saw Lucy and Claude standing together in the street. Lucy kissed him on the cheek and then broke away.

Arthur hung back so they reached the door to the hotel together.

'Oh, hi, Dad,' she said, too casually.

'Hello. Did you have a good evening?'

'Yes, very. And you?'

Arthur looked at the rising sun. 'Yes,' he said. 'Yes, I did. Though I don't think I will see Sylvie again. I . . . well, I . . . er, your mother . . . '

Lucy nodded and opened the door. 'I understand, Dad. Claude was for one night only too. Sometimes that's okay.'

Bookface

It felt good to be back in his own bed, in his own home. After his stay in a hostel, on Mike's sofa, in a boutique Parisian hotel, in a manor house with orange and black striped wallpaper, his own room was where he wanted to be. It was comforting, familiar, like being in a cocoon. He could have his cups of tea when he wanted them.

He lay and thought for a while about his kiss with Sylvie, replaying the moment their lips met over and over in his mind. He could still feel the softness of her waist, the warmth of her pressed against him. A pit of heat radiated in his stomach and he moved his hands to feel it there. When he closed his eyes he was transported back to Paris. He could still smell her perfume.

He didn't regret his decision not to have coffee with her, but he did wonder where it might have led. What would have happened if he had followed her upstairs and into her bedroom? Would they have made love or would he have scuttled away into the night, unable to go through with it? He would never know now. He had only ever spent the night with his wife. The idea of being with another woman made him feel both nauseous and curious. Opening his eyes, he rolled on his side and then got out of bed, flustered by his improper thoughts. Yet a small knot of longing remained in his heart.

He dressed in the trousers and shirt that he had bought with Lucy in Paris and stuffed the shirt that smelled of Sylvie into the wash basket. When he caught sight of himself in the mirror he was surprised to see that he looked good. His hair had grown longer on top. By now Miriam would insist he visit the barber in the village, but he quite liked it. He reached up and gave it a ruffle.

For just a moment he considered taking up his old routine, to make sense of the day. He caught himself looking at his watch, to see if it was time to make his toast yet. But then he thought, *Sod it.* He was going to go with the flow today, see what happened.

In the kitchen, he ate an apple while he stood barefoot looking out of the window over the garden. He was surprised to see that the fencing around the garden looked much too high. Why had he and Miriam ever chosen such a tall structure that blocked out the view of their neighbours' gardens? A small picket-style fence would be better.

There were only three charms left to discover the stories behind. His only lead, however, was a name. Sonny Yardley. Even though he racked his brains he couldn't recall Miriam ever mentioning anyone called Sonny.

He started his search with the phone directory, running his finger carefully down the Ys. There were two S. Yardleys listed but when he phoned, one was a Steve and the other was a Stuart. He supposed she could have married and changed her name, or she might not even be alive any longer. Frustrated that he didn't have the resources to carry on his search, he cleaned the house from top to bottom. This wasn't as part of his routine, but because it needed it. Having been out and about for the best part of two weeks, there was a thin layer of dust covering every surface. He sang the tune played by the accordionist in the little bar that he had visited with Sylvie. He watered Frederica and placed her outside in the rockery so she could get some fresh air.

He had just made himself a ham sandwich and glass of milk when the doorbell rang. *Bernadette.* He jumped to his feet then ran a hand over his new shirt. He didn't even think about going into National Trust statue mode. It would be really good to see her. He was sure she would like to hear about Paris. He had even bought her a small gift — a cotton lavender bag with a bird carrying an envelope embroidered on it. Smiling, he opened the door. He was most surprised to find that it was Nathan rather than Bernadette who stood on his doorstep.

'All right, Tiger Man.'

'Oh. Nathan. Hello.'

'You weren't expecting me, right?'

'No, er, I thought it might be your mum.'

'Is she not here?' Nathan said. He wiped his nose with the back of his hand. His white T-shirt was printed with large black capital letters: PARENTAL ADVICE.

'No. I haven't seen her. I've been to France with my daughter.'

He expected the young man to shrug and shuffle off, to mumble that he'd find her elsewhere, but he stayed put as if rooted to the doorstep. They looked at each other. 'Would you perhaps like to come in for a cup of tea?' Arthur asked.

Nathan shrugged but came inside.

'Go through. Please. Make yourself at home.'

'Your house is a bit like ours.' Nathan walked into the sitting room. He sank into the sofa and swung his legs over the arm. 'It's the same layout, except Mum likes loud colours obviously.' He rolled his eyes. 'Yours is kind of all neutral and calm.'

'Really? It's looking kind of old-fashioned to me.'

Nathan shrugged. 'Looks fine.'

Again there was a strange silence as if they were both waiting for the other to speak, or as if they realised that they actually had nothing to say. 'I'll put the kettle on,' Arthur said.

He bustled out and made a pot of tea in the kitchen and then added a saucer of biscuits to the tray. When he carried it through, he found Nathan was studying his photographs on the mantelpiece. There were a couple of the kids when they were toddlers and a family shot taken on Lucy's eighteenth when they had hired the local community hall and Vera from the post office turned up even though she hadn't been invited.

'Did you find François De Chauffant?' Nathan asked.

240

'Yes. I visited his house.' Arthur set the tea tray down. 'It was the address you gave me.'

'A big white mansiony thing?'

'That's the one.'

Nathan clicked his tongue and sat back down. 'That's pretty cool, you know, visiting a living legend. Was his house, like, lined with loads of books? Did he swan around in a velvet dressing gown while smoking those thin cigar things? I bet he had a girlfriend and she was only twenty-one or something.'

Arthur thought about the wizened old man who sat alone in the attic. However he didn't want to shatter Nathan's illusions. 'It was a most enlightening visit,' he said. 'Yes, he had lots of books. He was rather, er, busy so I only stayed a short while.'

'Did you get his autograph?'

'No. I didn't. But I did get a book of his poetry.'

'Cool. Can I take a look?'

Arthur then remembered when he'd last seen it, glowing orange under a street lamp on a bench in London. 'I'm afraid that I promptly lost it.'

'Oh.' Nathan looked down. His fringe flopped over his face.

Arthur poured the tea and held a cup out. 'I was actually going to call on your help.'

'Yeah?'

'I once overheard Vera in the post office talking about something called Bookface. Apparently you can look people's names up, to try and find them.' Or stalk them, in the case of Vera,

241

who was trying to locate an ex from her school days. 'I need to find another person.'

'You mean Facebook?'

'Oh, do I? Facebook then. What does it do?'

'Like the biddy at the post office says, you can look people up and friend them online, post statuses, upload pics and stuff.'

This was like a foreign language but Arthur nodded as if he understood.

'It was, like, sick once but now everyone is so over it, unless you're ancient. All the thirty-pluses use it.'

'I'm trying to find a Sonny Yardley. Could you use your computer skills to help me?'

Nathan slurped his tea noisily. 'I'll look tonight for you. My phone is playing up. Do you know that everyone who has an iPhone drops it? Mine went down the bog this morning. Do you have any more on this Sonny? How old?'

'Around my age.'

'Jurassic period, ha ha.'

'Definitely prehistoric.'

'Leave it with me.'

They drank their tea and Nathan ate all the biscuits. 'So you can't find your mum,' Arthur said.

'No. She's probably in the village, looking out for her lost causes.'

'She's a very kind lady, your mum.'

'I know.' He hesitated with his mouth open, and then gave a toss of his head. 'I wonder sometimes why she wants me to go to a university so far away. I mean, I suppose I'm an awkward git sometimes, but . . . you know, it's like she wants to get rid of me.'

'I think she's just looking at the best place for you, what is best for you.'

'I did think she might want me to go to a uni close by, so I could live at home with her, but . . . ' He shrugged.

'Have you told her that?'

'Nah. She's got it in her head that I'm going to university and that it should be to study a proper subject. So I can get a good job when I leave, blah blah, so I get on the housing ladder blah blah. I have no idea what I am going to do with an English degree. I mean, I can speak English so what is the point of learning about it?'

'Well,' Arthur said, aware that he probably wasn't best placed to give advice to an eighteen-year-old. 'What do you want to study then?'

Nathan shook his head. 'If I tell you, you won't believe me.'

'Why wouldn't I?'

'Because you wouldn't. Because my mum won't listen to me either.'

Arthur thought of sitting with Lucy in the garden when he had promised to listen, how it had been the catalyst to start building bridges and becoming a family again.

'I'm a good listener,' he said. 'I have all day.'

Nathan bit his bottom lip. 'Do you have any more biscuits?'

'Bourbons?'

'I prefer custard creams.'

'I'll see what I've got.'

In the kitchen Arthur purposefully gave

243

Nathan longer to think about whether he wanted to talk or not. He always seemed to have so few words. Back in the sitting room, he handed over the refreshed saucer with Jammie Dodgers and Party Rings.

'Party Rings,' Nathan exclaimed. 'I love those.' He then seemed to remember that it wasn't cool to get so excited over iced biscuits. 'Okay then, Tiger Man . . . You want to know what I want to do at college. Well, I want to bake cakes.'

Arthur digested this information. He took great care not to smile or look surprised. 'Cakes?' he said without expression.

'Told you.' Nathan blew into his fringe. 'When I told Mum she looked at me like I'd gone mad.'

Arthur placed a hand on his shoulder. 'I don't think you've gone mad. I'm not judging you.'

Nathan gave a deep breath. 'I know. Sorry about that. I like baking though. Always have done. I help Mum in the kitchen sometimes. She tells me that baking is not a real subject, that I have to do something useful. When I speak to her, she won't listen. It's okay for her to make her sausage rolls and her pies, but not me.'

'Baking is useful. You could be a chef, or own a cake shop . . . '

'Or have my own restaurant or range of products. I know this. She just doesn't get it. She's always so busy looking after other people.'

'She cares about you more than anyone.'

Nathan looked away. 'I know. I suppose. Look, do you think that . . . er . . . you could have another word with her, Arthur? Get her on my side.'

244

'I don't think she'd listen to me.'

'No. She would,' Nathan said quickly. 'She thinks a lot of you. I can tell.'

Arthur felt his chest puff up a little. 'I can try.' He nodded. Bernadette was asking him to be a good influence for her son, and now, vice versa, Nathan was asking for his help too.

'Thanks. Do you mind if I ask you another question? I want you to be honest with me though,' Nathan said.

Arthur lowered his teacup. 'Yes of course.'

Nathan rubbed his nose. 'Is my mum going to die?'

Arthur spluttered. Tea slopped over the side of his cup and onto his lap. He leaped up and jerked backwards, the tea spilling over his groin so it looked as if he'd had an accident. 'Is she going to do what?'

Nathan spoke without any emotion. 'I just want to be more prepared this time. When my dad died it was a shock. I found her hospital appointments . . .'

What hospital appointments? Arthur didn't know anything about them. Bernadette hadn't confided in him. When she visited it was always about him, how he was feeling, what he was up to. He never asked about her. 'You really shouldn't read other people's things.' He dabbed at his trousers with a tissue.

Nathan shrugged. 'She should have hid it better, not left them lying around. She has to go to the cancer unit. Is that what it is?' He didn't wait for Arthur's response. 'I figured I should know more so I can look after her. She thinks by keeping things secret it protects me, but it just makes things worse. I thought that you'd know. She must have told you something . . . '

'No. Nothing.' Maybe if he had been here to listen. How had Bernadette put up with his maudlin moping around, his hiding from her? He had taken her for granted. 'I think you need to speak to her,' he said quietly. 'You should be honest with each other. Tell her how you feel about uni. Tell her that you're worried about her. Have a proper conversation.'

Nathan stared into the bottom of his cup as if he was reading tea leaves even though Arthur made the brew with a tea bag. 'I think I'd get upset. It would be so embarrassing. I don't want her to see that.'

'She won't mind. Please, just talk. I should have talked to my children more. I'm only just unravelling the past now. Don't leave it as long as I did. You won't regret it.'

Nathan nodded, taking in his words. He stood up. 'Thanks, Tiger Man. You're all right, yeah.' He directed a punch at Arthur's arm, directly connecting with the tiger scratches.

Arthur smiled through the pain.

Later that day he went to the post office. Vera gave him a cheery wave as he entered. He asked if she had seen Bernadette that day but she reported that she hadn't. However, she said, there was a new widow over on Bridge Street who was in need of feeding up so Bernadette was probably there.

★ ★ ★

246

When he got back to the house, Arthur found the red light flashing on his answer machine. He pressed the button and listened to the message.

'Tiger Man. I've looked up this Sonny Yardley person. It's a lady! Anyways, not sure why I'm surprised by that. There are two on Facebook, but one is, like, eighteen. She has a nose ring and pink hair. I think the one you're looking for is a lecturer at Scarborough College. She teaches jewellery. There's not much else on her home page. It's pretty basic. She only has five friends, ha ha. Hope that helps. Okay. Laters.'

The Paint Palette

Arthur phoned Bernadette that evening but there was no reply. He considered calling around but that might raise her suspicions and Nathan made him swear not to mention the hospital appointments.

She'll probably be at her belly dancing class, he told himself. He thought that actually she might look rather nice dressed in jewel colours and small brass bells, shaking off her worries. He wrote himself a note to phone her the next day.

While watching *NCIS*, which he rather enjoyed even though it was more grisly than it needed to be, he looked up the number for Scarborough College in the phone book. There wasn't a number for a jewellery department listed but there was one for Art and Design.

He sat with the phone receiver in his hand for fifteen minutes before he plucked up the courage to make the call. When he phoned Mr Mehra in India it had sparked the start of a long journey of discoveries about his wife's life. Sylvie's words about him not liking what he might find out rang in his head. If Miriam and Sonny were friends, why would he not like what he heard?

His heart thumped as he dialled the number. Don't worry, there will be no one there at this time of evening, he told himself.

He expelled his breath when an answerphone message announced the college was open between the hours of nine and five and would he like to leave a message stating the department and person he wanted to contact.

He asked that Sonny Yardley phone Arthur Pepper as soon as possible. He left his home and mobile numbers.

At ten-thirty the next day, when he had received no reply, he left another message and then one at just past four also. In between he rang Bernadette, but again she wasn't there.

The day after that he decided to call round to Bernadette's in person. When he left the house, Terry was mowing his lawn.

'How are things with your daughter, Arthur?'

'All good, thanks. We went to Paris for a long weekend.'

'Ah yes, she said you had. It sounds fantastic.'

'She told you about our break?' Arthur frowned. He hadn't realised that Lucy and Terry were acquainted. 'When?'

'I bumped into her at school. I was looking after my niece and we got chatting.' He gazed off into the distance for a moment then refocused on Arthur. 'Is she coming round for tea soon then?'

'Probably.'

'So, does she live far?'

'Oh. No. Not too far.'

'That's good. It's nice for family to live close together.'

Arthur nodded at the lawn. 'Why do you keep

mowing it?' he asked. 'It doesn't need doing that often.'

'No. It keeps me busy. I like things neat and tidy. My wife used to have me doing it this often, when we were together.'

'I didn't know you were married.'

'We moved back up here from the Midlands and things didn't work out. I've been divorced for over a year now. I've been single long enough. It would be nice to meet someone new to share things with. Is Lucy, er, with anyone at the moment?'

'She split up with her husband a while back.'

Terry shook his head. 'That's tough.'

'It was. She's a lovely girl.'

'She seems very caring, Arthur. Families should be like that, shouldn't they? Looking out for one another. We moved to look after my mum when she had her fall. I wanted to do it. I couldn't let her struggle on her own or have a stranger doing it. My ex-wife had a bit of a grumble about relocating, but she liked it here after all.' He gave a wry smile. 'She met someone else and left me for him.'

'Oh. I'm sorry to hear that.'

Terry shrugged. 'I tried hard to make it work, but it wasn't to be.'

'And your mum . . . ?' Arthur said cautiously.

'Oh, she's as right as rain,' Terry laughed. 'I see her most days. She's even got a boyfriend. He's a lovely fella who lives two doors down from her. We all go for lunch most Sundays. Anyway, I'd better get back to work, mowing my lawn, hunting for tortoises. Will you tell Lucy

250

that I asked after her?'

'Yes. Will do. Cheerio.' As Arthur started to walk away he wondered if Terry's well wishes for Lucy were more than just friendly, and he decided that he didn't mind if they were.

At Bernadette's house he knocked on the door. The windows to the sitting room were open so he would imagine that someone was inside. He pictured her in the hallway, her back pressed against the wall, hiding from him. How had he been so cruel and ridiculous? He could hear the faint tinny sound of rock music and he stood and shouted out, 'Nathan?' But there was no reply.

Feeling it was too forward to go round the back of the house, he returned home. The red light on his answer machine was unblinking. Sonny Yardley still hadn't returned his call.

He would have to take matters into his own hands.

★   ★   ★

Scarborough College was a swarm of students. They moved as if one, through the reception area and into the corridors that led off it, like a termite mound. The youth and vitality surrounding Arthur made him feel very, very old. These young people would think they had their whole lives in front of them, unaware that it would pass in the blink of an eye.

It was easy to picture Miriam among them. Some of the fashions were the same — dark eyes, heavy fringes kissing eyelashes, short neat skirts.

251

She had started to wear more grown-up clothes when they started dating, as if she had shelved part of her personality when they met. There were some trends that surprised him too — holes through eyebrows, tattoos everywhere.

He asked at reception after Ms Yardley in the art or jewellery department. The lady behind the desk had a phone glued to one ear and a mobile phone to the other. She spoke into them in turn. At the same time she had a file opened in front of her and she studied it. When she had hung up both the phones, Arthur said, 'You need another arm.'

'Huh?' She glared at him, as if poised to deal with yet another student who had lost their iPhone.

'Like an octopus, so you can do all the stuff you need to do.'

'Tell me about it.' The woman popped a piece of chewing gum in her mouth. She had a round face and her platinum hair was pulled into a tight bun. 'Are you here for the silver surfer's club?'

'Surfing? They do that here?'

'Are you trying to be funny?'

'No.' He had no idea what she was talking about. 'I'm looking for the jewellery department. I'm hoping to find a Sonny Yardley.'

'Not today you won't. She's off sick. Been off for a few weeks now.'

Arthur's hopes sank. 'But she does work here?'

'She does, but she only does part-time. It's her last term and she's about to retire. You could try Adam. He's been taking her classes. Room 304.'

The receptionist directed him to the room, which was in an old part of the college. When he had arrived, the foyer had been modern, lined with glass. A long walkway connected that building to another red-brick Victorian one. The windows were tall with lots of small panes and the walls were tiled in bottle green and cream shiny slabs. It reminded him of being back at school. Any moment now his old teacher, Mrs Clanchard, would appear from a classroom, threateningly slapping a wooden ruler against her palm. He shuddered and carried on, reading the signs on the doors. Ceramics studio, sculpture, papermaking, glass. He finally found 304.

There was a circle of students in the room. Some stood at easels and others sat on wooden benches. All were facing blank white sheets of paper. A man stood in the centre of the room. He was older than the others and wore a red-checked shirt and jeans through which his knees poked. He dug a hand into his hair.

Arthur tapped him on the shoulder. 'Adam?'

'Yes!' the man said as if his football team had scored. 'Oh, thank God you're here. We've been waiting.'

The reception lady must have phoned ahead. 'I'm Arthur Pepper. I . . . '

'Arthur. Yes. That's fine.' Adam twitched. 'Look. I need to make a call. My wife is threatening to leave me again. If I don't phone, she will cut off my balls. Come into this room. I'll only be five minutes.' He moved swiftly and Arthur followed.

Arthur thought that five minutes seemed like rather a short period of time to win round a spouse, especially if she had a knife, but he did as he was told.

'Stay here for a moment,' Adam said.

The room was wood panelled. Arthur had watched a Harry Potter film on TV once and it reminded him of Hogwarts. There was an old oak desk with a green leather top and artwork lined the walls. He strolled around and admired the work. After studying the third work (a charcoal drawing, very expressive) he realised that all the subjects were naked. Both men and women. They stretched, stood and sat for their portraits. With an amateur eye, he classed some as very good studies with clear brushstrokes, a nice use of colour and the faces and expressions were well done. Others, he didn't really understand. They seemed to be little more than a collection of angry brushstrokes, scribbles and splashes of paint. Each was dated and the dates ran in succession. It appeared that a piece of artwork was added to the room each year.

He was working round the room the wrong way so he looked at the recent work first before he found his way to the seventies then the sixties. There was a painting at the end of the row that drew his eye. Unlike the other works, this lady was smiling, as if she knew the artist and was posing especially for them rather than as a job. Her breasts jutted proudly outward. Her lips were parted. She looked more than a little like Miriam. He smiled at the resemblance.

Then his smile faded.

He studied the portrait again, stepping closer to the frame. He took in the aquamarine of the sitter's eyes, then the birthmark on her left hip. She had always hated that birthmark. It resembled a hot air balloon with a large circular shape and then a small square beneath it.

Arthur found himself staring at a naked painting of his wife.

'Right.' Adam burst back into the room. He knitted his hand into his hair. 'She won't bloody listen to me. Hung up in fact. I have to call her back. She doesn't usually respond until I've rung her at least fifteen times. She judges how much I want her back by the number of calls I make. It's a game but if I want to keep her then I have to play it. God, I could do without this. Anyway, the students are getting restless. Follow me.'

Arthur followed him to the original room. The students were still standing around, chatting and looking bored.

The portrait of his wife was stuck in his head. When had she posed? Who had she posed for? Why was she naked? He felt dazed, unable to focus on where he was and what he was here to ask. He put one foot in front of the other but felt as if he was floating rather than walking. He had expected a conversation, a mere yes or no that someone could tell him about the paint palette charm, but now he had discovered this. Just who had Miriam Pepper been?

'Go over there behind the screen. Then we can get started.' Adam clapped his hands.

Arthur stared blankly, his mind not functioning. Another waiting room? Where? Oh there.

Yes, okay then. His feet moved again. He was aware only of himself and his discomfort.

It wasn't a room as such, more of a wooden screen but there was a plastic chair and a glass of water on a low table. There was a towelling robe. He sat and waited for Adam. He thought of how at the beach with the kids Miriam clutched a towel around her in a series of Houdini-like moves as she removed her wet swimsuit and wriggled back into her underwear. On their wedding night she had insisted on the lights off. Yet, here she was naked. An image of her bare body had hung on the wall in a room for over forty years for all to admire it. He didn't know how to feel. Should he march back in there and pull it from the wall? Or would Miriam have been proud of the painting; that it wasn't about her at all but about the person who had painted it?

Who *had* painted it?

He felt the now fanriliar emotions of jealousy and confusion invading his body again. Between each charm he raised his hopes that the next thing he found out about his wife would be normal, it would be understandable. It would tell him that everything had been fine between them. And each time he felt even more bewildered. Everything had once been so simple but his curiosity had spoiled that.

The chattering slowed down. A few minutes passed. Adam poked his head around the screen. 'Are you ready yet?'

'Yes,' Arthur said. 'Ready when you are.' He took a sip of the water. He reached out and felt the robe. It was white towelling and had gone stiff from being washed too many times. A few more minutes passed.

A girl appeared this time. She had black hair with a fuchsia fringe and wore a tartan kilt and biker boots. 'Adam's had to make another call,' she said. 'We were wondering if you're ready?'

'Yes. I told Adam. I've been waiting here for him.'

'But you're still dressed.'

It was the strangest and most obvious observation. 'Well, yes.'

'Er, did Adam not tell you? We're studying the human form.'

Arthur frowned, not sure of the connection.

'Our drawings will influence a piece of body jewellery.'

'That's nice.'

'We only have an hour and a quarter left, so if you're ready . . . the fire is on and it's pretty warm out here.'

It took a few moments for what she was suggesting to sink in. He gulped. 'You th — think I'm a life model . . . ?' he stuttered.

'Well, yes.'

'Well, *no*.' He shook his head furiously. 'Definitely not. I came to see Ms. Yardley. She's off sick so the receptionist told me to see Adam. I wanted to speak to him about a piece of jewellery. He asked me to wait in the room with the paintings and now in here.'

'So, you're not our model?'

'Most certainly not.'

'So, he's not turned up?' The girl opened her

eyes wide. Arthur saw they had become glassy, as if she was about to cry. 'But you *have* to do this. If we don't do this work then we fail our final.'

'I'm sorry but I really don't think I can help you . . .'

The girl shook her head but then she reconsidered and straightened her back. 'I did it once. I'd do it now but I have to be in the class. All you have to do is sit there. It's simple. You sit and we draw.'

'But you want someone who is naked?'

'Well, yes.'

'I am not a model.'

'It doesn't matter.'

'What about Adam? Can't he . . . ?'

The girl rolled her eyes. 'We'll be lucky to see him again. He disappears for entire lessons sometimes. His wife is a real cow. I'm Edith by the way.' She held out her hand. When he took it, she said, 'Please help us.'

'I'm Arthur. Arthur Pepper.'

The painting of Miriam flashed in his mind again. How had she felt when she sat for her portrait? Did she feel free? Had she done it to help someone out? For money? He might have been worried that she had been coerced into something that she didn't want to do, but there was her smile. It looked as if she had enjoyed it. Putting himself in this same position could bring him closer to understanding how she felt.

Miriam had a beautiful and young body. His was sagging, as if his skin was sliding away from his bones and muscle, no longer wanting to cling on.

But indeed what did he have to hide away from? There would probably be no more lovers in his life, no more trips to the beach to paddle. The next glimpses of his naked body might be by nurses in the hospital as they gave him a bed bath on his deathbed. What exactly did he have to be scared of?

The memory came flooding back to him, sweet and painful. He and Miriam had taken a picnic to a National Trust property. The kids were in school and he'd had an unexpected day off work when an appointment was cancelled. Miriam made sandwiches and they walked into the woods and found a field overgrown with poppies. When they sat down the grasses were taller than their heads. They ate their lunch and Miriam had complained that her dress was sticking to her in the heat.

'Take it off then,' he had quipped as he delved into her basket for an orange. He dug in his thumbnails and peeled it. When he looked up she sat there naked except for her white cotton knickers.

'Good idea,' she laughed. But then her smile faded.

They had moved together urgently, unable to resist the force. He had groaned as he touched her skin, so warm and glowing from the sun. They made love quickly, Arthur still dressed with her on top. For a few moments afterwards, she had lain there in the grass, on her back and completely naked and natural. She was the most beautiful thing that he had ever seen.

'Miriam, we . . . ' His usual reserve returned.

'Someone might come.'

'I know.' She reached for her dress, shpped it back over her head and kissed him on the tip of his nose. 'Did you remember to bring cake?'

They had eaten Battenberg as they stole coy but knowing glances with each other and as they bid hello to a passing dog walker.

Although this sort of thing didn't happen very often, he knew that she could be spontaneous and abandoned.

But he had thought it was just for him.

'So, are you going to do this?' Edith asked. She scratched her nose, leaving a smudge of charcoal on the end. She had thick black eyelashes like Miriam and wrung her hands together. 'Purrleee-ase, Arthur.'

He found that he was trembling. If Edith hadn't been there he would have held his head in his hands and cried — for those tender days with his wife, for the never-ending feeling of loss. 'If I do this, can I keep my undergarments on?' he asked distractedly.

She shook her head. 'I'm afraid not. Ben is planning a piece of body armour based on the male genitalia. He needs detail. You do go swimming? People have seen you naked before?'

'Yes, but . . . not posed.'

'It's just natural.'

'It's *not* natural for me.'

'It's not like we're going to be lusting after your body.'

She was right. It was more likely that his naked body would provoke wincing or hunching of shoulders.

'You'll never see any of us again.' She gave him a smile.

'That doesn't exactly help.' He lifted up one of his trouser legs by a couple of inches to display his ankle. He'd always had brown legs even in the winter. He closed his eyes and pictured his wife again on the day of the picnic. *Take it off*, he repeated in his head, mimicking his words to her. He thought of how she had undressed within seconds, how she had been so unselfconscious. *Take it off*. He *could* do this. 'Okay,' he said quietly.

'Great.' Edith vanished back around the screen before he could change his mind.

Arthur hesitated, wondering what he had just done, but then undid his shirt. His chest was okay, firm even. It was tanned with a few wires of grey hair. Miriam said he had a good body. He didn't think at that time she had anything to compare it to. He shook his trousers down then peeled off his socks and underpants. Finally, he was naked. He held the dressing gown to his groin and side-stepped from behind the screen and into the room. Had his wife posed for one sitter, or a room full of people? A few of the students looked up. They wore expressions that could best be described as fed up. He moved to the chair, sat down and crossed his legs, covering his dignity. Edith nodded and he reluctantly allowed the dressing gown to slip to the floor.

There was a sudden pleasing sound of scribbling pencils and charcoal and rubbers scrubbing at paper. He stared straight ahead and focused his gaze on a lightshade. It was dusty and a maggot wriggled in the light bulb. Edith was right. He felt quite free, like he was a Neanderthal who had wandered out of his cave and into an art studio, which he supposed was a bit like what had actually happened.

At one point he thought he saw Adam poke his head round the door but he didn't want to move and disturb his pose. He was warm from the small electric fire that cast an orange glow on his shins and he allowed his thoughts to drift away, back to the day of the picnic. He relived every single second of that delicious day and he was glad that he had his legs crossed.

After ten minutes someone shouted out, 'Can we have a new pose?'

Without worrying about his nakedness, he stood up and let his arms hang by his side. He stared straight ahead.

'Er, can't you like pose or something? You look kind of sad.'

'Tell me what to do.'

A young man strode over. He took hold of Arthur's arms and manoeuvred them so that one was outstretched and one was crooked. 'Pretend that you're firing a bow and arrow. I'm creating a piece of body jewellery based on war.'

'You're Ben?'

'Yes. I am.'

'Just tell me exactly what you want, Ben.'

These kids were going to create a brilliant piece of jewellery or art with his help. When he had gone, his memory might live on, as a jewelled codpiece or armband, just as Miriam's memory was doing in the panelled room.

It was then a thought hit him, and it was a strange one. He realised that he wanted her portrait to stay hanging in that room, even if she was naked. Even if she might not have known when she posed that the work would remain on display for so many years. It was a beautiful piece of art. It wasn't part of his life but it was part of hers. People should be able to see it.

★　★　★

'You did good, man,' Ben said at the end of the class. 'Do you want to see?'

Arthur got dressed and followed Ben and Edith around the room. It was strange to see himself depicted in twenty or so different pieces of artwork. He saw his body in charcoal, pastels, as smears, in paint strokes. These young artists hadn't seen him as an old man. They had viewed him as a model, a warrior, an archer, as something beautiful and useful. He wondered what would happen to the art now. It would no doubt be displayed in portfolios, or proudly on walls. In twenty years from now, when he might no longer be here, his form might still be admired. Tears pricked his eyes. He recognised himself in some and not others. His face looked peaceful, at odds with the wrinkled, tired apparition that greeted him in the mirror each morning.

'Happy?' Edith said.

'They're rather wonderful.'

'My wife says she's giving me a second chance.' Adam shuffled back into the room. His face was ashen and his shoulders drooped. 'Oh, is the lesson over?' He glanced around the room and then at his watch. 'Some good work here, students,' he shouted out.

Ben and Edith gave him a disdainful stare and walked out.

'What's up with those two?' Adam said incredulously. 'What's been going on?'

'The model didn't turn up.'

'But their work. They've . . . ' His words tailed away as he saw the subject in their art. 'Oh . . . '

Arthur straightened his collar. 'My name is Arthur Pepper. Now perhaps we can talk about what I came here for. I want to ask you about a gold charm in the shape of a paint palette. It's engraved with the initials S. Y. I believe they may stand for Sonny Yardley.'

The college didn't keep full records of students' work, Adam explained. But they did keep some sketches and photos from some of the most promising students by year. Arthur said that he was looking for a piece of jewellery created around the mid-sixties and Adam pulled some heavy books off the shelves, opened them and set them in front of him.

'You should have said that you were here to find a piece of work,' Adam said. 'I am *so* sorry that you had to strip off. This is the second time this has happened. If anyone finds out then I will be fired. I'll never get my wife back then. You won't tell anyone, will you?'

Arthur said that he would not. 'Why does she keep threatening to go?'

'Because, just look at me. I'm a bloody college

264

lecturer. She's a lawyer and way out of my league. She can run rings round me. Most of the time her work keeps her mind occupied. But she likes to keep me on my toes by threatening to leave. I can't keep doing this.'

'It sounds exhausting.'

'It is. But we both love it. The sex afterwards, when we make up, is astounding.'

'Oh.' Arthur flipped the pages and studied the sketches even more closely.

'They must have made charms that year,' Adam said. 'This year it's a piece of armour or body jewellery.'

'Ben told me. My penis may become a nose guard or something.' He said it without thinking and then gave a burst of laughter, that he had said the word 'penis' and that he had stood for over an hour naked for students. It was absurd. Adam gave him a confused stare, which made Arthur laugh even more. A tear ran down his cheek and he wiped it away. His stomach muscles ached as he thought of Ben crafting a piece of brass into the shape of his dangly bits. He used his fingers to blot under his eyes. He was losing it. His life with his wife was a lie.

'Have you found anything yet?' Adam said. 'What date are you at?'

'Um. 1964. I'm sorry, I just got hysterical for a moment.'

And then he found it. The next page he turned showed an intricate line drawing. It was of a palette with six blobs of paint and a fine brush. 'This is the one.' He took the bracelet from his pocket and laid it out on the paper.

Adam peered at the page. 'Ah yes, it was Sonny Yardley herself who made it. She's a wonderful artist. Very inspiring. How wonderful that you have this actual piece.'

'I believe that Sonny's been ill, but I want to find out the story behind this charm and how my wife came to own it.'

'Well, when she's back, I'll ask her to call you.'

Arthur walked back over to the painting of his wife. They smiled at each other.

Adam joined him. 'That's my favourite too. There's something about her eyes, isn't there?'

Arthur nodded.

'It's by Martin Yardley, Sonny's brother. He only painted for a short time. I'm not sure why.' Adam lowered his voice. 'I've never told anyone before, but that painting inspired me to become a teacher. I didn't know what I wanted to do when I was at school. I loved art but didn't think of it as a career. Then we came to visit the college. I remember Sonny. She wore these huge orange trousers and had a headscarf in her hair. You can imagine the sniggers of us fifteen-year-old lads as we looked at these nudie paintings of women. I tried to pretend to be mature but touring a room full of painted breasts was the most exciting thing that had ever happened to me. I thought how amazing it would be to paint naked women for a living. I used to visit this gallery and look at the brushstrokes, especially on this piece of work.'

'She's my wife,' Arthur said quietly, thinking how strange this sounded, standing with a young man admiring this naked portrait.

266

'Really? That is so incredible. You must bring her here to see this. Tell her that her painting helped me to paint, and meet lots of lovely young ladies too. She'll know Sonny then?'

Arthur stared at him. He was about to say sorry but Miriam had passed on, but then he reconsidered. He didn't want to hear another expression of sorrow for him, for his wife. He didn't know her. She felt like a stranger to him now. 'They were friends once, I think,' he said.

He said goodbye to Adam and walked out of the college, shielding his eyes against the bright light of the afternoon and unsure which direction to head in.

Bernadette

When Bernadette rang his doorbell it didn't seem as loud as usual. It was a subdued brrriiing. Arthur was in the kitchen making a cup of tea. He automatically reached to the cupboard and took out another cup. He still hadn't managed to have a conversation with her about Nathan's yearning to bake and about her hospital appointments.

Before he made his way to the front door, he stole a look at his *Stunning Scarborough* calendar. Tomorrow was his birthday. He had seen the date circled for weeks but hadn't taken any real notice. He was going to be seventy. It was no cause for celebration, another year closer to his death.

After his visit to the college, he was feeling foolish. He needed his head to be quiet, still. All his thoughts were running riot, like rowdy children, and he wanted them to stop and leave him alone. He had forgotten what it was like to have nothing on his mind other than cleaning and watering Frederica, and he was beginning to miss those days.

He couldn't understand how Miriam could be so close to someone as to pose nude for them, and then to never mention that person to him.

He racked his brains for if he had ever met anyone called Sonny. Had Miriam ever written letters to her? But he came to the conclusion that this lady was a stranger to him.

The doorbell rang again. 'Yes, yes,' he called out.

It was a lovely sunny day and yellow light flooded the hallway and the dust motes shone like glitter in the air. He thought of how Miriam loved the sunshine then dismissed it from his mind. Did she love it? How could he be sure what was right or wrong, what he knew and didn't know any longer?

Sonny Yardley was going to be phoning into work this week to discuss her return and Adam promised to remind her to get in touch with Arthur. He might even find a lead for the last of the charms — the ring and the heart. He just wanted to get this mission over with now, done and dusted.

'Hello, Arthur.' Bernadette stood on the doorstep.

'Hello.' He half expected her to stride inside, to inspect his hallway for dust, but she stood very still. He thought of Nathan's words about the cancer unit appointments. He instinctively avoided eye contact in case she could sense he knew something. 'Come on in,' he said.

She shook her head. 'You're probably busy. I made you this.' She proffered a pie in a paper bag on the flat of her hand. 'It's wimberry.'

He found himself listening to her tone of voice. Did she sound upset or sad? He decided to make an extra-special effort with her today.

'Ooh wimberry. How lovely. That's one of my favourites.'

'Good. Well, hope you enjoy it.' She made to leave.

Arthur stared after her. If she went then he would be alone and he couldn't trust himself not to get out the wipes and clean his worktops. He also wanted to know that she was okay. 'I'm not very busy at all,' he said. 'Will you join me?'

Bernadette remained still but then followed him inside.

Arthur stole a glance at her. Her eyes had dark circles under them. Her hair was a darker shade of red, almost mahogany. He couldn't mention the appointments as it would break Nathan's trust in him. He tried not to think about losing Miriam and how it would feel to lose someone else in his life. He supposed he was at the age now when friends and family started to get older and grow weaker. He felt the same feeling of dread as when the Graystocks' tiger had stood over him, a dreadful churning of his stomach.

But he told himself he was being overdramatic. This might be just a scare, a routine check. He tried to think of something cheery to say. 'Nathan said that he enjoys baking too,' he said lightly, as he looked inside the bag at the pie.

Bernadette gave a distracted, 'Yes, he does.'

Arthur slid the pie onto a baking tray and switched on the oven, choosing a lowish temperature so that it wouldn't take off. 'You don't need to bring me things any longer, you know. I'm out of the woods now. I'm not going to kill myself or sink into a sea of despair. I'm not a lost cause any longer. I'm doing good.' He turned and beamed, expecting her to do the same, to congratulate him.

'A lost cause? Is that how you see yourself?' she said crossly.

Arthur felt his cheeks grow a little pink. 'Well, no. I don't think that. It was something I overheard at the post office. Vera says that you like to look after people who are down on their luck. She calls them your lost causes.'

Bernadette lifted her chin. 'Well, that silly woman has nothing else better to do than to gossip about others,' she snapped. 'I prefer to spend my time being useful and helping others than to stand around being of no use to anyone.'

He could see that he'd offended her. She rarely took the hump at anything. 'I'm sorry,' he said, his spirits fading. 'I shouldn't have said anything. It was thoughtless of me.'

'I'm glad you did. And I have never seen you as a lost cause. I saw you as a lovely man who'd lost his wife and who could do with a little looking after. Is *that* a crime? Is it a crime when I help other people with a little bit of attention? I will not be using that post office again. That Vera can be a cruel woman sometimes.'

Arthur had never seen Bernadette so flustered. Her smile, which was usually always present, had gone. She was wearing more eyeliner than usual. The thick black lines had cracked and flaked. He didn't want to think of them as bad signs. 'The pie smells good,' he said weakly. 'We could eat outside. The weather is fine.'

271

'It's going to break soon.' Bernadette sniffed. 'They've forecast storms over the next few days. Black clouds and rain.' She stood up and moved over to the cooker, studied what temperature the knob was turned to then turned it higher. She took hold of the baking tray and opened the oven door. The pie began to slide off the tray. It glided until it hung precariously, half on and half off. They both watched as it wobbled on the edge. Slowly half began to break away. It creaked to a right angle and then dropped to the floor. The pastry smashed, scattering crumbs over the lino. Purple wimberry filling oozed from the half that remained on the tray. Bernadette's hand trembled. Arthur moved quickly and took the tray from her.

'Whoop-sa-daisy,' he said. 'You sit down and I'll clean up this little mess. I'll get the dustpan and brush.' He fetched it and his back cracked as he bent over. It was then he noticed that Bernadette's eyes were swimming with tears. 'Don't worry,' he said. 'There's still a good half left. You know, I've never actually known what wimberries are.'

He saw Bernadette bite her cheek. 'They're also called blueberries or bilberries.' Her voice shook. 'I used to pick them when I was a girl. My mother could always tell what I'd been up to when I went home with a purple tongue and purple fingers. They tasted so good, fresh from the bush. We used to put them in salt water and all these little worms came wriggling out. I used to wonder when I ate the pie if any of them were still left in there.'

'They'd have been in the oven,' Arthur said gently.

'I suppose they'd have burned rather than drowned. Not a good death either way.'

'I don't suppose any death is a good one.' This was not a good conversation to be having.

'No.' She stared out of the window.

Arthur looked outside too. Frederica was still sitting happily in the rockery. The fences were still too high. He thought that Bernadette might mention the garden or the weather, but she didn't. He racked his brain for something to say, especially as she seemed very upset over a broken pie. The only thing they really had in common was food. 'When I was in London,' he said, 'I ate a sausage sandwich while I was sat on the grass. It was greasy, it was covered in ketchup and it had these stringy, brown onions on it. It was the best thing I'd tasted in ages. Apart from your pies, of course. Miriam thought it was the height of bad manners to eat hot food outside in public, especially walking and eating. I felt guilty but a certain sense of freedom too.'

Bernadette turned away from the window. 'Carl insisted on roast beef every Sunday. He used to have it when he was a kid. I did turkey once and he was so upset. To him I was insulting his family tradition. Beef on a Sunday was a comfort. I was questioning his whole upbringing when I cooked that turkey. When he died, I carried on making roast beef in his memory, but I never liked it. Then, one day, I couldn't face it. I made myself a cheddar and pickled onion sandwich instead. I could hardly swallow it

273

because it felt like I was betraying his memory. But the next week I made it again. And it was the best sandwich I'd ever tasted. Now I eat what I want whenever I want it. But I'd never have changed all those roast beef lunches because, although the food wasn't what I wanted, Carl was the man I wanted to eat it with.'

They were both silent for a few moments, thinking about their spouses.

'I've got some nice cheddar from the village,' Arthur said. 'And I always have pickled onions in. I can make us both a sandwich and we could have your wimberry pie for afters.'

Bernadette stared at him. He couldn't read her expression. 'You know this is the first time you've ever invited me to eat with you?'

'*Is* it?'

'Yes. It's very nice of you, Arthur. But I don't want to take up your time.'

'You're not taking up my time. I thought it would be nice to eat lunch together.'

'It's a breakthrough that you're doing this. That you're thinking about socialising.'

'It isn't a scientific experiment. I thought you might be hungry.'

'Then I shall accept your invitation.'

There was something different about her today. She usually moved quickly and with purpose. Today she seemed slower and reflective, as if she was thinking about everything too much. He had expected a battle for control of the kitchen with her insisting on peering through the oven door every few minutes while he sat and read the paper. But when he got the cheese

274

out of the fridge she said she would look around the garden. She wandered around while he cut a couple of oven-bottom muffins in half and applied a thick layer of butter.

It was the first time he had eaten with anyone in the house since Miriam had gone, and it actually felt nice to have company. Bernadette usually stood guard to make sure he ate the sausage rolls and pies she brought. She didn't join him.

He again recalled guiltily the number of times he had hidden from her, cursing as her produce landed on his doormat as he posed like a National Trust statue. She was a saint. How she had put up with his behaviour and not given up on him, he didn't know.

'Lunch is ready,' he called from the back door when he had cut the muffins in four and put them on a plate with a few plain crisps. But Bernadette didn't move. She stared out over the fields, her eyes fixed on the spire of York Minster.

He pulled on his slippers and walked out onto the gravel. 'Bernadette? Lunch is ready.'

'Lunch?' For a moment she frowned, her thoughts elsewhere. 'Oh yes.'

They sat at the table. Since Miriam had died he didn't usually bother how food looked, he just tipped it on a plate and ate it, but he was pleased with how the sandwiches had turned out. He had cut them evenly and left a small gap between each quarter. Bernadette sat in the seat that used to be Miriam's. She took up more room than his wife. She was colourful too, reminding him of a parrot with her red hair and purple blouse. She had green nails today, the colour of the emerald

275

in the elephant charm's howdah.

'So, you went to Paris?'

Arthur nodded. He told her about Sylvie and the wedding boutique and how Lucy had met a nice waiter. He had wrapped Bernadette's lavender bag in pink tissue paper and he handed it to her now, before they had finished.

'What is this?' She seemed genuinely surprised.

'It's just a small gift, to say thanks.'

'For what?'

Arthur shrugged. 'You're always so helpful.'

She opened it, turned it round in her hands and held it to her nose. 'It's a lovely gift,' she said.

He had expected her to give him a big smile and squeeze his arm. Something ebbed away inside him when she did not. It was only a small present but a big gesture for him to give it to her. He wanted to show that he appreciated her, that he liked her, that he valued her friendship. He had invested a lot of his feelings into that little bag. But how was she to know that? He wished that he had added a thoughtful note, especially as she might be going through a difficult time. His mouth grew dry as he tried to find the words instead. 'You're a very kind person,' he managed.

'Thank you, Arthur.'

They finished their lunch. However his mind wasn't still. His insides felt churned up and he wasn't sure if the sandwich and pie would stay put in his stomach for long. He found that as well as worrying about Bernadette he was also itching for Sonny to ring him, to answer all his questions.

'Did you ever wonder what Carl's life was like before you met?' he asked, as casually as he could as he cleared the plates.

Bernadette raised an eyebrow but answered anyway. 'He was thirty-five when we met so of course there'd been other women. He had been married before too. I didn't question him, as I didn't want to know, if that's what you mean. I don't suppose it mattered if he'd been with two women before me or twenty. It's Nathan I feel sorry for. He was so young to lose his father.'

Arthur knew he could confide in this dignified woman; his friend, even if she was a little distant today. It didn't yet seem the right time to mention her appointments.

'Is there something you want to say to me?' she prompted.

Arthur closed his eyes and saw himself sitting naked on a stool, his body white and crinkled. He saw Miriam smiling seductively for her portrait painter. 'I . . . ' he started then broke off, unable to find the words, unsure if he wanted to speak them. 'I just wonder why Miriam stayed with me. I mean, look at me. I'm nothing to look at. I had no ambitions, no drive. I don't paint or write or create. I was a bloody locksmith. She must have been so bored.'

Bernadette frowned, surprised by his outpour. 'Why would she be bored? Whatever gave you that idea?'

'Oh, I don't know,' he sighed. He was fed up of this now, fed up of this mystery. 'She had such an exciting life before she met me. And she didn't tell me about it. She hid it away from me.

All the time we were together, I wonder if she was thinking back to her life of India, tigers, artists and novelists and she was stuck with boring old me. She got pregnant and had to settle for the life that I gave her when really she wanted to be doing something else.' Embarrassingly, he found tears pricking his eyes.

Bernadette was still, her voice calm. 'You're never boring, Arthur. Having kids and being a grown-up is an adventure in itself. I saw the two of you once at a church fair. I saw the way you looked at each other. She saw you as her protector. I remember thinking that you belonged together.'

'When was that?' he challenged.

'A few years ago.'

'You were probably mistaken.'

'No,' she said firmly. 'I know what I saw.'

Arthur jerked his head. He knew that nothing she could say would make things better. He would be better keeping his thoughts to himself and his mouth shut, rather than passing on his maudlin mood.

'You never know what is round the corner.' Bernadette stood and carried the plates into the kitchen. She began to rinse them under the tap, even though she hadn't finished her food.

'Leave them,' he called after her. 'I'll do them.'

'It's fine.' Her voice wobbled.

Arthur froze. It sounded as if she was crying. He should not have mentioned Carl, or argued with her about the church fair. Now what was he supposed to do? He sat stock-still, his shoulders stiff. Bernadette sniffed. He stared straight ahead pretending that this wasn't happening. He wasn't good at this emotional stuff. 'Are you okay?' he asked quietly.

'Me? Yes, of course.' She spun on the tap. But as she moved to retrieve the tea towel he saw that her eyes were wet.

He recalled a conversation with Miriam once. He had asked what she wanted for her birthday and she told him not to bother getting her anything, there was nothing she wanted. So he just got her a card and a small bunch of white freesias. That evening she barely spoke to him and when he finally asked why she was so snippy, she told him that she had expected a gift.

'But you told me not to get you anything,' he protested.

'Yes, but it's a figure of speech. Like when you see a woman is upset and you ask her what's wrong and she says, 'Nothing'. She doesn't mean it. She means that something is wrong and that she wants you to ask her again what it is, and to keep on asking until you get an answer. You should have wanted to buy me a present, even if I told you I didn't want anything. It was your chance to show you care.'

So Arthur knew that when women said things it could sometimes mean the opposite. 'I don't think that you are okay,' he said. He stood and walked over to her. He reached out and patted her shoulder.

Bernadette's body grew stiff. 'I might be. I might not.' She picked up a plate and wiped it with the dishcloth then set it on the draining board.

Arthur reached out and took the cloth from her. He wrung it out and put it on the worktop.

279

'What is it? What's wrong?'

She looked down, considering whether to tell him anything. 'I went to my belly dancing class last month and, as I was changing, I found a lump in my . . . boob. I went to the doctor and he referred me to the hospital to check for breast cancer. I get my results tomorrow.'

'I see . . . I, er . . . ' He didn't know what to say. Nathan was right.

'The doctor says it's routine and it's best to get things checked out. But my mother died from it and my sister had it. In all likelihood, I have it too.' She began to speak more quickly. 'I'm not sure how I'll cope with Nathan leaving for university and Carl gone. I've not told Nathan. I don't want to worry him.'

'I could drive you to the appointment . . . '

'You've not driven for a year.'

'I used to drive for my job. I'm sure I'll be okay.'

Bernadette smiled. 'It's kind of you, but no.'

'You've done a lot for me.'

'I don't need repaying.'

'I'm not trying to repay you. I'm offering you a lift. And my friendship.'

She didn't seem to hear him. 'Nathan is only eighteen . . . Imagine if there was something wrong. First Carl and now me.'

'Try not to worry. You can't possibly know until you get the results. All will be clear tomorrow.'

She took a deep breath and held it in her chest before exhaling through her nose. 'You're right. Thanks, Arthur.'

'I can pick you up in a taxi. You don't have to go through this on your own.'

'You're very kind. But I want to keep this to myself. I'll go to the hospital alone.'

'Nathan is probably very worried.'

'I've kept it from him. He doesn't know anything.'

Arthur didn't know whether to tell her about Nathan's visit and that he was worried sick. As he mused over what to say, his phone rang.

'You get your call,' Bernadette said. 'I'm going anyway.'

'Are you sure? They can phone back.'

She shook her head. 'I'll let myself out. Thanks for lunch. It was very nice.'

'What time is your appointment?'

'It's in the afternoon sometime. Your phone is ringing. In the kitchen.'

'Tell me how it goes.'

'Your phone . . . you should get it.'

Arthur reluctantly opened the front door. Bernadette stepped out. He watched her walk along the garden path as he distractedly picked up the receiver.

The woman's voice was clear and controlled. Her tone was so cold that it made him shiver. 'Arthur Pepper?'

'Yes?'

'I believe that you've been looking for me. My name is Sonny Yardley.'

The Ring

'I am really not happy that you turned up at my place of work unannounced,' Sonny said. 'It is most unprofessional. I might have been in the middle of taking a class. As it was, I was on sick leave so I really do not need this intrusion. It was on my return that Adam informed me that you had turned up in person looking for me.'

'I'm sorry. I did ring first, and left messages.'

'And I got them. That does not invite you to stalk me.'

Arthur reeled at the venom in her voice. He hadn't realised his actions would cause such offence. 'I really didn't mean any harm, Ms. Yardley.'

'Well. It is done now. Did you find what you were looking for through Adam?' Her manner was still sharp.

'I have a piece of jewellery, a charm bracelet. I believe you might have designed a charm in the shape of a paint palette for it.'

'Yes.'

'Well, as I said in the messages I left, I think you knew my wife, Miriam Kempster. I think you may have given her the charm.'

Sonny didn't speak. It made him feel uncomfortable. He carried the phone over to the

282

kitchen table and tried to fill the silence. 'Sylvie Bourdin gave me your name.'

'I don't know of a Sylvie Bourdin.'

'She was also a friend of my wife's. Miriam stayed with her in Paris. She suggested I get in touch.'

'Really,' Sonny said witheringly.

Arthur began to feel cross that she was being so inhospitable. 'Ms. Yardley, my wife died. Twelve months ago now. I don't know if you're aware of that. I've been trying to find out some things about her past.'

He kind of expected her to apologise, to say that she was sorry for her manner, but again she didn't speak. He thought that she must be very angry or was withdrawing her words as some kind of show of power. Perhaps she was still feeling poorly after her illness. So he began to witter again. Words tumbled off his tongue. He told her about the charm bracelet and how tracing the charms had led him to Paris, London and Bath. There were just two charms left for him to discover more about — the ring and the heart.

He could tell that she was still there from the occasional clicking noise, like earrings clinking against the side of the phone. When he had finished, he added, 'So that's the story.'

'I don't know why I shouldn't hang up on you, Mr Pepper,' she said frostily.

'Why on earth would you do that?'

'Did your wife ever mention me to you?'

'No. I don't believe she did. My memory can be a bit rusty though . . . '

'I wonder how many other skeletons she kept in her closet. Do you know?'

'I, er, no.' They seemed to be speaking different languages and he was tired of playing games, following leads and not knowing where they were taking him.

'No. It doesn't sound like you do,' Sonny said. 'I shall take pity on you then.'

'I went to the art college to find you. I saw a painting by your brother while I was there. It was of Miriam. He was a fine artist.'

'Yes, he *was*.'

'He no longer paints?'

'He is no longer with us. You really don't know anything, do you?'

Arthur wasn't sure what she meant. 'I'm sorry to hear that. It's a wonderful way to remember him, for his work to be on display.'

'I *hate* that painting. It's far too whimsical for my taste. If I had my way, and if my brother wasn't the artist, it would be removed. Or even burned.'

'Oh, I thought it was rather lovely.'

'Don't humour me. I really do not have time for this conversation, Mr Pepper.'

Arthur stood his ground. 'I'm just trying to find out about my wife. I feel that there are things I don't know, stories I've never heard.'

'It might be best if you don't know them. We can end this call. Feel free to throw away the paint palette charm. It is a part of history I'd rather forget.'

Arthur's mind reeled. His hand holding the phone trembled. It was so tempting to do as she bade him. It was something he'd thought of too, to get rid of the bracelet and try to return to normal. But he had come so far. 'Were you and my wife very good friends, once?' he asked gently.

Sonny hesitated. 'Yes. Yes, we were. A long time ago.'

'And Martin too, if he painted her?'

'It was a long time ago . . . '

'I need to know what happened.'

'No you don't. Leave this be.'

'I can't, Ms. Yardley. I thought Miriam and I knew everything about each other, but now I feel I don't know anything. There's a big hole and I have to find out how to fill it, even if I hear things I don't like.'

'I don't think you *will* like it.'

'But I have to know.'

'Very well, Mr Pepper. You asked for the truth. Well, here it is. Your wife was *a murderess*. How do you like that?'

Arthur felt as if he was falling down a giant hole. His stomach plunged. His limbs felt as if they were flailing. 'Forgive me. I don't understand,' he gasped.

'She killed my brother, Martin.'

'That can't be.'

'It is.'

'Tell me what happened.'

Sonny swallowed. 'We'd been friends for a long time, Miriam and I. We played together and did our homework together. When she was having trouble at home, it was me she confided in. I'm the one who listened and offered advice.

285

I encouraged her to follow the Mehra family to India. I bought her the bracelet as a good luck present before she left. I was there to support her when she stayed in Paris. This Sylvie Bourdin's name is vaguely familiar to me. Miriam and I wrote to each other all the time throughout her travels. We were as close as two friends could be.

'But then, after she'd travelled to Paris and India and London, when she was tired of moving around, she came home. But instead of turning her attention to me, picking up on our friendship, she set her sights on Martin. She batted her eyelashes at him. They started to go out without me. Within a couple of months, they were engaged to be married. Did you know that?'

'No,' Arthur whispered.

'Martin wanted to buy her a diamond ring, to do things properly. So he began to save every penny he could. In the meantime, he bought her a charm in the shape of a ring to go on her bracelet.'

'I have it here.' When he spoke the words did not sound like his own. 'And you made the paint palette charm?'

'Yes. It was a birthday present.'

'And you say that Miriam and Martin were engaged?' He thought that *he* had been her first love.

'For a short while. Until he died. The car he was driving ploughed head-first into a tree.'

'I am so sorry. But you said my wife was a murder — '

'They were in my father's car. Martin hadn't

passed his driving test yet but he wanted to impress Miriam so much that he took the keys without asking when my parents were out for the evening. Miriam goaded him on. I heard her saying that she wanted another adventure. Miriam with her black-lined eyes and her shiny beehive, her fancy clothes and pearls. A young lad like him didn't stand a chance when she turned her attention on him. He painted, but he really wanted to be a writer you see, a journalist. When he found out that she had a friendship with that French author De Chauffant, he was smitten. He wanted to impress her.

'It was a sunny evening. I remember hearing the birds singing as they headed out, arm in arm. I told Martin that he mustn't take the car, but they both laughed at me. Miriam told me not to fuss, but I'm sure I saw Martin hesitate, just for a second. Still, she tugged him out of the door and I watched as they drove away.

'An eyewitness said that Martin took a bend too tightly. He lost control and crashed into a tree. They were both taken to the hospital. Miriam escaped with a minor cut to her forehead. My brother was in a coma for three weeks. He didn't stand a chance. All because he wanted to show off to Miriam, to prove he was good enough for her. If she hadn't turned her attention to him he would be here now. He'd be married to someone else. He might have had children. My parents might have had grandchildren. I couldn't give them that but he might have been able to.'

'But your brother was driving . . . you said that Miriam — '

'She as good as killed him.'

He thought of a tiny scar his wife had on her temple. She had said it was from a childhood fall.

'So, she never told you about Martin? She never even spoke his name?' Sonny asked.

'No. I didn't know about an engagement before ours.'

'Well, so now you know that your wife was a liar.'

'She didn't *lie*. She just didn't tell me. Miriam closed off her past. She didn't speak about her life before we met. I thought it was because it had been uneventful, that there was nothing to tell me about. But it sounds as if it's the opposite. Would she be married to Martin now if this dreadful thing hadn't happened? Was she with me but thinking about him? Even though, I still love her so much. Sometimes I feel I can't live without her.'

Sonny cleared her throat. 'I'd say sorry for the way I speak about her, but I'm not. She ruined my life and the life of my family.'

'Then I will say I'm sorry. For what happened; if that's worth anything.'

'She visited Martin every day; sat by his bedside. I couldn't bear the sight of her then. She made my flesh crawl. We'd always both treated him as my annoying brother and then suddenly she's attracted to him, telling me that he might be the man she's looking for. She wanted to settle down. I wanted him to meet someone else, someone who wasn't so flighty. It's like she threw me over for him.'

Arthur felt his body beginning to quake. Whatever stories he had uncovered about his wife, he was not going to listen to her ex-friend bad-mouth her. 'Whatever you think of Miriam, Ms. Yardley, she was the gentlest, kindest woman I ever met. We were married for over forty years. I am very sorry for what happened to your brother, but you are talking about years and years ago. The woman you describe sounds nothing like my wife. People change. It sounds as if you were jealous of your own brother's happiness.'

'Well, yes I was. I admit it.' Sonny's words quickened. '*I* was her friend, not Martin. We shared everything. Then she came home and took him. She threw me over. She wanted to see Martin more than me . . . '

Arthur let her words hang. He used silence in the same way that Sonny had.

'Are you still there, Mr Pepper?'

'Yes, I'm still here.'

'She killed him. I don't care who was driving that bloody car. As far as I'm concerned, Miriam killed him. She deprived my family of their son and me of my brother. She came to the funeral and I never saw her again after that. I didn't want to see her and I made sure she knew that. I heard that she had got married to someone else. She wrote to tell me, another of her bloody letters. She moved on, but the Yardleys never could. I hope that answers all your questions, Mr Pepper. Now you know the truth.'

Arthur moved the receiver away from his ear. He couldn't bear to hear any more of Sonny's

289

words. 'I loved her, no matter what,' he said. 'I really loved her.'

He put the phone down and sobbed.

Crappy Birthday

Today was his birthday. He was seventy years old. It was supposed to be a landmark. Miriam would have bought him a small gift, maybe some new stripy socks or a book. They would have gone to the Crown and Anchor in the village for haddock and chips or perhaps a ham and mustard sandwich. They'd have had a couple of shandies and maybe apple pie and custard as a treat. His wife didn't like anything fancy. Except that's what he used to think.

Lucy hadn't been in touch yet. He didn't expect Dan to remember and Bernadette had more important things on her mind. He was sure that there would be no cards falling on his mat today.

He had gone to bed thinking about Sonny and Martin and had woken through the night thinking about them. His sleep was fitful and he wasn't sure which thoughts were true and which were in his dreams. He saw Miriam laughing in a car with Martin's arm hanging over her shoulders, as if he owned her, protecting her from harm. He pictured a car, a bottle-green one with a roll-top roof. It shot across both lanes of a road and ploughed into a tree. He imagined himself at the scene, running over to help.

Miriam lay there, her head lolling, a trickle of blood from her forehead. But the man driving had his head against the steering wheel. The angle of his neck wasn't quite right, like he was a piece of origami folded the wrong way. He saw his own hand reaching out to touch the man's head and saw blood like black treacle in his hair. Then Martin raised his head. He laughed manically and his teeth were smeared red. 'She killed me. Your wife killed me. Happy birthday, Arthur.'

He sat bolt upright in bed. His clothes were wet and clung to him like a second skin. At first he plucked at them and then peeled them off. After throwing them in a pile on the bathroom floor, he got into the shower, even though it wasn't yet five in the morning.

Letting the water trickle down his face, he stood stock-still trying to block out the thoughts and images in his head. Miriam wasn't here. She had killed a man. How could he spend a lifetime with someone and not know them? Did she ever consider telling him? He must be an idiot not to sense it, not to ask her anything about her past. Instead, he had assumed that they were similar, that there had been nothing significant in their lives until they had met. He was wrong.

He dried himself and automatically put on one of his old shirts and Graystock's blue trousers. It was still dark outside. He felt listless. Hopeless, helpless and useless; a lost cause. Nothing he could think of doing had any meaning. This should be a happy day, a celebration. His birthday. Yet he was here alone, bereft.

He sat on Miriam's side of the bed. He opened up the drawer in the bedside cabinet, took out a lined pad and pen and, without thinking, began to write a letter. His wife had written to Sonny, now he would write to her too. Although Miriam may have been involved in Martin's death, he had loved her for many years and always would, even if she hadn't confided in him.

He felt the need to do this. He was confused and hurt but he wouldn't allow himself to become bitter. He had to fight it. In his shock during the conversation with Sonny yesterday there were things he hadn't said.

Dear Ms. Yardley,

I loved my wife with all my heart. She wasn't perfect, but no-one is. I am certainly not.

I am a quiet man, not particularly bright, not particularly handsome. I did wonder for a long time what Miriam saw in me, but she did see something and we were happy.

I have discovered things about her life that I didn't know. I wasn't aware of you or Martin, or of India or Paris. I could sit here and spend the rest of my life mulling over why she didn't tell me. But she had her reasons and I honestly don't think those reasons were selfish, or to hide anything. I think she kept them from me because of love.

You may think of me as a silly deluded

293

old man, but I want you to know and remember me as the person who loved Miriam and who was loved by Miriam. I feel like the luckiest man alive to have had that. She made me a better person.

It sounds as if she loved you and Martin too, dearly . . .

He carried on writing unaware of what was spilling from him. All the anger, and frustration and love he felt for his wife went into his words.

When he was finished he held four completed pages in his hands. His wrist ached and he was teary from emotion and as empty as an egg with no yolk. He didn't read through the letter knowing that he had said all he needed to. He added to the bottom of the last page . . .

After all these years, I implore you to search your heart to forgive her. If you cannot forgive, then to at least remember the friendship you once shared.

Yours sincerely

Arthur Pepper

He ripped the pages out of the pad and folded them into an envelope. Then he wrote *Ms. Sonny Yardley* on the front.

He rolled up his sleeve and exposed his forearm, then he gave his skin a firm pinch and watched as his flesh slowly moved back into place, leaving pink fingerprints. He didn't even

294

feel it. So he tried again, this time digging in his nails. He just wanted to feel something, physical pain, to tell him that he was alive, that this was all happening.

The weather was miserable. From his bedroom window, he could see that the sky was the colour of ink-soaked cotton wool. The good weather had broken as Bernadette said it would. But he couldn't stay in the house. The thought of being surrounded by four walls made him feel claustrophobic. It would be miserable to spend his birthday here. He would only sit thinking what might have been, what could have been. Had his wife spent over forty years mourning Martin and wishing she was with him, instead of Arthur?

The questions in his head made him feel woozy and he placed his hands flat against the walls to steady himself as he went downstairs. He had to get out of here.

In the hallway, he pulled on a coat and some shoes, not thinking if they were suitable for the weather. As he walked out of the door he shoved the envelope in his pocket.

The stars and the moon were still in the sky. No one would remember that seventy years ago a cheeky, chubby baby named Arthur had been born. Today was a non-day like any other. The only thing of any meaning was that this afternoon his friend Bernadette would find out if she had cancer.

At that thought he stopped dead in the street. He wished with all his heart that she was going to be okay. How could he cope if he lost someone else who was dear to him? He realised that Bernadette had been more than a helping hand to him in his time of need. She was a friend. She was a *dear* friend.

Terry was leaving his house. 'It's nasty, isn't it, Arthur? Do you want a lift?' he shouted out, pulling up the hood of his anorak.

'No thank you.'

'Where are you going so early in the morning?'

'Out for the day.'

'To Lucy's?'

He didn't want to make conversation so he pretended not to hear Terry's question and ploughed on. He walked and stopped at the third bus stop he came to and waited for a bus to York centre. Then he took the train to Scarborough. For the fifty-minute journey he stared out of the window. Clouds were thick inky blankets and the sky was a fluorescent white.

When he got off the train, rain dripped off the trees. But he didn't stop. He strode through the streets toward the college. He arrived dripping wet and handed the envelope to the silver-haired receptionist.

'Look at the state of you,' she said, recognising him. 'Don't you have an umbrella?'

He didn't reply. 'I want you to give this to Ms Sonny Yardley as soon as she arrives for work. It is most important.' He turned and walked back to the glass entrance doors, not hearing as she shouted after him offering him her jacket.

He walked past the students, smoking, chatting, browsing on their phones and making their way to begin college for the day. He didn't

296

notice the cafés where families sheltered from the rain under striped canopies, or hear the electronic jingles and rattle of pennies from the arcades just opening up for the day. When he reached the beach, he was alone. No one else was stupid enough to come out in this weather, especially down to the sea.

It stretched out before him like a grey carpet, moving, rippling. He stood at the edge and watched, letting the shush of the waves hypnotise him. Water soaked through the toes of his shoes. The wind nipped his thighs. His ankles grew red and sore as he stood.

In the space of a few weeks he had gone from being a grieving widower, pining for his lost wife, to his mind becoming a mass of suspicion.

They had known each other so well. That's what he had loved about their marriage. They were soul mates who were in tune with each other's thoughts and emotions and likes. Except they hadn't known each other's story. Why had he never asked his wife about her life before him? Because he hadn't expected her to have one, that's why.

Without her, he had — what? He had Lucy. He had Bernadette. He had his son on the other side of the world. But there was a hole inside him that ached, which would never be filled again. It ached for the woman he loved, the woman he didn't know. His house wasn't a home without her. It was just walls and carpet and a silly old man rattling around inside.

How could he live without again feeling her cheek pressed against his shoulder? Without the sound of her singing as they made breakfast together. Things could never be as they were, when they were a family unit. The thought pulled him down like quicksand.

It began to rain more now. A spatter at first, flecking his eyelids. And then it began to fall heavily so it looked as if drinking straws were firing down from the sky. The water hit his face, rolled down his cheeks. His trousers were sodden, stuck to his legs. He cupped his hands around his mouth and shouted, 'Miriam!' His voice was captured and taken by the wind and blown elsewhere. '*Miriam*.' He shouted her name over and over, knowing that she couldn't hear him, that his words were futile. '*Miriam*.'

When those words were gone he felt empty, as if they were the only things holding him together. The sea rolled over his feet and filled his shoes. He stumbled backwards over a rock and he hit the wet sand with a thud. His knees crunched and his hands and backside slapped against the sand. A wave crashed over his legs, soaking him again and surrounding him with a halo of white foam. 'Miriam,' he said again weakly, digging his fingers into the sand. He felt it suck and slide away from him. He wished he had left her alone, perfect in his memory, instead of prying and pursuing her. He had opened doors that he wished had remained unlocked. How he wished he hadn't sunk his hand into the boot. Someone buying them from a charity shop would have had a nice surprise in finding the charm bracelet. It might have brought them good luck.

He took it from his pocket. He hated it now,

detested what it had done to his memories. The grey stretch of sea beckoned. He raised his hand to shoulder height, feeling the weight of it in his palm. He imagined it spinning through the air and then plopping down into the water. It would sink and drift down and then lie on the seabed for centuries waiting to be discovered, when someone might find it and wonder about the origins of the charms. Except to that person the bracelet would be anonymous. Its only significance would be its curiosity value or worth in gold.

Arthur wondered if it would make him feel better to be rid of it, but there was still the one charm he knew nothing about — the heart. The heart-shaped box, the heart-shaped lock and the heart-shaped charm. Perhaps it could tell him that his wife did really love him, that their time together hadn't been a compromise for her. It might hold the answers.

It had to.

But it was so tempting to walk into the sea with the bracelet. The waves lulled him into their midst. If he carried it in he could be sure it was gone. His feet were wet, and his ankles, so why not his groin, his waist, his chest, his shoulders? Why shouldn't the sea cover his mouth, his nose, his eyes, until all that was left was a tuft of white hair, which the sea could sweep over and claim?

Who would care?

A few months ago, he would say that no one would care. But then he and Lucy had reconnected. He and Sylvie had kissed. Bernadette cared for him.

It was when he thought of Lucy that he forced himself to stand up. She needed him. He needed her. It was a relief to hear the shingle crunch under his feet; that he hadn't carried out what the sea willed him to do. Lucy. She had been through enough with her miscarriage, her marriage ending, losing her mother. He would have to be a selfish old fool to kill himself and bring more tragedy to her door. He stepped backwards again and again until his feet hit a bank of pebbles. He sat back on a rock and stared at the bracelet in his hand. It shone so brightly against the dark grey of the pebbles and sea and inky sky. The heart seemed to glow.

There was a halo of water around his feet as he sat next to a rock pool. A tiny grey crab swayed, suspended in the seawater, still enough to be dead. Arthur watched it for a while. It was trapped. The tide would go out. The sun might come out and dry up the water. The crab's little body would dry to a crisp.

He dipped his fingertips into the water. The crab moved one claw and then was still. It was as if it was waving at him. Arthur slid his hand in further. His little friend was acting out its own variation of a National Trust statue routine.

'You might die if you stay in that rock pool,' he said out loud. 'You'll be stranded. You'll be safer in the sea.' He cupped his hand and the crab drifted into his palm. Arthur gently lifted up his hand. He and the crab stared at each other for a while. It had black pinprick eyes. 'Don't be scared,' he said.

He carried it to the sea and waited until a

small wave crept up onto the beach. Then he deposited it at the water's edge. It paused for a moment as if to say thanks and goodbye, then it sidestepped toward the water. A gentle wave swept over it and when the water eased away, the crab was gone.

Arthur stared at its vacant spot on the beach. *Perhaps I've been stuck in a rock pool too,* he thought. *I need to be in the sea, even if it's scary and unknown. If I don't do it then I will shrivel and die.*

He imagined what Lucy would say if she saw him here, soaked to the skin, rescuing a crab. 'You'll catch your death. Come and get warm.' It's what he would have said to her when she was a child. The idea of their roles being reversed was strange. He thought that Miriam would find it funny too.

It didn't matter what he did now. He was a widower. There was no one to tell him how to live. Why, if he wanted to perform a silly jig in the sea, he could do. In fact, why shouldn't he? He kicked up his feet and waited until waves rushed toward him and he kicked and danced. 'Look at me, Miriam.' He laughed hysterically as the tears rolled down his cheeks mingled with the raindrops. 'I'm being silly. I forgive you. You didn't tell me things because you thought it was for the best. I have to trust that you did it for the right reasons. And I'm still alive. I wish you were too, but you're not. And I want to live even though it hurts. I don't want to be a dried-up crab.'

He broke into a jog and then intermittently

strolled and ran along the water's edge, dipping in and out of the sea, the icy water reminding him that he was alive. He flung out his arms and embraced the wind, letting it whistle through his clothes and sting his eyes.

He had to forgive and forget. There was no other way.

He hugged himself and walked into the wind until he reached a beach café. He saw that the dark clouds were blowing over. The sun peeked through. Raindrops sparkled along the edge of the blue and white striped canopy. Puddles on the pavement shone like mirrors.

A couple opened the door and made their way inside. They had a fox terrier with them, its fur wet and curled. Water dribbled down their waterproof trousers and coats. *I'm just as wet as they are*, he told himself but thought what Miriam might say. *You can't go in in that state.* But he *could* go in. He shivered as a welcome jet of warm air blasted his cheeks as he stepped inside.

'Gosh. Just look at you,' a lady in a cheerful yellow apron said to him. 'Let's dry you off a bit.' She disappeared behind the counter then brought him a fluffy sky-blue towel. 'Rub yourself down.' She handed the couple a scruffier towel for their dog. 'It's as miserable as sin out there. Did you get caught out while you were walking? The weather can just turn like that.' She snapped her fingers. 'One minute everything is lovely and then it all goes dark and gloomy. The sun always comes out though, love. I think we're at that stage now. It will be bright soon.'

Arthur used the towel to blot and wipe and

rub himself. He was still soaking wet but his face was dry. He saw a young couple share a hot chocolate. The girl had dark hair like Miriam and the boy was skinny with too much hair. Their drink was in a tall glass and topped with whipped cream and chocolate sprinkles. When the lady in the yellow apron came to take his order he asked for one too. It arrived with a chocolate flake on the side and a long spoon. He sat in the window and watched the raindrops on the glass. He scooped up the cream and savoured every mouthful, blowing and sipping at the hot syrupy liquid.

When he was finished, he jumped on the train at the station, and then onto the bus home. His clothes clung to him, swishing as he walked. As he neared the house, his mobile vibrated in his pocket. Bernadette had left a text message. 'Call me,' it said.

Memories

Arthur's hallway was dark, chilly. He stared at Bernadette's text message. It was stark and to the point. Oh God, no, was his first thought. He hoped she was okay. He would strip off his wet clothes and then ring her.

As he had predicted there were no birthday cards waiting for him. Lucy would be at school marking books. Bernadette might still be at the hospital. He was on his own.

Placing his keys on the shelf near the fabric pot pourri leaf, he paused. He thought he heard a rustling sound. Strange. He stood still for a while, listening. After blaming his age on hearing things that weren't there, he pushed the door to the front room open in small increments. But then something made his heart almost stop.

In silhouette against the window he saw a shape. It was hulky — a man. It didn't move.

A burglar.

Arthur opened his mouth to shout, to scream, whatever sound he could make, but nothing came out. He had locked the door behind him and didn't want to turn and fiddle for his keys. *Why me?* He thought. *I don't have anything. I'm a silly old man*.

But then his resilience kicked in. He had been

through too much to let a stranger in his house ruin things further. He was glad that Miriam wasn't there. She would have been scared. He stepped forward and spoke loudly into the darkness. 'I have nothing here of value. If you leave now then I won't call the police.'

There was a thump from the kitchen. An accomplice. Arthur's mouth grew dry. He was surely defeated. Two intruders were not going to listen to him, be reasoned with. He felt around for something heavy with which to arm himself. All he could find was an umbrella and he clutched the pointed end ready to thwack the strangers with the handle. He strained forwards to peer through the gap in the door and braced himself for a blow to the head.

Behind him, the light in the kitchen flicked on. He blinked, feeling thrown off balance.

'Surprise!' A chorus of voices rang out. There was a group of people in his dining room. He stumbled and tried to focus on their faces, to see who his intruders were. Then he saw Bernadette wearing a white apron. Terry was there, without the tortoise. The two red-haired kids who didn't wear shoes were there. 'Happy birthday, Dad.' Lucy appeared and enveloped him in her arms.

Arthur dropped his weapon. 'I thought that you'd forgotten.'

'We've been here waiting for ages in the dark. I texted you,' Bernadette said.

'I was just about to ring you. Is everything okay?'

'Let's talk later,' she said. 'It's your birthday.'

'You're soaking wet,' Lucy gasped. 'Terry said

he saw you go out for the day. We thought you'd be home by now.'

'I needed to get out. I . . . Oh, Lucy.' He hugged her again. 'I miss your mum . . .'

'I know, Dad. Me too.'

Their foreheads touched.

Rings of water had formed around Arthur's feet on the carpet. His blue trousers were cling-filmed to his legs. His coat was heavy with water. 'I went for a walk. I got caught out with the weather.'

'Come on. Get out of those clothes and join us,' Lucy said. 'But don't go into the front room yet.'

'There's a man in there,' he said. 'I thought he was a burglar.'

'That was going to be your big birthday surprise,' Lucy said. She looked over her father's shoulder. 'But I suppose you can have it now.'

'Hello, Dad.'

Arthur couldn't believe his ears. He turned mechanically to see his son standing with his arms outstretched. 'Dan . . .' he stuttered. 'Is it really you?'

Dan nodded. 'Lucy called me. I wanted to come.'

Time fell away. Arthur just wanted to hold his son again, be close to him. When Dan had left for Australia the two men had only managed to give each other a friendly slap on the back. Now they held each other tightly, there in the hallway. Arthur relished the feel of his son's bristled chin on top of his head, his strong arms. The guests were quiet, allowing father and son to savour the moment.

Dan broke away and held Arthur at arm's length. 'What the hell are you wearing, Dad?'

Arthur looked down at his blue trousers and laughed. 'It's a long story,' he said.

'I'm here for a week. I wish it could be longer.'

'That should just be about long enough to tell you what I've been up to.'

When he went upstairs to change, he could hear chattering and laughter downstairs. He had never really enjoyed parties or family gatherings, feeling uncomfortable that he had nothing amusing or interesting to say. He would stand in the kitchen and top up people's drinks or attack the nibbles while Miriam did the socialising. But now, he liked the sound of other people in the house. It was friendly, warm. It was what he had been yearning for.

From his wardrobe he instinctively took out his usual slacks and a shirt. He lay them on the bed and peeled off his wet outfit. But then he stared at the clothes on the bed. Those old man trousers scratched his ankles and cut into his waist when he sat down. The way he dressed was yet another routine, a widower's uniform. The clothes he had bought in Paris with Lucy were a little formal so he rummaged at the bottom of the wardrobe. There he found an old pair of Dan's jeans from before he grew Popeye legs, and a sweatshirt with *Superdry* written on the front. He found this amusing because he was actually still super wet. He dried himself off with his towel, rubbed his hair, pulled on the clothes and went downstairs.

In the dining room the farmhouse kitchen

table had been laid with a buffet — sausage rolls, crisps, grapes, sandwiches and salad. A shiny seventieth birthday banner was taped across the wall. On his chair sat a small pile of cards and presents.

'Happy birthday, Arthur.' Bernadette planted a kiss on his cheek. 'Are you going to open your pressies?'

'I'll do it later.' He always felt embarrassed opening gifts in front of others, having to act out delight or surprise. He liked to peel off the paper slowly and consider the contents. 'Did you do all this?'

She smiled. 'Some of it. Dan and Lucy have been great too. Your neighbour Terry offered to look after the red-haired kids while their parents went to the cinema, so they joined in too.'

'But . . . ' Arthur hesitated. 'Your appointment at the hospital . . . you left me a message. What happened?'

'Tsk. Let's talk about it later. It's *your* day.'

'This is important. I want more than anything to hear that you're okay.'

Bernadette patted his arm. 'I'm okay, Arthur. The results were fine. The lump was benign. It's been such a worry so it's been good to be busy, helping to plan this surprise for you. Lucy called me. She called all of us.'

Arthur grinned.

'Nathan told me that he confided in you,' Bernadette said. 'He read my hospital appointments so I'm glad he had you to speak to. Anyway. Yes, I am fine.'

'Oh, God.' The relief he felt was immense. It

made his knees wobble and his throat constrict. He stretched out his arms, circled them around her and held her close. 'I am so glad you're okay.' She felt soft and warm and she smelled of violets.

'Me, too.' Her voice trembled a little. 'Me too.'

The doorbell rang and Lucy shouted out, 'I'll get it.'

A few seconds later, the kitchen door opened. 'Hey, put my mum down, Tiger Man,' Nathan said.

Arthur shot his hands to his sides but he saw that Nathan was laughing.

He'd had his hair cropped short, which displayed his china-blue eyes. He was holding something covered with foil in his outstretched hands. 'For you.'

'Me?' Arthur took it from him. He removed the foil. Underneath sat a chocolate cake so beautiful it looked like it came from an exclusive shop. It was covered in shiny icing and had piped icing words saying, 'Happy 65th Birthday, Arthur.'

'I made it,' Nathan said. 'Me and Mum are back on track. We've talked. She's happy that I want to bake. Has she told you that her results are clear?'

'Yes. I am so pleased for you both. And just look at this cake.' He would not tell the boy that he was seventy, not sixty-five. 'That's incredible. It looks delicious.'

Arthur was almost knocked off his feet by the two red-haired kids from over the road. One bashed into his elbow. 'Oi, you two,' Nathan said as he set down the cake. 'Watch what you're doing and put your socks and shoes on.'

The two kids stopped and immediately did what they were told. 'They just need someone to pay attention to them,' Nathan said. 'Terry's a saint for looking after them.'

Lucy appeared. 'Dad? We want to show you something. It's your present.'

'I have a pile of presents here. I've not opened them yet.'

'It's your big one from me and Dan. It's in the front room.' She pushed open the door.

Arthur shook his head. 'You shouldn't have bothered,' he said, but he followed her in.

He was confronted by an explosion of colour, of people. Each wall was covered with photographs. They had been neatly stuck in rows and columns like paint swatch colours. But, as he stepped closer, faces came into view. His face, Miriam's, Dan, Lucy. 'What is this?' he said.

'This is your life, Dad,' Lucy said. 'You wouldn't look inside the pink and white striped box so I've brought the photos to you. I want you to take a close look. I want you to study these photos and remember what a fantastic life you had with Mum.'

'But, there are things you don't know. Things that I've found out . . .'

'Whatever those things are, they don't change what you had together. You had many years of happiness. You've become obsessed with the past, Dad. You're hooked on finding out about a time you weren't in Mum's life. And you have built that time up in your head and heart to be

310

bigger and brighter and better than what you and Mum had together.'

Arthur turned on the spot. There were hundreds of images of him and Miriam, together.

'Look at your life. Look at how Mum is smiling, how you are smiling. You were made for each other. You were happy. And there may not have been tigers or dreadful poems, or shopping in Paris. You might not have travelled to exotic climes, but you had an entire life together. Look at it and cherish it.'

The photos looked like tiny windows in a sprawling tower block, each giving him a glimpse to a past time. Lucy and Dan had pinned them in chronological order, so the ones nearest the door on his left-hand side were black and white; the time when he and Miriam had met. He remembered seeing her for the first time, strolling into the butcher's shop with her huge basket swinging from the crook of her arm. He could even recall what was in that basket — a string of pork sausages in paper sat on top of a block of butter. He remembered that the wicker was frayed and broken. He slowly circled the room gazing, studying the photographs, seeing his life played out before his eyes.

Bernadette, Nathan and Terry tactfully retreated to the kitchen, ushering the red-haired kids with them.

Arthur reached out to touch a photograph. There was their wedding day. He looked so proud and Miriam was gazing at him in adoration. There was a photo of Miriam pushing

311

a pram. Lucy gurgled inside. Then he saw something shiny dangling from his wife's wrist.

'Where are you going, Dad?' Lucy called out as he scuttled out of the room and upstairs.

'Be back in a mo.' He reappeared seconds later with his box of tricks and took out his eyeglass. He pointed at the photo and then screwed the eyeglass into his eye socket. From Miriam's wrist hung the gold charm bracelet.

'So it wasn't a secret. She did wear it,' Lucy said, peering closer. 'I don't remember it.'

'Nor do I.'

'It doesn't suit her, does it?'

'No, it doesn't.'

'Can you see though that you were happy? It doesn't matter about a silly gold bracelet.'

Arthur stood with his arms by his side. He felt dizzy with love and pride. It had taken his children a few hours and lots of packets of Blu-Tack to prove it to him. He had been blind. The past twelve months of living alone, of devising his strict routines, had made the colour fade from his life. He had needed something to fill the void and he had done so with an obsession for an old gold charm bracelet. He felt so sorry for Sonny Yardley, losing her brother. But it had been a terrible accident. Miriam had recognised that she needed to move on with her life and she had done. He was glad that she had chosen to do it with him.

He strolled around the room twice, remembering, laughing. Recalling the first time he held Lucy in his arms, how proud he felt pushing the kids in their prams. He saw how beautiful

Miriam had been at his fortieth birthday party, how her eyes shone with love for him.

'Are we ready then?' Dan shouted out.

'*Dan!*' Lucy shouted. 'You are so impatient. Dad is still looking.'

Dan shrugged. 'I just thought that . . . '

Lucy shook her head. 'Oh, go on then,' she relented.

'What?' Arthur said. 'What's going on?'

The lights dimmed. Bernadette struck a match and lit the candles on the cake.

Arthur's heart began to thump in his chest. Everyone sang 'Happy Birthday' and he liked how different words were sung when it came to his name. Lucy and Dan sang 'Dad', and the red-haired kids sang 'Neighbour'. Bernadette sang 'Arthur' and Nathan just mumbled a bit. Arthur hadn't expected to ever feel this happy again.

He sat in his armchair with a cocktail in his hand. Bernadette insisted on making him a Sex on the Beach. It tasted nice, sweet and warm. He wasn't a mingler but that was fine because one by one his guests came to him. Dan crouched and whispered how much he missed England. He missed Heinz baked beans and the countryside. Terry said he hoped that Arthur didn't mind, but he had asked Lucy to the cinema next week and she had said yes. There was a film on that they both fancied. Arthur said that was great. He watched them talking and they looked relaxed together. Lucy was laughing and he realised that he had never seen her laugh with Anthony.

'I've been talking to Luce. She's told me about Mum's bracelet,' Dan said.

The bracelet sat in the pocket of Arthur's soggy trousers, on the bedroom floor. He didn't want to think about the bloody thing. Perhaps he should have flung it out to sea. It belonged in the past now where he wanted to leave it. 'I don't really want to talk about it tonight.'

Dan opened his mouth to speak but then Bernadette bustled over. She thrust a plate with a slab of chocolate cake on it into Arthur's hand. 'Did Nathan tell you he made this? What do you think?'

Arthur dug in his fork and sampled the cake. 'It's very tasty. Your son has a talent. He takes after you.'

Bernadette beamed and then insisted she was going to get Dan a slice too, even though he said he didn't want one.

Lucy sidled up to Dan. 'Have you told him yet?'

'Told me what?' His two children stood in front of him, both with their lips pursed as if they had bad news for him. 'What is it?' he said.

'Here we are. Lovely cake for us all.' Bernadette reappeared with her arm laden with plates. 'Enough for everyone.'

'Dan?' Arthur said, as his son was forced to take a plate.

'I'll speak to you tomorrow.'

'Perhaps we can sleep at yours tonight?' Lucy said.

Arthur felt his chest swell with happiness. 'Of course.'

'But tomorrow morning,' Lucy continued, 'we need a family meeting. Dan has something to tell you.'

The Heart

Arthur had a hangover. It felt as if his brain was banging. The house was still but he could hear strange yet familiar noises. Dan was snoring in his old room. He could tell that Lucy was awake and reading. If he strained his ears he could hear her turning over the pages of a book. He turned on his side to see the empty expanse of mattress beside him. 'The kids are back home, Miriam,' he whispered. 'We're still the Peppers. We still all love you.'

He had forgotten how much cereal they ate and how much space Dan took up at the kitchen table. Dan and Lucy insisted on rustling up his breakfast even though Arthur didn't really feel like eating. He swallowed two paracetamol with his cup of tea. The three of them ate and laughed. Dan knocked over the milk and Lucy tutted, wiped it up and called him a numpty.

Arthur looked at his son and caught only glimpses of the young boy with the round face, chocolate button eyes and tufty hair, who used to jump up with excitement when *The Muppet Show* came on TV. 'You said you had something you wanted to tell me,' he prompted.

Lucy and Dan looked at each other.

'I told Dan about your travels around the

country,' Lucy said.

'You're a real adventurer, Dad.'

'I also told him about the charm bracelet.'

'I remember Mum showing it to me when I was a kid,' Dan said.

'She showed it to you?'

'I remember once when Lucy was at school and I was at home with Mum. I'd got a stomach ache and she let me stay off and watch TV. After a while I was so bored. So we went to your bedroom. Mum crouched and got something out of her wardrobe. It was the charm bracelet. She showed me all the charms and she told me a little story about each one. Of course, I've always had cloth ears, so I can't remember any of them. But I played with it all afternoon. Then she put it back and I never saw it again. I asked her on a couple more occasions if I could play with it but she said she had 'put it away'. I always remembered it though. I liked the elephant best. I remember his green stone.'

'Me too. He's a noble beast.' Arthur looked at his son. 'So what did you have to tell me?'

'There's the story of one charm left to discover?'

'Yes, the heart.'

'I bought it,' said Dan.

Arthur dropped his cup. It smashed on the floor and tea and china spattered everywhere. Lucy went to find a cloth and a dustpan and brush. 'What did you say?'

'I bought the heart charm. Well, Kyle and Marina picked it out. We were in a shop in Sydney. Mum told me that I should make more

317

effort with my gifts to you.'

'I used to think that you should try harder with gifts to your mum.'

'Well, this time I did. We walked past a jewellery shop and the trays in the window were lined with gold charms. Marina wanted to stop and look and I remembered Mum's charm bracelet. I'd totally forgotten but then the memory was so clear. It was as if I was a kid again, playing with the tiger, the elephant. I said that Marina could pick a charm and that we'd send it to Grandma in England. She was so excited. She chose the heart straight away. I didn't know if Mum still had the bracelet, but it was a nice present anyway.'

'I took the bracelet to a jewellery shop in London and the owner said that the heart charm was more modern,' Arthur said. 'It wasn't soldered onto the bracelet properly.'

'Maybe Mum used your box of tricks to nip it in place herself.'

'But she didn't mention it to me. She didn't show me,' Arthur said.

'We only sent it a couple of weeks before she died. She might have planned to show you another time . . .'

Or perhaps if she had showed me then I would have asked questions, Arthur thought. *I would have asked her the stories behind the charms and it was too late for her to tell me. It would have brought up bad memories of Martin. Maybe the heart charm helped to bring happiness to the bracelet.* 'That's probably the case.' He nodded. 'Of course she would have told me about it.'

318

★ ★ ★

Dan drove Arthur and Lucy up to Whitby in his hire car. It was a sunny but windy day and Arthur had dressed appropriately this time in a padded waterproof jacket and lace-up boots. He had lent Dan some clothes. His son had forgotten what the British weather could be like.

They walked through the old town and up the one hundred and ninety-nine steps to the old abbey. Arthur took it steady, stopping to sit on benches en route and look out over the orange-tiled roofs of the houses and B and Bs. Lucy rescued strands of hair from her mouth and Dan flung out his arms and ran into the wind when they reached the top. 'Whooo,' he shouted out. 'Kyle and Marina would love it up here.'

'Do you think you might bring them over one day?' Arthur asked tentatively. He hadn't seen them for a long time.

'I will do, Dad. I promise. We'll try to come over each year from now on. I didn't realise how much Mum's passing away would affect me . . . I also want to say that I'm sorry.'

'Whatever for?'

'I used to give you a hard time sometimes, when you wanted to read to me, when you were late home from work. I didn't appreciate how hard it is to be a parent, until I had the kids myself. I was a total pain in the backside.' He turned to his sister. 'To you too, Luce.'

Arthur shook his head. 'No need to apologise, son.'

'Nobody's perfect.' Lucy gave Dan's arm a punch. 'And you certainly aren't.'

Dan gave a mock *ouch* and laughed.

They strolled around the graveyard and circled the crumbling abbey and then walked over to the hillside overlooking the sea.

'Do you remember that time that me and Lucy went to the ice-cream van with Mum?' Dan said. 'We were playing tig and ran into the road? That big lorry was rumbling toward us, but we hadn't noticed. You appeared out of nowhere and yanked our arms out of the sockets. The lorry thundered past. You saved our lives. I almost peed with terror.'

'You remember that?'

'Yeah. I thought you were like Superman. I told all my friends at school. It was like you had superhuman powers.'

'You just ran off and had your ice cream.'

'I think I was in shock. You were my hero.'

Arthur blushed.

'This is it.' Lucy stopped. 'This was one of Mum's favourite places. I remember, there's a rock over there shaped like a dog's head.'

'And one over there shaped like a volcano,' Dan added. 'We always sat on that bench and looked out to sea.'

Memories gradually began to emerge in Arthur's mind, like friends appearing out of the mist. His curiosity about the stories behind the charms was beginning to fade. They were almost like fairy stories, things that had happened in a time past. He was pleased that his head was becoming full of his own stories again, ones about his wife and children.

'I remember one day and we were begging you, begging you to come in the sea,' Lucy said. 'And you kept saying that you were happy to stay and read your paper. So me, Mum and Dan went into the sea, and then suddenly you were beside us and laughing and scooping up water and throwing it at us. Mum was wearing that white dress that went see-through in the sun.'

'I remember,' Arthur said. 'But I thought that I stayed on the sand and watched you.'

'No. You came in,' Dan said. 'We nagged you into submission.'

Arthur thought about how it was possible for memories to shift and change with time. To be forgotten and resumed, to be enhanced or darkened as the mind and mood commanded. He had conjured up emotions, of how Miriam had felt about the people who gave the charms to her. He didn't know. He couldn't know. But he did know that she had loved him, that Dan and Lucy loved him, that he had lots of reasons to carry on.

'Come on, Superman.' Dan patted him on the arm. 'Shall we head down to the beach for a paddle?'

'Yes,' Arthur said and he took both of his children's hands in his. 'Come on, let's go.'

Letters Home

When Arthur returned from his outing to Whitby with Dan and Lucy, he found a bundle of letters on his doormat. They were bound with a piece of yellowing string. All had been written on lavender-coloured paper. All were open and from the look of them had been read many times, except the top one which was almost pristine. They were in his wife's handwriting.

On top, and sealed, was a manila envelope. He tore it open.

Dear Mr Pepper.

I enclose here some letters sent to me by Miriam many years ago. They are probably more use to you than they are to me.

Sometimes you hold on to things, not because you want to keep them, but because they are difficult to let go. I hope they answer some of your questions about your wife.

I would appreciate it if you do not contact me again, but I am sorry for you and your family's loss.

Sonny Yardley

'What are those?' Lucy asked, as she and Dan tugged off their boots in the hallway.

'Oh, nothing,' Arthur said lightly. 'Just something for me to read later.' He tucked the letters into his pocket. His wife had kept her past secret because that's what she'd felt the need to do. He had been too curious to let her secret lie. But there were some things that should remain in the past, that his children didn't need to know about — about Sonny and Martin Yardley.

'Come on,' he said. 'Let's get inside the house properly and get warm. Does anyone fancy a sausage butty with ketchup and a game of snakes and ladders?'

'Yes please,' Lucy and Dan said in unison.

★ ★ ★

That night Arthur put on his pyjamas and sat on the bed. The bundle of letters sat beside him. He tentatively picked them up. For only the briefest moment he considered not opening them, of letting them be.

He flicked through them, reading the dates on the postmarks. The one on top was the most recent. It looked as if it could have been mailed just yesterday. His hands shook as he opened the envelope, took out the letter and unfolded it.

January 1969
Dearest Sonny

This letter is terribly difficult to write. Is it really over two years since I last put pen to paper to you? We used to write so often.

I do so miss our friendship and think about you often. However I have to accept that you no longer want me to be part of your life. Although this makes me terribly sad, I take comfort in that it is what you want.

Throughout all my life, you and Martin were a constant. You were there for me when I was growing up, then shared in my troubles and travels. It is so hard to believe that Martin is gone. I am so truly sorry for my part in his death. I have tried to contact you so many times to convey my condolences and sorrow.

I still think of Martin and what might have been. The memories are both sweet and painful. I miss you both so very much.

After mourning for a long time, I am trying to move forwards. And that is why I am writing to you one more time, my friend. I would not want you to hear my news from anyone else.

I have met a lovely man. His name is Arthur Pepper. We are engaged and will be married in York in May this year.

He is quiet and kind. He is steady and he loves me. We share a quiet kind of love. The simple things in life now bring me pleasure. My days of searching are over. I no longer have a desire to be anywhere but home. And my home shall be with him.

I have not told Arthur about Martin and I have decided not to do so. This is no disrespect to your brother's memory, but rather an effort for me to not live in the past and to take small steps toward the future. I do not want to forget the past, only to move on from it.

I ask once again if you would like to meet, to talk and remember our friendship. If I do not hear from you, then I know your answer is 'no' and I shall leave you be. I hope that your family are well and that you have found some peace.

Your friend
Miriam

Arthur stayed up until two in the morning reading his wife's letters to Sonny.

He finally reread the first letter in which Miriam told Sonny of her love for him.

After that, he took each letter in turn and tore it into tiny squares. He swept them off the duvet, into his hand, and then wrapped them in a handkerchief ready to deposit in the bin the following day.

He knew his wife well. They had shared their lives for over forty years. It was time to let her past go.

Finders Keepers

Six weeks later

Before he entered Jeff's shop in London, Arthur stood for a while and looked at the gold bracelets, necklaces and rings in the window. What stories they could tell of love and happiness and death. And here they were waiting for new people to buy them and to create new stories.

He pushed open the door and waited for his eyes to adjust to the darkness.

'Just a second,' Jeff's gravelly voice called out. He then pushed through the beaded curtain. He removed his eyeglass. 'Oh hello there. It's . . . '

'Arthur.' He held out his hand and Jeff shook it.

'Yes of course it is. You came in with Mike and brought that incredible gold bracelet; the one with the charms that I fell in love with. It was your wife's, wasn't it?'

'You have a good memory.'

'I see a lot of jewellery in my job. Of course I do. I sell the stuff. But that bracelet, well there was something special about it.'

Arthur swallowed. 'I've decided to sell it and thought you might be interested.'

'You betcha. Can I take another look?'

326

Arthur stuck his hand in his backpack and handed over the heart-shaped box. Jeff opened it. 'Just beautiful,' he said. 'It's even more magnificent than I remembered.' He picked it out and turned it over in his hands, just as Arthur had done the first time he had found it. 'It will be a confident lady who buys this. This won't be about showing off, or about an investment. She will buy it because she loves the charms and that they have stories to tell. You definitely want to sell?'

'Yes.'

'I know a lady in Bayswater who would love this. She's a film producer, a real bohemian type. This is right up her street.'

'I'd like it to go to a good home.' Arthur heard his own voice waver.

Jeff rearranged the bracelet back in the heart-shaped box. 'Are you sure about this, mate? It's a big decision.'

'It has no sentimental value for me. It was hidden away and forgotten for years.'

'It's up to you. I'm not going anywhere. I've been here for forty years, as was my father before me, so I'm going to be here next week or next month or next year if you want to think about it.'

Arthur swallowed. He pushed the box with one finger back toward Jeff. 'No. I want to sell it, but I do want to keep one of the charms. Would you still be interested if I kept the elephant?'

'It's your bracelet. If you want the elephant, you keep it. I'll just reposition the other charms to fill the gap.'

'He's the little fellow that started off my journey.'

Arthur sat on a stool at the counter as Jeff went into the back of the shop. He pulled a magazine toward him. On the back was a jewellery advertisement for a new kind of charm bracelet. Instead of dangling charms there were beads that fed onto a chain. The advert suggested that they should mark occasions, just as Miriam's bracelet did. It was funny how some things didn't really change.

Arthur pushed it away and surveyed all the gold and silver surrounding him. There were rings that must have been worn for decades and meant so much in people's lives, then they were sold or given away. But the jewellery would get a new life, go to a new person who would love and use it. He tried to imagine the film producer that Jeff knew. In his head she wore a red silk turban and a flowing paisley dress. He pictured Miriam's bracelet dangling from her wrist and it looked good.

'Here he is.' Jeff pressed the elephant into Arthur's palm. Away from the other charms he looked majestic, as if he was supposed to march alone. Arthur turned the emerald with his finger.

Jeff handed over a roll of money. 'It's what we discussed. It's worth that even without the elephant.'

'Are you sure?'

Jeff nodded. 'Thanks for thinking of me. What have you got planned for today then? Are you calling in on Mike?'

'I'm going to try and find him. Do you still see him?'

'Only every day.' Jeff rolled his eyes. 'He's such

a sweetheart calling in to make sure I'm okay. I had a bit of a heart scare a while back. Mike has taken on the role of my guardian angel, whether I like it not. Every day I get questioned about what I've eaten and if I've been exercising enough.'

'He's a caring young man.'

'He is that. Heart of gold that one. He'll be back on his feet soon. He just needs to stay away from wrong 'uns and he'll be fine. So, what are you going to do with this money, Arthur?'

'My son lives in Australia. He's invited me out there.'

'Well, you should spend that cash. Blow it all on something that makes you happy. You can make memories out of money but you can't make money out of memories, unless you're an antique dealer. Bear that in mind, Arthur, my old son.'

★   ★   ★

Next, Arthur took the Tube across London. He knocked on the door of De Chauffant's house but there was no reply. The upstairs curtains were closed. He had separated off some money in his pocket for Sebastian.

A woman appeared on the doorstep next door. She carried a briefcase under one arm and a Chihuahua under the other. 'I hope you're not a bloody journalist,' she snapped, setting both dog and case down on the ground.

'No. Not at all. I have a friend who lives here.'

'The writer?'

'No. Sebastian.'

329

The woman jerked her head. 'Young lad with a European accent?'

'Yes. That's him.'

'He moved out a couple of weeks back.'

'Oh.'

'He had a lucky escape if you ask me. He was arm in arm with an older man. Smartly dressed. They seemed very much together, if you know what I mean.'

Arthur nodded. He had visions of Sebastian still being locked in servitude. It sounded as if he had met someone else.

'Better than looking after that narcissistic old bastard,' the woman said.

'So you knew them both?'

'The walls are paper thin. I heard their rows often enough. The way that writer shouted at that poor young boy was despicable. He died this morning. It's not been on the news yet.'

'De Chauffant? He's dead?'

The woman nodded. 'A cleaner found him. He was a young thing, terribly shocked. He knocked on my door and we phoned for an ambulance. He vanished as soon as it arrived. So now I'm waiting for the journos and fans to turn up. I thought you were one of them.'

'No. I'm just Arthur. Arthur Pepper.'

'Well, Arthur Pepper, it goes to show that you never know what goes on in people's lives, huh?'

'No. That's right. May I trouble you for an envelope and paper?'

The lady shrugged, re-entered her house, and then handed over the stationery. 'There's a stamp there too if you need it.'

Arthur sat on De Chauffant's top step and put four fifty pound notes in the envelope. He wrote a brief note:

For tiger food, from Arthur Pepper.

He wrote out the address for Lord and Lady Graystock and dropped the envelope into a post box.

For his next port of call, Arthur headed first to the Tube station where he had encountered Mike for the first time. He felt like a seasoned traveller now with his training shoes, backpack and wallet wedged firmly into his pocket. He listened for the lilting sound of flute music but instead all he heard was a guitar. A girl with a face full of piercings sat cross-legged on the ground. Her stripy woollen scarf doubled as a guitar strap. Her rendition of 'Bridge Over Troubled Water' was hauntingly beautiful. Arthur dropped twenty pounds into her guitar case and then took the bus to Mike's apartment.

His friend wasn't there.

Arthur stood in the corridor in National Trust statue mode. He listened carefully and looked around him to ensure he was alone. The corridor was empty. He could hear the faint noise of a television from one of the upstairs apartments. It sounded like a game show. His heart pounded as he rang the doorbell on the apartment next door to Mike's. He waited but no one answered. Good. Just what he had hoped for. He pressed the buzzer again for good measure. He crouched and took his box of tricks out of his rucksack.

After sifting through it, he took out a set of picks. Studying each in turn, he then selected the most apt one for the job. He used to be a good locksmith. He jiggled it into the keyhole, listening, turning, feeling. There was a click, then a louder one. He had done it.

'Hello,' he called gently, sticking his head around the door. He thought back to how scared he had felt the night of his surprise party when he thought intruders were in the house and hoped that no one was home. He wasn't here to scare or confront. He just wanted to do what was right.

The layout of the apartment was the mirror image to Mike's next door. Firstly, he pulled a chair and wedged it under the handle. If anyone did come home it would give him time. The flat was on the second floor of the building and, with his weak ankle, he could hardly risk jumping out. He had to move quickly.

As he moved around the apartment, he slid out books and opened drawers. He stood on tiptoes to look on top of cupboards and slid his hand under the mattress and felt around. His search yielded a pile of *Nuts* magazines. Perhaps Mike was wrong when he thought his neighbour had stolen his gold Rolex. If it was here, he would find it.

He did find suspicious piles of jewellery dotted around. There was a clump of gold chains on the bathroom windowsill, a stack of laptops on the kitchen table. The bedroom yielded an array of designer handbags neatly laid out on the duvet as if ready to be photographed. Then he spotted a small black box in the bedside cabinet. Inside sat a gold Rolex. He took it out and looked on the back. The engraving was as Mike had described: 'Gerald'. He slipped it into his pocket. In the front room, he picked up his rucksack, zipped it up and slung it on his back.

It was then that he heard a noise. A rattle. The sound of keys sliding into a keyhole and then trying to open the lock. Oh, God. His body froze. Only his eyes moved, sliding from one side to the other as he thought what to do.

'Damn door is stuck.' He heard a man's voice and another rattle of the lock.

He looked around him. The chair was still wedged under the door.

'I can't get the bleedin' door open,' he heard.

There was no response so he figured that the man must be speaking to himself. He heard footsteps moving away and the muffled sound of a doorbell as the man tried a neighbour.

Arthur swept the chair away and then scanned the apartment. He had to get out of here. But how? He moved swiftly to the window. He saw that the drop must be at least ten feet. He would surely snap his ankles. But there was no other way out. All he could do was jump, hide, or leave the way he came. The man's wardrobe was a tiny Victorian thing. He couldn't cram himself inside that, and how would he cope if he broke both of his legs from the jump?

There was only one way left . . .

Slowly opening the door, he half expected to come eye to eye with Mike's neighbour. If he was capable of stealing a watch and all the loot then what else might he do? Arthur opened the door by a few inches and peered out. At the end of the corridor the man stood. He wore a dirty string vest over too-big trousers. His hair was matted and dyed black. If Arthur left now then the man would surely see him. He cursed himself for even having this madcap idea. He should have left Mike to sort out his own battles. But even so he was glad to have the Rolex stashed in his pocket. He stepped quickly into the corridor and pulled the door shut behind him. The click wasn't loud enough for the man to hear. Arthur's heart thumped. Badum, badum. It seemed so loud he was surprised that no one else could hear it.

He walked speedily away in the opposite direction.

'Hey!' a man's voice shouted after him. 'Wait.'

Arthur speeded up. He could see the exit door now, just a few more strides and he would be out of here. 'Hey.' The shout came again and he could hear footsteps quickening behind him. Then a hand grabbed his shoulder. 'Hey, mate.'

Arthur turned round. The man handed him the plastic lid of his ice cream box. 'I think you dropped this.'

'Thanks.' He was still carrying his box of tricks. The lock picks lay on the top. 'I didn't realise I dropped it.'

'No probs.' The man was about to move away. 'Are those lock picks?' he said.

Arthur looked down and nodded. 'Yes.' He waited for the punch in the nose, or for his arm to be grabbed as the man marched him to his apartment.

'Great. I'm locked out of my flat. Can you let me in?'

Arthur swallowed. 'I can try.'

He made the job look more difficult than it was. He wriggled a pick in the lock. He huffed and puffed. Finally, he opened the door. 'Fantastic. I'll make you a brew,' the man said. 'To say thanks.'

Arthur recalled Mike saying the man seemed like a charmer until you knew he was a thief. 'That's fine,' he said. 'I really must be off.'

As he left the flat, he was sure he heard the man muttering to himself, asking why the chair wasn't where he'd left it.

He considered writing a note or posting through some money, but he knew how proud Mike was. Instead, he lifted Mike's letterbox and pushed the watch through. The small thud it made when it landed on the doormat gave him a feeling of satisfaction like no other.

Journey's End?

'Factor forty?' Lucy said, reading off her checklist.

'Yes,' Arthur replied.

'Lip balm?'

'Check.'

'Does it have an SPF?'

Arthur picked up the navy-blue stick and peered at the small white writing. 'Yes. Factor fifteen.'

'Hmmm,' Lucy said. 'You could do with a higher one.'

'It'll be fine.'

'I'll see what I've got in my make-up bag.'

'It's fine. I *have* been on holiday before, you know.'

'Not anywhere as far, or as hot,' Lucy said firmly. 'I do not want a phone call telling me that you have sunstroke.'

Arthur changed the subject. 'Did you go to the cinema with Terry?'

Lucy smiled. 'We had a lovely time. We're going for a meal on Friday, to that new restaurant in town. He absolutely loves kids too,' she added.

Arthur had asked Terry to keep an eye on the house. 'Frederica likes watering first thing in the morning so she has moisture for the full day.'

'You've told me five times,' Terry said. 'And I will switch your lights on every night and close your curtains so that people will think you're still at home.'

'Good. And if ever you want me to look out for the tortoise, that's fine.' Really, he had no idea what he would do with the little fella, but he felt good for offering.

'Have you packed your sunglasses?' Lucy started again.

'Yes.'

'Hold on. Are those the ones you wore when I was little?'

'I've only ever had one pair. They're quality ones. Tortoiseshell.' He put them on.

'I suppose they're quite fashionable again now.'

Arthur flipped the lid on his suitcase shut. 'I have everything. If I've forgotten anything I can pick it up at the airport.'

'You've never actually been to an airport before, except to see Dan off.'

'I'm not a child.'

They both laughed. It was something Lucy used to say when she was a teenager.

'Seriously though, Dad. A month abroad is a long time. You need to be prepared. It's not going to be like your holidays to Bridlington with Mum.'

'I hope not,' he laughed. 'I want to try new food and culture.'

'You certainly have changed. I wonder what Mum would say if she could see you now.'

Arthur picked up his sunglasses. 'I think she'd be pleased.' He glanced at his watch. 'The taxi is ten minutes late,' he said.

'You have plenty of time.'

As another ten minutes ticked past, Arthur began to worry. 'I'll phone them,' Lucy said. She carried the phone into the kitchen. 'Right. They said they didn't have a note of your booking. They're going to get someone here as soon as possible but they're short-staffed. It's rush hour and so it might be an hour.'

'An hour?'

'I know. It's not good enough. We need to get you on the road now. If you get stuck in traffic . . . Is there anyone you can ask for a lift?'

'No,' Arthur said, but then he did know someone, a friend he could rely on for life.

Bernadette and Nathan arrived at the house ten minutes later. 'You do know the way, don't you?' He could hear her voice before the doorbell sounded. Briiiiing.

'How does she make it sound so loud?' Lucy asked.

Arthur shrugged and opened the door.

'Don't worry, Arthur.' Bernadette bustled in. She pressed a carrier bag into his hand. 'Some fresh sausage rolls for the journey. Nathan will get you there on time.'

Nathan nodded. He obediently picked up Arthur's case and travel bag and put them in the boot. Then he got into the car and waited. Lucy and Bernadette stood in the hallway. Arthur felt like a schoolboy with two aunts waving him goodbye.

'I always take some cereal bars,' Bernadette added. 'In case I'm not keen on the food when I get there.'

Arthur gave Lucy a huge hug and a kiss. 'I'll send you a postcard.'

'You'd better do.' She nodded and then left the house. 'Love you, Dad.'

'Love you too.'

Bernadette seemed quite choked up. 'I'll kind of miss you, Arthur Pepper,' she said.

'You have plenty of other lost causes to attend to.'

'You were never a lost cause, Arthur. Just one who had lost direction a bit.'

'Who will I hide from now?'

They both chuckled and he noticed for the first time how clear her eyes were and that they were a kind of olive green with brown speckles. He loved how she embraced life and held it tight against her ample bosom, never letting it go.

'You never gave up on me,' he said. 'Even though I gave up on myself.' He reached out to hug her. Bernadette hesitated for a moment and then stepped forwards. They held each other for a few seconds before pulling away. He would have liked to have held her for longer and the feeling took him by surprise. She fitted against his body well, as if it was a place that she was meant to be. 'See you in a month,' he said brightly.

'Yes,' she said. 'You will.'

Nathan commanded the traffic. He nipped in gaps, took side roads, skipped a couple of traffic lights on amber. All the time he was calm. He hummed and tapped his finger on the steering wheel to the music that was so quiet Arthur could hardly hear it. 'I'll get you there, no worries,' he said. 'My friends are well jell of you, y'know. Everyone wishes their granddads were like you, y'know, adventurous and stuff. I sort of told them you were like a surrogate granddad to me, seeing as I don't have one of my own.'

It was a role that Arthur was keen to develop further. He had already made a mental note to stock up on icing, flour and those edible shiny balls when he got back, in case Nathan fancied a spot of cake making together one day.

He sat back and marvelled at this transformation in the young man. He had judged him by his hair, and that was a mere fashion that disguised a sensitive nature. 'Is your mum okay now?'

'Yeah, thank God. I was worried that I was, you know, going to be an eighteen-year-old orphan. That would have sucked. Thanks for being there for her. It's good to know that when I go to catering college she has a good friend to look out for her. Scarborough's not too far away either.'

'I've been to the college,' Arthur said, smiling about the life-drawing class. 'The art department is lovely.'

'I can cook for you as well as my mum.'

'That's great. Though please don't make me marzipan cake.'

'Don't worry. I hate it.'

'Me too. I don't know how to tell your mum that though.'

'Me neither.'

340

★　★　★

The airport was as bright as a dentist's studio and the shops were stuffed with jewellery, teddies, clothes, perfumes, alcohol. He wandered around and bought some marbles and a cuddly elephant and a travel book for himself. He opened the front page and there was a map of the world. England was a tiny smudge. There is so much to see, he thought.

When his gate number was called, he felt as if he had grasshoppers in his stomach. He joined a line of people and held his passport opened on the correct page as instructed. He shuffled away along the queue. A small shuttle bus took him to the aeroplane. He hadn't imagined it would be so huge — a shiny white beast with a Roman nose and red tail. A friendly lady with a blonde bob welcomed him aboard and he found his seat. He sat down and strapped himself in, then absorbed himself in the activity around him: people finding their seats, announcements, a free magazine in a pocket of the seat in front. The lady next to him offered him her spare inflatable neck cushion and a humbug. The engine roared up. He watched the cabin crew's emergency instructions intently, then he leaned back in his seat and gripped his armrests as the plane tilted upward.

He was on his way. On his next journey.

The Future

Arthur sat on the edge of his sun lounger and dug his bare toes deep into the hot white sand. His cream linen trousers were rolled to the knee and his loose-fitting white cotton shirt was half-tucked into his waistband. The heat enveloped him tightly. It made him feel lethargic, slower. Sweat prickled under his arms and formed on his forehead like tiny glass beads. He liked it, this feeling of being in an oven.

He watched the blue sea lap against the shore, depositing a stripe of white foam. A group of small boys ran in fully dressed, splashing one another. There were wooden boats around him, upturned; the fishermen having already been out to sea and returned with their haul of fish. He could smell it on the barbecues in the shacks along the beach. Soon the tourists would descend, in their brightly coloured beach wraps and beads, to eat supper and drink beer from the bottle.

The sun was setting and the sky was already striped with ribbons of fuchsia and orange, like a woven sari. Palm trees reached out like hands to touch the magnificent sky. A rainbow of scarves, sarongs and towels hanging from the beach huts billowed in the breeze.

Arthur stood and walked to the edge of the water. The sand felt like warm dust beneath his feet. In one hand he clasped the elephant charm tightly, and in the other he held his half-read book: *A Rough Guide to India*.

It had been a difficult decision to choose Goa over Australia. But he needed to come to where his journey began, from the phone call he had made to Mr Mehra. It had changed how he saw his wife, how he saw himself.

He and Lucy had already arranged to go and spend Christmas with Dan. That suited his daughter better, when she could travel in the school holidays.

He opened his hand and the gold elephant shone. As the sun began to dip further, sinking into the sea, the light slid over the charm and Arthur could swear that the elephant winked at him. 'You are getting old,' he said aloud to himself. 'Seeing things.' Then he noticed that he hadn't said *You are old*. He had said, *You are getting old*. He was just on the way there.

'Mr Arthur Pepper. Mr Pepper.' A small boy, no more than six years old, ran toward him. He had ears that looked like cup handles and a thatch of black hair. 'Sir. It is time for tea back at the house.'

Arthur nodded. He made his way back to the sun lounger, slipped on his sandals and followed the boy off the beach. They passed a cow that stood chewing the frayed leather on the seat of a rusting red motorbike. 'Follow me, sir.' The boy led them both through a heavy turquoise iron gate and into a courtyard garden. Having arrived

343

in darkness the previous night, Arthur was glad for an escort back to his host.

Rajesh Mehra stood waiting by a small fountain that was studded with mosaics. Water trickled and looked like flowing silver. A small round table had been laid with a silver teapot and two china cups. He was dressed all in white and didn't have one hair on his head. His eyes were hooded and kind. 'I still cannot believe that you are here, my friend. I am so glad you came to stay with me. Are you enjoying your sunbathing?'

'Yes. Very much so. I've never been quite so warm before.'

'It can be stifling. Now, it is not so bad. Miriam used to like the sun. She said that she was like a lizard and she needed the sun to warm her bones.'

Arthur smiled. She said the same thing to him. At even a hint of sun, she would lie in the garden with a magazine and soak up the rays.

They took their tea in the courtyard. 'I am a creature of habit,' Rajesh said. 'I like to have my tea at the same time each day. I like my newspaper folded in the same way and I take precisely thirty minutes to sit and read.'

'Then I am spoiling your routine.'

'You are not spoiling it. You are enhancing it. It is good to shake things up.'

Arthur told Rajesh about his own routines, how they had started as a comfort and became a prison. He was about to say that a very nice lady named Bernadette had helped him out of it. But it was he himself who had done it. He had found the bracelet. He had called Mr Mehra. He was responsible for the change in his life.

'I remember that Miriam was not one for routines. I think she was a free spirit,' Rajesh said. 'I think she was a special lady. Did she have a good life?'

Arthur didn't hesitate. 'Yes,' he said proudly. 'She looked after you. She played with tigers. She inspired a poem. She influenced great art. She was a fantastic mother. We truly loved each other. She was remarkable.'

He waited for Rajesh to pour his tea then he took a sip. The china cup was dainty and painted with tiny pink roses. Miriam would have loved it.

He and she had lived their lives in opposite directions. Miriam's had been colourful and lively and vibrant but then quietened and calmed when she met him. He in turn had never wished for more than his wife and the children, yet here he was, his sandals white from sand and his ankles suntanned. It was unexpected, invigorating. And his wife had led him here.

'I shall take you to see her room, yes?'

Arthur nodded, a lump rising in his throat.

Her room was small, no longer than eight feet and around five feet in width. There was a simple low wooden bed and a writing desk. The walls were white plaster and there were holes where photos and paintings had been pinned over the years. He imagined her sitting at the desk, looking out of the window and laughing at the children playing in the courtyard, rolling marbles between her fingers. She could have optimistically written a letter to Sonny here, not knowing what terrible events would unfold when she got home.

He stood at the window and closed his eyes, allowing the falling sun to warm his face. The back of his neck was already pink and tingly, just as he liked it.

Just then his mobile phone vibrated in his pocket. 'Hello, Arthur Pepper. How may I help you?' he said without looking at the screen. 'Oh, hello, Lucy. I'm fine. Please don't stay on too long. These mobile phones are very costly. Don't worry about me, really. It is very beautiful here and Mr Mehra and his family are very welcoming. I can imagine your mother here as a young woman. She must have felt so happy and free, her life ahead of her, like yours is now. Like mine is. We must enjoy it. It's what she would have wanted. Okay, well, goodbye, darling. It's so lovely to hear from you. Love you.'

He slipped the phone back into his pocket. Then he gave a small smile and left the elephant charm on the bed, back where he belonged. He walked back into the courtyard. 'My daughter was on the phone,' he said. 'She worries about me.'

'We worry about our children and then they worry about us,' Rajesh replied. 'It is a circle of life. Enjoy it.'

'I will.'

'Did you know that Miriam and I walked to the village together each day? Our treat was to buy a fresh bread roll each and to pull the soft bread out of the centre and eat it on the way back. One day I proclaimed my love for her and

346

she was very sweet. She told me that, when I grew older, I would meet the love of my life and it would be the real thing. She was right, of course. Miriam said that she longed to find her own true love, too. 'I won't compromise,' she told me. 'I will only marry once. I will take it seriously and marry the man that I will spend the rest of my life with.' I remembered her words when I met Priya and I felt that lightning bolt of love strike me in the chest. And I hoped that Miriam had found it, too. And of course she did, when she met you. She followed her heart.'

Arthur closed his eyes. He pictured the rows and columns of photographs that Dan and Lucy had arranged in his front room. He saw Miriam smiling, happy. He saw the words in her letter to Sonny. 'I'm proud that I was the one for her, just as she was the one for me. I believe that her life was the one she chose to lead.'

Rajesh nodded. 'Come. Let us walk.'

The two men walked back to the edge of the quicksilver sea. Behind them a line of fires shone from the beach shacks. The smell of barbecued fish hung in the air. Two dogs chased each other along the beach. Arthur kicked off his shoes and let the sea kiss his toes.

'To Miriam.' Rajesh raised his cup of tea in a toast.

'To my wonderful wife,' Arthur said.

Then they stood and watched as the orange sky darkened to indigo and the sun finally sank into the sea.

We do hope that you have enjoyed reading
this large print book.

Did you know that all of our titles
are available for purchase?

We publish a wide range of high quality
large print books including:
Romances, Mysteries, Classics
General Fiction
Non Fiction and Westerns

Special interest titles available in
large print are:
The Little Oxford Dictionary
Music Book
Song Book
Hymn Book
Service Book

Also available from us courtesy of
Oxford University Press:
Young Readers' Dictionary
(large print edition)
Young Readers' Thesaurus
(large print edition)

For further information or a free
brochure, please contact us at:
Ulverscroft Large Print Books Ltd.,
The Green, Bradgate Road, Anstey,
Leicester, LE7 7FU, England.
Tel: (00 44) 0116 236 4325
Fax: (00 44) 0116 234 0205

HAG-SEED

Margaret Atwood

Felix is at the top of his game as Artistic Director of the Makeshiweg Theatre Festival. His productions have amazed and confounded. Now he's staging a *Tempest* like no other: not only will it boost his reputation, but it will heal emotional wounds as well. Or that was the plan. Instead, after an act of unforeseen treachery, Felix is living in exile in a backwoods hovel, haunted by memories of his beloved lost daughter, Miranda — and also brewing revenge. After twelve years, his chance finally arrives in the shape of a theatre course at a nearby prison. Here, Felix and his inmate actors will put on his *Tempest* and snare the traitors who destroyed him. It's magic! But will it remake Felix as his enemies fall?

BLUEPRINTS

Barbara Delinsky

Jamie MacAfee's life is almost perfect. She loves her fiancé, and adores her job as an architect on her family's home renovation TV show. Her beloved mother Caroline has built up her own confidence after a painful divorce, working as the very successful host of the show. Everything is going to plan . . . and then the lives of both women are changed overnight. When the TV network decides to replace her with Jamie as the show's host, Caroline is left feeling horribly betrayed. Then tragedy strikes, leaving Jamie guardian to her small orphaned half-brother, and fiancée to a man who doesn't want the child. *Who am I?* both women ask, as the blueprints they've built their lives around break down. It's time to find out what they really want, and where their future lies . . .

THE DAY I LOST YOU

Fionnuala Kearney

Contentedly sipping a cup of tea at home after a fun-filled afternoon at a Christmas fair, Jess receives the most terrible news a mother can get: her daughter Anna has been reported missing after an avalanche while on a ski trip. Though she's heartbroken, Jess knows she must be strong for Anna's five-year-old daughter Rose, who is now her responsibility. As she waits for more news, Jess starts to uncover details about Anna's other life — unearthing a secret that alters their whole world irrevocably . . .

THE OUTSIDE LANDS

Hannah Kohler

Jeannie is nineteen when the world changes. The sudden accident that robs her and her brother Kip of their mother leaves them adrift, with only their father to guide them. Jeannie seeks escape in work and later marriage to a man whose social connections propel her into an unfamiliar world of wealth and politics. Ill-equipped and unprepared, she finds comfort where she can. Meanwhile, Kip's descent into a life of petty crime is halted only when he volunteers for the Marines. By 1968, the conflict in Vietnam is at its height; and with the anti-war movement raging at home, Jeannie and Kip are swept along by events larger than themselves, driven by disillusionment to commit unforgiveable acts of betrayal that will leave permanent scars.